CIA KIBITZERS

CIA KIBITZERS

James Benedict

PAPERBACK: 978-1-970066-53-1
EBOOK: 978-1-970066-54-8

Ordering Information:

For orders and inquiries, please contact:
1-888-375-9818
www.toplinkpublishing.com
bookorder@toplinkpublishing.com

Printed in the United States of America

CONTENTS

DEDICATION

This book is dedicated to the brave men and women who covertly serve and die for their country.

Our talents are for God.

Proceeds from this book go to charity.

CHAPTER 1

THE BEGINNING

Top of the Morning!

My name is Jackson McKenna, from the Gaelic Irish surname, "Mac Cionaodha." My folks immigrated during harsh times from the Irish Emerald Isle and I was born in this great country of the United States of America!

Chelsea became our home, one of the toughest suburbs of Boston and my dad worked as a dock-hand in East Boston. I came along in 1921 and learned to fight before I knew how to blow my nose. As a young pup, one had to learn how to scuffle if one wanted to survive. The scrapes and knocks in life teach us to grow strong not only in body but in our mind and volition. I had enough of education after high school and enlisted in the Army where I served in Europe during WW II. After the war, I was recruited by the CIA, the central intelligence agency, which was formed to prevent another Pearl Harbor from ever happening again.

The United States in the early seventies was well immersed to the Stature of Liberty's eye brows, in the esoteric world of counter-espionage. Russia, the dastardly nemesis, orchestrated a plot to manufacture bombs in Lagos, Nigeria and smuggle them into the United States through Mexico to disrupt our electrical and communications grid. One bomb can disrupt life but multiple bombs can cause pandemonium. The plot included blowing-up bridges to cause traffic jams and mayhem along with assassins from death squads of the Philippines to assassinate our top leaders. Then the nightmarish, dreaded all out push for WW III. But now I am getting ahead of myself!

This is a story not so much about myself as it is about four, young kibitzers, observers, hired to gather covert information for the CIA long before the advent of computers. Each came from a strong background of a college education and regimentation of either military or merchant marine academies. This background milieu is vital to understand the era that the United States is in because our nemesis then, is still our enemy today. Make no mistake about that! Any naivety about our foe, will cause our total destruction!

I became their mentor on various missions. The old dog and the young educated pups that became a mutual education for survival. I got to know each of them, but one in particular fairly well, and admired this lad's solid faith and convictions. His name is Rick, and from what I learned from our conversations, this is where our story begins.

He had an uncanny way to express himself and described the vicissitudes of life as crossroads to either choose or ignore, as he once said to me, "Bang, Life!"

He went on to say, "We are ushered into this world from birth where God knows each of us by name long before our parents acknowledge us. This is because He endows each one of us with a soul. A soul to make choices with our gift of life!"

When Rick told me this on one of our many conversations, I was amazed how enamored he was with the beauty of life considering the lad had no formal education in either philosophy or theology. He continued with saying, "Our odyssey actually begins in the womb of our mother and if the mother is happy, then the child will most likely be happy. Because once we are in this world, the race is on!"

I remember him rambling on in his thought provoking ways about how from infancy we learn to crawl, walk and run. Then we jump into childhood where we learn and learn or else face discipline. Before we have both of our feet firmly planted on the ground, we are catapulted into puberty and the adolescence years.

The passion years where one learns of the spiritual passion in church but prefers the physical passion of our hormones doing the wave in our bodies. Halleluiah for the sexual years. Puberty is barely over and the bridge from adolescence to adulthood is like hitting a brick wall with questions, many choices and very few answers.

The maturity of our choices isn't forth coming just yet. The crossroads of life inundate us with pivotal options of college, service, marriage and that dramatic question where your country comes to you and says, "Your country needs you now, boy!"

Like I said, he didn't express himself like most people and always had these questions about this or that. Then he went on to hypothetically ask.

"Now what do you do?"

He continued by philosophizing about the high school years and what they are about. He talked about harmony, a harmony of life where everything fits into a need glove of learning, family, faith, sports, and dating. He was very retrospective for a young pup.

Then he said something that hit me as he continued, "It is very simple, safe and innocent but service is compelling and something we must do!"

Right then and there I knew he was gutsy. This young youth had a strong, driving impulse to enter the merchant marine academy and from that point on, nothing was simple ever again. I felt the same way about the army.

He described that his reckoning began as a "MUG," midshipman under guidance, and you are mine boy! That first year was a blur as one goes through indoctrination, military boot-camp, continual hazing and double-time routine. The regimentation, discipline, physical dexterity and mental adeptness forges them into a lean, quick thinking, agile robot.

Needless to say, I grew fond of this lad. Throughout the next few years over a cup of coffee or some drinks, acquired a genuine enjoyment listening to his stories as he described to me some of his shenanigans that led him to the CIA.

The commands are barked out, **"What time is it MUG?"**

As quickly as the question is proposed their answer better be quick, concise or pay the forfeit.

"The chronometer of precision workmanship through its mainspring, which is the source of energy; the gear train, which transmits the energy; the dial train, which governs the movement of the hands; the winding and setting mechanism; the escapement and balance unit, which controls the release of energy; and the plates which enclose and protect the movement shows 0800, Sir!"

Their responses had to be instantaneous and no matter how ludicrous the replies became, it sharpened their mental dexterity.

From what he said, it reminded me of my days in boot camp! Rick went on with his stores and described a different life of existence.

Midshipmen lived on the training ship as a dormitory and if one was caught sleeping pass reveille, then all hell broke loose with, **"Down for a hundred push-ups MUG!"**

This was followed by a run on open deck in your skivvies. It is mid-January and damn cold outside with Northern winds whipping down from Canada across the bay of Castine, Maine.

The yell is shouted, **"How cold is it Mug?"**

And again, their reply better be quick, "Colder than the nipple on a witches' tit!

> Colder than a pile of penguin shit!
> Colder than the hair on a polar bear's ass!
> Colder than the balls of a snake in the grass!
> It's cold Sir!"

What an era, Lyndon Baines Johnson is president of the United States following the assassination of President Kennedy, Vietnam is in full escalation of war with continual bombing of Hanoi, the cold war gets even colder with Aleksei Kosygin as the

Soviet Premier of Russia, Thurgood Marshall is sworn in as the first black U.S. Supreme Court Justice and the Tet offensive is in full swing. This is followed by the assassinations of Reverend Martin Luther King Jr. and Senator Robert F. Kennedy.

Your perception on life, faith and duty changes abruptly as the world is infested with so many transgressions, so much infamy that it boggles the mind. One wonders where are the core values in life and do they exist anymore? Some are raised to believe in reverence for God, respect for life and honor to do what is right. Then as his dad always tried to instill in him as he was growing-up, he would always say, "Son with those core values one needs the courage to follow through and do good!"

His dad sounded allot like mine and learned that he was a marine serving his entire campaign in the pacific during world war II for those four harrowing years. He must have lived by those core values that he instilled into his son. This is the same time that I served my tour in Europe. As Rick continued with his stories about the academy, it reminded me of my hazing days in the army.

Hazing, bilge parties where one is thrust down in the lower bowels of the ship to crawl through the bunker-C oil, standing watches, attending classes to earn a degree and military commission in the USNR, training cruises and endless repetitiousness; he lived to the words of the school song, "We're a bunch of bastards, bastards are we."

As the song went on in decaying stanzas, the academy owned them from reveille to taps! There were only two choices to make and those were whether one decided to go deck or engine. He went engine and so along with his engineering classes, one pursued naval science classes throughout the four years to qualify for their commission. The calisthenics kept one in shape, classes educated their minds and their attitudes became callous with the double-time, military routine. The first two years can be epitomized as the hellion years, for they lived up to their school song which by the way was banded in six countries.

I got a kick out of that story when Rick explained it to me.

Not all progress to lead, for the true leadership qualities come from within; but given the proper discipline and guidance, one's inner qualities would mature and develop. MUG year, from Queen Anne Chairs, sitting position without a chair, arms extended fully out for ten minutes doesn't sound like much of a strain, but one would sweat and the legs would shake. This torment was followed with doing push-ups over a knife blade, running up agony hill with rifles fully extended over your head at high-port arms and those endless horror shows. Believe it or not, this bullshit taught them perseverance and above all, not to show any fear.

At this point I recognized where Rick got his strong will. From a father that served in the marines and instilled in him discipline and a mother with a strong faith. Together, his parents raised him properly as his story continues.

One night, during his third-class year, while standing watches on the training ship in the engine room, he got the mischievous idea to call the bridge and ask for permission to turn over the props. It was December in Maine and the boilers were lit to give heat for the ship. Both he and his roommate traced out the lines and decided to see just how far they could proceed to start-up the entire engine room.

The senior in charge had left his post, and he knew that a fellow classmate was standing watch on the bridge. The full procedure to light-off a marine power plant from boilers to superheaters, lube oil system, turbines, condensers, ejectors, evaporators and the list goes on and on needs to be learned and understood like the back of your hand. Grabbing the ship's phone and ringing to the bridge,

"Ber-ring, Ber-ring."

The ship's phone on the bridge is answered by Commander Billingsworth who was making an un-announced inspection as he heard, "Permission to disengage the jacking gear and turn over the props."

A very eloquent, **"Who the hell is this speaking?"** barked Commander Billingsworth.

I just slapped my leg and laughed when Rick told me that, as he continued telling the story.

He quickly slammed the phone down and yelled to his roommate, **We're in deep shit!"**

Within seconds, a commander with vehement blasphemy raced down the ladder to the engine room yelling, **"Who the hell is in charge here!"**

The first classman hadn't return yet and he was probably in deeper doo-doo than the both of them as they came to attention. Both were sweating profusely and Commander Billingsworth sized up the situation rather quickly.

"Boilers, Turbines, Reduction Gears, a multi-million-dollar power plant and you two nincompoops' decide to play chief engineer!"

Now they are really sweating!

Commander Billingsworth took off his piss-cutter, side cap, and is walking back and forth while hitting his piss-cutter against his leg.

His eyes are bulging as he looks around and sees that the upper classman isn't present. He scratches his bald head and smoke appears to be emerging from both of his ears as the way I heard it. Then Rick continued his story with,

"This is what I'm going to do," explained a perturbed Commander, "I will trace out the complete start-up of the power plant and if any one thing is left out or missed, if I find one valve not opened or a drain line not used, then the both of you along with the First classman will be expelled from the academy!"

The old man didn't miss a thing, and thank God, they didn't either in the start-up procedure as he scrutinized every pump, valve and gage and finally after two exhausting hours turned to them and said, "I'll be damned, I've got first classmen that can't do a complete start-up!"

He took down their names and said to the both of them, "When you get to be in my turbine class, I will expect nothing but the best from each one of you! Now do a complete shutdown, and I will be watching!"

In unison, they replied, "Yes Sir!"

They both appropriately reversed their steps and shut down the equipment, all except the boilers which were needed for heat, finished their watch and returned to quarters.

And may I add, that they slept well with the relief of not being expelled.

It seems that in every rambunctious youth, they have to learn some things the hard way. Come to think of it, I did too. Through the stress and the strain of making the grade, he relied on his faith, friendships, sports, sailing and the game of chess to be his relief valves. Mighty admirable, and yes, I, Jackson McKenna have some faith but I'm afraid that I turned to Jack Daniels too often, instead of Him above.

I envied that in him for his self-confidence and resilience at such a young age, for it took me longer to gain my self-confidence through the school of hard knocks. I guess I enjoyed his stories due to his enthusiasm and because I never went to the academy or any formal education.

He had two other roommates that year, Walter and Danny. Walt taught him how to play chess and Danny was always his sailing partner. During those first two years, strong friendships were gained and bonds cemented for life and it seemed that he did everything to beat the system. Then during the upperclassmen years, there was a pride that radiated and he started working for the system. He was maturing. The tradition of the academy became more important than their adolescent pranks.

The annual cruises engendered camaraderie and opened a whole new horizon of friendships, places, and opportunities as they were being trained as midshipmen to become commissioned officers and engineers.

The upper classmen years symbolized a transformation from a mug to obey orders, to a leader to take command. Subjects intensified in both their engineering and naval science classes and as they approached their first-class year, there was little time for any leisure.

Naval qualification exams for commissions as reserve officers, fire fighting school, finals for professional degrees and those week-long exams for the third engineers license by the Coast Guard rounded out their final year. It was principally firefighting school that taught him an invaluable lesson. Whenever a person is faced with imminent danger, one has to flex the mind, extend the will and allow courage to bolster you from within.

When Rick told me this story about when the entire first-class, or seniors for you land-lovers, went to firefighting school at the Philadelphia Naval Shipyard, it revealed his inner strength of character.

A prerequisite for any third engineer's or third mate's license is to complete firefighting school. Not just the classroom boredom of instructions but hands-on experience in all phases of firefighting from combustible fluids including napalm, to electrical and combustible materials. One particular morning, Rick was assigned with the group that proceeded to the smoke house.

They suited up in fireproof gear and were issued OBA's, oxygen breathing apparatus. One of the instructors led them to a three-story brick building that didn't have any windows, only steel grating for floors. Climbing the outside of the building to the rooftop, the cadets formed a semicircle around the instructor. He meticulously drew the floor plan on a blackboard to outline the maze to the basement of the building. The cadets climbed through the Bilco Roof Hatch and down the stairs with their OBA's activated.

Pine boughs were heaped in the basement under the grating, sprayed with gasoline and torched. Then more green boughs were heaped on top of the fire to cause thick, white smoke billowing throughout each floor. The thick, putrid smoke permeated throughout the building and out the rooftop. The instructor yelled, "Party time!"

A human chain was formed with their right hand on the shoulder of the person in front of them for you couldn't see anything through the smoke. Once all were on the first floor, each of them had to remove their OBA's and feel their way back through the maze and to the rooftop.

The agonizing smell, the putrid taste, the irritation to the eyes and one's mind racing with the very thought, "What the hell am I doing?"

They learned that day, that there is no reason for anyone to die from smoke inhalation. Just remain calm, keep one's mouth shut and breath shallow through your nose. A good lesson in life for all.

When Rick told me that, I knew then he would be a good fit for the CIA.

Upon successfully completing all requirements there was an added dimension to the gear train, covert interviews by the CIA. Candidates with diversified attributes were required to meet off campus for classified interviews.

The first thought that ran through his mind is, what the hell are diversified attributes?

It is odd, perhaps even funny, but that is one of the thoughts that ran through my mind when I was approached to enter the CIA. A different era, a different time but the same thoughts.

He never did get an answer to that question, neither did I. Arrangements were made that at a designated time, he would be chauffeured to a stately looking house at some designated area. The drive took approximately thirty-five minutes; therefore, it wasn't far from Castine, Maine. A very handsome, distinguished home that had both character and charm. It reminded him of a captain's home who had sailed the seas due to all the nautical paraphernalia from many ports of call.

The interview took three hours by four individuals of various backgrounds. The first was an aide from Senator Margaret Chase Smith's staff who was quite amicable and direct. The next two characters could be from a Perry Mason movie and weren't detracted from his presence, as they read over his file.

The last person, to Rick's surprise, was a Mr. Gardner Pope, his high school principal. Apparently, he was one of the original kibitzers for the CIA and now recommends future candidates for the agency. I don't recall any Gardner Pope during my tenure but too many agents have come and gone through the CIA and the Jack Daniels has dulled my memory.

The aide, who was quite pompous and full of himself, began the process of interviewing Rick, "State your full name for the record."

He gave his full name and then the aide reiterated what the other three were reading from his file.

"You graduated with a 3.64 average and possess:

- Bachelor of Science degree
- Third Engineer's License
- Commission as Ensign in the United States Navy

But what we are mostly interested in, are your diversified attributes!"

Dexter, the aide, continued, "Fourth class year you challenged a first classman to a boxing match. Is that true?"

He simply replied, "Yes Sir!"

"Now on your freshman cruise you reported aboard from liberty out of uniform in Acapulco?"

Again, he replied, "Yes Sir!"

Dexter continued the questioning process with, "Third class year while shipping out on a commercial vessel to Africa, you were AWOL for better than a week missing your ship in Takoradi, Ghana?"

Thinking to himself that this is getting a little boring for he knew these things, he again replied, "Yes Sir!"

Now continuing through his files, "It states here that during your first-class year, your senior year, that you participated in the regular hazing to mugs but not in the horror shows or bilge parties. Is this correct?"

The monotony continued and once again, he replied, "Yes Sir."

"May I ask why?"

He replied emphatically, that he didn't believe in them.

Now the four of them are conferring together but out of ear shot so he could not clearly hear what they are saying. One of the elder gentleman from the CIA who looks older than most, summarizes what the group were discussing and from that surmises his diversified attributes, "You appear to:

- Think on your feet
- Don't cave under pressure
- Have strong beliefs
- Determined
- Strong attitude to make the grade

Have I left anything out?"

He hesitated before smiling and replied, "No Sir!"

Now the other character from the CIA who appeared to be in his mid-fifties spoke up and said, "Would you be interested in serving your country, for your country needs your service?"

He replied, "I wouldn't have accepted my commission, if I didn't want to serve!"

I found it peculiar that Rick answered that question precisely the same way I did, when I was questioned about my patriotism.

Rick then explained how Senator Margaret Chase Smith walked into the room, as he came to attention on deck, out of respect for her. She walked over to her aide and gave him a file. And then as prestigious as she was, she glanced towards Rick, smiled and exited the room. She graciously served the great state of Maine as a U.S. Senator from 1949 to 1973 and was instrumental in our patriotic country as she gave her Declaration of Conscience speech to the U.S. Senate in 1950, four months after Senator Joseph McCarthy accused the State Department of harboring communists. In 1954 Senator Smith cast a vote for McCarthy's censure which effectively ended his political career. Rick remembered reading about her illustrious career in their military code of ethics class as Senator Smith was an active member of both the Naval Affairs and Armed Services Committees.

As the CIA associate continued, Rick was beginning to get the whole picture. It seems that our country long before the advent of computers and cell phones needed people in the field as observers or kibitzers to gather useful data concerning global threats.

Different skill levels are needed as different threats evolve. Current events do not change how the CIA recruits its next generation of people but due to existing global threats of espionage, weapons, drugs and human trafficking many eyes and ears were needed as spectators to intercept the many threads of information of crime.

Before the adjournment of the interview, he was told that he would be notified at a future date for inception and for security reasons this meeting never took place. Each successive decade has seen caustic times and a toxic organization is necessary to deter perilous coercion.

One event that Rick talked about intrigued McKenna. It was the traditional ceremony at the merchant marine academy known as a Ring-Dance. An event where the young ladies wear their beautiful gowns and the cadets their dress whites for an evening that is special, formal and exhilarating. He had invited a young, charming girl that upon graduation from high school wrote in his year book that if he ever had mail box blues to write to her. Well, by the end of his mug year he did write and enjoyed a three-year bliss dating her.

Upon making graduation he did not have the money to buy a class ring and so borrowed his roommate's ring for the gala festivities of the ring dance, since the roommate wasn't attending the formal ceremony. The evening was beautiful, and their feelings deepened with each passing moment.

True love in life is rare to find and when one finds it, one needs to become more retrospective and perceive things from all sides. Once he entered the realm of the CIA, he knew down deep that it would be difficult to explain the inexplicable and forever lost touch with her. He always felt gilt-ridden about that, and I for one could empathize with him. For I never married, one of the facets for serving with the CIA.

Graduation was not the culmination of four strenuous years of training and studies but only the beginning path of a diverse, intricate career. His flight to Dulles International Airport was short, dull and monotonous; barely enough time to gather his thoughts of, "am I doing the right thing?"

His folks were under the impression that he was on his way to New York to board a ship bound for Africa. He never told them of the side-stop at Langley, Virginia at the CIA Headquarters.

Each candidate was assigned a mentor who was more than just a coach but continually evaluated their mental psyche to foresee any hidden agendas or problems. From the very first day of signing the line it was made crystal clear that once you sign up, you better suck it up! His mentor's nickname was, "checkmate," for he was always a move ahead of him.

As we talked, I told Rick that my mentor's name was, "dynamite," for if anyone pissed him off, he exploded. I remember on one occasion five of the green recruits sneaking out one night for a few drinks. That was a big mistake for upon their return, they had to run around the athletic field 365 times, one lap for each day of the year. Dynamite told the green recruits that he was being kind because it wasn't leap year. Needless to say, no one finished the 365 laps and five individuals were dismissed from the program. One either learns or dies from discipline!

We both had a good laugh over that!

Indoctrination has been the same since the agencies inception that covered:

- History of the CIA
- Mission
- Law Enforcement
- Paper Work
- Polygraph Testing
- Assignments

There were nineteen of them in the, "Welcome to the Kibitzer Class", a class without any ceremony or graduation. It doesn't even exist as far as the outside world is concerned. To his surprise there were two other midshipmen from his class at the merchant marine academy. He presumed that the others were from the various military academies across the country. He never found out their names or where they were from. None of them were allowed to associate with the other candidates but interacted only with mentors and instructors.

Twelve intense weeks of taking a snapshot of our trouble world and learning to be an intricate commodity to gather and transmit valuable information for the sole purpose of national security. Then, if they passed the psyche evaluation, transferred to a military base outside of the United States for rapid information skill kibitzer training known as RISK.

The Central Intelligence Agency was created on July 26, 1947 when then President Harry S. Truman signed the National Security Act into law. Back then the major impetus for the creation of the CIA was the unforeseen attack on Pearl Harbor. A few years later the first training facility was established as a clearinghouse for foreign policy intelligence and have been expanding their roles ever since.

When Rick took any break from the classes, he would take a walk outside to get a breath of fresh air and always pass the statue of Nathan Hale which serves as a constant reminder of the duties and sacrifices for all. It is amazing that no matter how much United States History one studies, the richness of our foundation comes alive from the settlers, founding fathers and our constitution. For Hale was a captain in George Washington's Army during the Revolutionary War. He volunteered to collect information on the British forces. On his first and only mission, he was caught by the British, found guilty of espionage and executed. His last words were, "I regret that I have but one life to lose for my country."

If one is not inspired by those provocative words, then that person doesn't belong in the CIA training.

As one is being trained to become a vital asset, there are many thoughts rushing through your mind. The human being is a complex being of mind, soul and body. Our mind grasps and leads us one way while the soul and heart lead us in another direction with the body in the middle of the twist, turns and tugs of life.

Rick's mentor during those weeks also became his good friend and taught him the value to discern and overcome the impalpable. This advice became invaluable especially when he went through those stupid polygraph sessions where one is accused of lying, just so they can get your reaction.

He was fortunate, for my mentor was a back-stabbing bastard, that caused me, Jackson McKenna, to never trust anyone and always watch your back.

The indoctrination concluded successfully and Rick climbed aboard a Boeing C-17 military transport bound for the United States Army Garrison at Fort Buchanan in Puerto Rico. In a corner of the base there was a CIA training compound where they would advance their knowledge on how to listen, infiltrate, communicate and literary kidnap information known as LICK.

Four of them were sent to that island, to most a paradise to enjoy but not for them as another six weeks of vigorous training to see and retain everything.

From sunrise to sunset all they ever heard ringing in their ears is, "Snapshot, see with a snapshot and retain what you see!"

They would sit in a self-contained booth and watch a video clip. They were taught the dynamics of total concentration. Focus on a screen for twenty seconds. Then the fun would begin! The screen was shut off.

"What did you see?"

"How many people in the shot?"

"How many vehicles in the picture?"

"Did you see any weapons?"

"How many weapons?"

"The signs in the picture, what did they read?"

Get the picture, from what I understand from him, he failed miserably the first few times as the process was continually repeated. He was in snapshot hell!

I laughed at that comment of his, for our regimented trainings were as different as day and night. For agents concentrated on self-defense, marksmanship and liquidating the enemy. After my tour in the Army, I had no problem in doing just that!

But eventually he learned his lessons well and could see the pictures in his dreams and remember every detail to the last letter. Once they could write down every detail seen in the pictures, then they graduated to the real thing.

They were taken to a warehouse and once inside were allowed to study the premises for one whole minute. After a full minute they were removed and taken to a second place to observe and then the fun began. For each person had to recall what they had seen at both places.

"What is the setting?" the instructor asked.

Rick replied, "I am in a bank."

"How many people in the bank?"

He closed his eyes and concentrated as his mind raced through the people in the bank and replied, "There are twenty-four people in the bank that can be accounted for."

The instructor replied, "Good, now describe them and where they are positioned in the bank."

The training taught each kibitzer that when entering any room or building; take a snapshot with their brain and memorize clockwise from left to right.

"To the extreme left, an office with one person behind the desk speaking to two other people seated in front of the desk. Next is the bank vault with one personnel inside the safe. Three tellers with two people in the first line, three people in the next line and five people in the third line. On the right side, another office with two people inside the office. There are two center service tables with three people at the first one and two people at the second one. Finally, there are two offices upstairs and no one is in the left cubicle but there are some people in the right cubicle because I can hear them speak, but I could not see them."

Rick passed giving a detailed description of both places and some admiration from his instructors. He learned well and as time progressed the scenarios of multifarious environments, places and peoples changed.

Each new kibitzer needed to hone their skills to perceptive sharpness as to descriptions, numbers and colors. It is all about details. Details are missed by most people according to the police description records. Your brain is the best computer in the world and with the proper training, it is better than any camera or recording equipment for there is no residual evidence.

This is nothing like those "007 movies" with the fancy gadgets, weapons, cliff-hanging assaults and masterful escapes. This is tedious, mind-bending tactics to outfox the enemy wherever the crime may be; but with the same danger and harrowing consequences if caught. There will always exist people whom their God is money, greed and power; hence, every crime and infamy possible will be committed.

The training sessions changed from the orchestrated to the live actions of metropolitan life. With the recruitment, paperwork, briefing and initial training behind them, the next stage was the torture test.

The night before the trial of torment that better than half of the recruits fail, their first liberty was permitted. Puerto Rico is a lovely island known as the Gibraltar of the Caribbean. Have you ever seen a sunrise from Bayamon or a sunset from Mayaguez? Breath-taking, simply breath-taking. The drinks were a welcome relief, the food scrumptious and the camaraderie couldn't have been any better. The rules were broken for once as first names were shared, some memories of their previous lives discussed, and friendships solidified.

Danny was one of Rick's roommates from their academy days. He was colorful especially with his red hair but full of piss and vinegar and always eager to do the job.

Trevor and Sinclair were from different worlds and from different military academies. They came from affluent families and had no wants or needs for they had it all. Sports cars, yachts, best educations and what most would consider enviable lives, so why the CIA? Boredom with life! Sad but true. The caveat to the CIA is simply this, once you're in, owner beware! Before the end of the evening, friendships were made and Trevor cordially asked,

"What's your first name?"

"He simply replied, Rick!"

Trevor quickly said with a friendly reply, "Always watch your back!"

Dawn brought a new day, a slight hang-over and their first torture test to see if coercion would be a possibility. It was really a simple test that required one pair of channel-locks. Individually, they were led into a small room, seated and the terms of the exercise were explained.

The certitude of the CIA throughout the years has been structured from the nefarious facets of kidnappings, tortures and loss of life! Forged through the fires of deception, mayhem and wars; if any covert operator is captured then his resolve for valor not to buckle under coercion must be tested.

Simply, if one is squeamish or cannot bear the pain, there is no gain and one does not pass go! There is no fanfare, absolutely no reaction and no utterance of sound can be made. Mum is the word! Ignore the pain and you pass.

Rick sat there as the associate opened his mouth, grabbing for a pair of channel-locks and ripped out his upper molar, third on the right side without any Novocain. He sat there expressionless and did not utter a single sound, but as Rick explained it to me, wanted to kick that bastard in the groin more than anything else!

Before finishing phase two of the covert training, code names were given out to each successful candidate.

McKenna laughed as Rick told the story of code names. His code name became 274. Since kibitzers worked alone, and the CIA felt that friendships were a liability, each of them were sent to different military bases to complete their final phase of training. Rick hopped a flight to the Rodman Naval Air Station in Panama.

The United States, concurrent with the construction of the Panama Canal maintained numerous military bases to protect American-owned interest and maintain strategic control of Central America. Fort Sherman was the primary Caribbean-side infantry base, while Fort Amador protected the Pacific side. And again, he found himself being transported to Fort

Amador, a short trek from the Rodman Naval Air Station to begin his last phase of training. During this period, Richard Milhous Nixon was our President and the New York Times began publishing the classified Pentagon Papers on the U.S. involvement in Vietnam. Up to this point in his life, he never really considered the ubiquitous horrors from war and crime throughout the world. It seems neither one ever stops.

I told Rick on one of our conversations, that one has to fight in a war to fully comprehend all the horrors of war.

The training intensified for him, his perception was sharpened, and the necessary multiple codes were learned. He never realized how colorful our history was in Central America with the long-standing relations with General Noriega, who served as a kibitzer for the CIA and a paid informant from 1967 and beyond, including the period when Bush headed the CIA.

Noriega played the U.S. like a marionette; he pulled the strings and got paid from all sides. He received sums of money upwards of $100,000 per year from the 1960's and then an increase as he worked with the DEA and CIA sabotaging the forces of the Sandinista government in Nicaragua and the revolutionaries of the FMLN group in El Salvador. Although he worked with the DEA to restrict illegal drug shipments, the crafty bastard simultaneously accepted significant financial support from drug dealers for the laundering of their drug money. In due time, his two-faced shenanigans would backfire!

Many philosophers take intrinsic values to be crucial to a variety of moral judgements. The one that Rick should have made was not to get involved in the first place with the CIA. But the coercion of evil for;

- Human trafficking for organs
- Arms deals with Rogue Nations
- Espionage
- Drugs
- Assassination Squads

And the list goes on and on and never sleeps or allow the innocent to be safe.

In a world of so much infamy, our mind, eyes and ears are our best weapons to detect the unthinkable before the storm, as the questions intensify and our concentrated efforts improve.

Rick's training intensified for now there are snapshots and sound-shots as the instructor yells,

"How many people are carrying weapons and what do you hear?"

He found it more difficult for the ear to be in-tune with his surroundings, then the comprehension of sights to know what is happening. Multiple noises can camouflage each other from a gunshot, a car backfire and a small combustible explosion to trick your senses. Adjusting one's mind to comprehend what exactly one hears is no easy task but as each day passed, improvement was made. The simulation in a classroom training is one thing but genuine experience separates the mediocre kibitzer from the good ones. Progression to the real-life scene of one of the largest cargo ports in Balboa, Panama sharpened their adeptness.

Many ships passed under the Puente de las Americas, Bridge of the Americas, and thousands of containers were either off-loaded or loaded in one of the largest container ports in the world. First, one must look for signs or codes that trigger where to look. One of the symbols that all kibitzers were trained to look for was the symbol of the "Devil's Advocate" that looked like this image.

छिद्रान्वेषी

Used extensively in the black trade industry for human trafficking, with an "H" stamped beneath it or an "A" for arms or a "D" for drugs. One of the worlds largest crime syndicates based in Russia known as the "Kdy-10" which stood for "devil's claw" had global ramifications. The Kogot'd'yavola were notorious in all aspects of the black market shawdow economy.

Upon graduating from the merchant marine academy, the United States had thousands of ships on the high seas. Shipping on the high seas received a boost when Congress passed the Merchant Marine Act of 1970, which extended the terms of the 1936 act.

That initial vitality faltered when President Richard M. Nixon's "73" budget slashed all funding of the program. This was followed by the end of the Vietnam War and less need for a large merchant marine fleet. The downsizing continued with the disrupting dockside union strike.

The United States Merchant Marine dwindled to twenty-sixth place. The worlds leading commercial fleets were now Panama, Liberia, China and Russia. And along with a transition from cargo holds to containerized vessels, illegal trafficking boomed in the distribution of prohibited goods and services of drugs, arms and prostitution. Now a ship could make a turn-around in hours versus days which made the jobs to detect the contraband and apprehend the perpetratraors extremely difficult as the training instructor yelled.

"Scan with your eyes, snapshot and look for the signs, codes, anything out of the ordinary!"

There are many codes to distinguish but literally with 17 million shipping containers in the world and some 3500 containers per ship, the black market developed a system to code, access and distribute the contraband which law enforcement had to continually track and crack to beat their system known as CAD.

Law enforcements countermove was also known as CAD but stood for crack, assess and destroy. He learned to snapshot the view of the ship to remember the name and the country's flag that it was flying. And more importantly for his eyes to scan the many containers to catch the hidden codes of contraband. This along with listening for sounds to detect the unusual. Cracking, hissing, tapping, any sounds that would alert them to the contraband of arms, drugs and human trafficking.

Agents of the CIA were trained in espionage, self-defence and military tactics whereas kibitzers were trained in reconnaissance, surveillance and not to get caught. Jungle warfare was added to the agenda for if one was captured, then escape was essential within the first 24-48 hours or pay the price of death. The only thing that he could say about that is, "He hated poisonous snakes, spiders, scorpions and jaw snapping crocodiles. He was in jungle hell and couldn't do the Tarzan yell."

There is nothing alluring or romantic about this career except the need to stop the maliciousness of the crimes that undermines society. The strategy behind any capture was known as "CREED" where one was to remain calm, because a calm head comes up with a solution versus one that panics. Rally oneself to escape and evade recapture and then with the training received in jungle warfare, defend oneself. Whether it was hand to hand, use of one's belt or shoe lacings, survive the ordeal any which-way that you can. With the conclusion of the jungle warfare, it was time to put the investment of training to work. All assignments had one link in common, intercept any information that underminds the national security of the United States.

CHAPTER 2

LAGOS

His first assignment was on the Barrier Reef as a third engineer, bound for Africa and reported to the Captain who was aware of his status with the CIA. Throughout the merchant marine fleet, selected ships were used for covert operations depending on their ports-of-call. There were only two people on board that would know his status, the captain and sparks, the radio operator. CIA Kibitzers are not on the roster, for they don't even exist.

A kibitzer, as he learned, is a Yiddish term for a spectator or derived from the German kiebitzen, to look over a card-player's shoulder, an observer, but here lies the catch-22; one had to learn to blend-in without raising any suspicions or pay the price.

The transit across the Atlantic Ocean would take six days and the only leisure time, when not standing watches, were for playing cribbage or chess. He needed something more rigorous and as he climbed topside to the flying bridge, cheers and yelling were coming from the stern of the ship. A boxing ring was set up on one of the cargo hatch covers with some of the crew members sparring off.

"Perfect," he thought to himself, "Boxing is just what he needed."

He viewed the ring with great propensity and decided to head towards the aft end of the ship and get in line. This was a little different from his boxing days at the Boy's Club in Waterville, Maine where he grew-up. Even the boxing lessons learned at the Academy were different for there were rules; this was bashing and staying on your feet. No gloves, no rules, just last man standing! His previous experiences shipping out as a cadet, taught him one thing, always be prepared for the unexpected.

Rick has been tossed overboard, gotten his nose busted and his two front teeth broken from previous boxing excursions. In the merchant marine, there is no such thing as fighting but only what they call brawling. No one is worth their weight if you cannot handle four to five on-takers.

He got in line and his hands were taped while looking across the ring to size-up his opponent. A young German man about six-one and maybe between 30 to 32 years of age. He was just a bit taller and a might heavier. No rules meant bash, evade and survive any which way you can. The bell rang as they both danced to the middle of the ring. The German came out swinging, his left hook felt like a baseball bat and his right punch like a sludge hammer. Rick stayed away from his right and played to his left. The punches were fast, hard and relentless. His tactics to evade were useless because his opponent had a longer reach. The only recourse was to move in quickly with a left and then a right and stay away from his deadly right. With a quick punch of his right and a snap of the elbow to his opponent's jaw; the young German fighter was down for the count. Time and experience seasons all; Rick was no longer a boxer, but a merchant marine brawler.

The duration of the cruise allowed him to make a couple of good friends, one being the bosun mate who also boxed regularly and was an avid chess player along with the 1st Engineer who enjoyed a good game of cribbage.

Lagos, Nigeria's largest city, sprawls beautifully inland from the Gulf of Guinea overlooking Lagos Lagoon. Victoria Island, the financial center is well known for its beach resorts, boutiques and terrific nightlife.

He was fully briefed in Panama about the LL, Inc. company better known as Lagos Logistics, a joint venture between Lexington Group of Belgium and the Russian conglomerate Berezniki Global to manufacture machinery and aircraft parts. A front for weapons manufacture and distribution to the highest bidder. Berezniki Global with connections to the chemical industry masterminded the production of chemical bombs and drug smuggling.

Lagos Logistics, conveniently located between two airports and the police college, had the means and wherefore to smuggle and export products from either the Murtala Muhammed Airport or the Lagos Airport. Another caveat for the company, was the paid-off protection of the local police department.

Part of the conglomerate were the O'dua Investment Corporation and the Lexington Group which were world leaders in the manufacture of affordable and sustainable building solutions. Strategically located on a massive acreage spread with state-of-the-art production facilities. This along with administrative, recreational and residential centers; it was a major player in the Nigerian economy and number-one on the CIA's international smuggler's hit list.

Alamosa Osife, a friendly chap who possessed some panache and spoke with a British accent, was the covert contact in Lagos. A MI6 agent working with the CIA in Africa on scuttlebutt picked up by the NSA about some encrypted message known as **"SZESTU".**

The common question asked by all intelligence agencies was, "What the hell is SZESTU?"

Contrary to public opinion and those romanticized movies, spying is tedious and long hours of observation. One must be astute to connect the dots, put the pieces of the puzzle together with as few clues as possible, so not to alarm the opposition.

Alamosa being extremely fluent in Russian, frequented the establishments where liquor and entertainment loosened their lips and imbibed their morals. Ladies of the evening catered to their every whim of desire and there were a few courtesans that were on the payroll of MI6. Especially at the Galleria Dream and Drum Beat Coliseum which were renown lounges where the upper management of Lagos Logistics patronized.

Clue gathering is fastidious work. The information gathered over the next few months between the excursions within the ship yards, night clubs and especially Lagos Logistics laid the ground work for a major global investigation. This was only the tip of the iceberg and since Rick was stationed on the Barrier Reef, he had carte blanche access to the ship yards of many container ships.

What at first appeared to be a difficult assignment, unraveled an intricate plan as he identified the symbol of the "Devil's Advocate." On many of the containers which were loaded in Russia and bound for Lagos Logistics, had the one distinguishable mark that raised a red flag. There was the letter "C" under each symbol. When he told Alamosa about the distinguishing mark, a perturbed look came over his face as he questioned, "What do chemicals have to do with Lagos Logistics?"

Alamosa in-turn contacted his connections at MI6 to scrutinize which port of origin the containers of chemicals came from. The name of the ship that anchored in Lagos Lagoon was the Raevsky II. It didn't take long for the combined effects of agents from both MI6 and the CIA to close the net. All information pinpointed to the port of Novorossiysk, Russia.

Unaware that Trevor was the kibitzer sent to Istanbul to monitor ships sailing from the Black Sea, efforts were intensified to find the missing pieces to the puzzle. The difference between a professional and amateur covert agent is not simply the years of experience but being attentive vs careless, keeping your mouth shut vs brash lips and honor to do your duty instead of paid for hire.

One event that intrigued Rick about most subversive agents is their utter gullibility to divulge too much information with each drink. One must be patient and listen for the clues.

One night while patronizing the Galleria Dream, enjoying the exotic dancers and nonchalantly watching for signs, the clues started to surface. The amazement of the utter buffoonery of the male ego. That need to brag or impress the opposite sex. "Loose lips sink ships," is damn good advice not heeded by many. The questions in our line of work always remain the same; the five "W's" and that very important "H". All that we received was scuttlebutt about some term known as SZESTU, but were still oblivious as to what it is, who are the perpetrators, where will the event happen, when will it occur, why and how?

Eventually brash lips become loose and they trip over their own tongues. Alamosa had a sixth sense as whom to tail and waited for a signal from one of the young ladies of the evening as she gave him the nod on one drunken customer. He meandered over to the bar and listened to his banter as the customer bragged and said, "What a boom, this explosion will destroy anything within three hundred feet."

He continued to try and impress the young courtesan as he continued, "We will test another unit tomorrow and the world will be surprised!"

"Bingo," this is exactly what they have been waiting for as Alamosa followed the suspects and Rick headed back to the ship to await further instructions.

The suspects led Alamosa to one of the warehouses of Lagos Logistics with security guards stationed around the establishment. Alamosa thought to himself, "why would a machinery manufacturer have so many security guards for their warehouses?"

In the shadows of the night, Alamosa made his stealthy way to a mobile crane parked by the side of the warehouse with the crane fully extended. Inching his way down the side of the warehouse towards the crane, he heard the whining of guard dogs on the chase from a distance. He quickly surmised that time was of the essence and made a mad dash to the crane and found it difficult to climb the extended arm to the rooftop. The humid night air caused much condensation on the metal extension arm of the crane. Avoiding the dogs and security guards, he made his way along the rooftop to the dormer windows.

Peering through the windows, he noticed materials of C-4, and other components laid out on a table. There were about six people assembling what looked like generator units, but with an added feature. They were fabricating enough explosive material for one hell of a bomb!

The next day Rick kept himself busy with duties on the ship as he anticipated some news from Alamosa. Meanwhile, Alamosa kept a close surveillance on the suspects that loaded a semi-trailer with generator units bound for a mining complex just north of Ibadan.

It was a two-hour drive to the destination and a fifteen-minute drive on an abandoned road that alerted the terrorist of a tail. Alamosa previously alerted MI6 for some satellite observations of the Ibadan area. Fortuitous for them that he did, for satellite detection picked up a huge explosion which alerted the free world of prep-work for possible terrorism.

Alamosa wasn't so fortunate, as two thugs apprehended him, bound him to a tree and slowly tortured him. They began with his extremities and cut off his arms and legs while he screamed in agonizing pain. It is unimaginable to understand the excruciating pain he must have endured. Then before he expiated, they beheaded Alamosa. The message of such gruesome acts is to intimidate and coerce horror throughout the free world. But the truth of the matter, it provokes our resolve to stop such acts of aggression.

One of the attributes of evil is terrorism, which creates a complete pandemonium. Journalists from around the world call it mayhem, extreme violence, fear and panic. It doesn't matter which descriptions they use, because the utter chaos that terrorism causes, solidifies the efforts to completely eradicate the evil!

This is where Rick meets the callous CIA agent for the first time, Jackson McKenna, rough, tough and an old Master Sergeant from WW–II, who hand delivers his new orders.

Unshaven, unkempt but sharp and had a memory like a hawk, he introduced himself with, “You’re a young pup!”

He continued by saying, “No time for any melancholy crape, one good agent is down and we need to finish this job!”

The startling news upset Rick, as the grimace on his face and the melancholy stare in his eyes showed some grief. Reality has no time for emotions, it just plows forward! The jolts in life either inspires our courage or deters it.

Jackson McKenna would eventually become mentor for all four greenhorn kibitzers; that is if each of them could survive his unorthodox style and the various nuances of espionage.

That evening they took a drive to a construction site just Northwest of Ibadan. The kibitzer did the driving and I did all the talking. Always scanning the horizon for trouble and constantly giving warnings to the kibitzer, “watch the rear-view mirror for a tail.”

About a mile from the construction site, two trucks appeared from no-where and Jackson told the kibitzer to shut off the car lights and keep driving. Squinting his eyes and trying to avoid hitting those damn huge baobab trees, Jackson yelled, “Turn off this road and shut off the engine!”

The kibitzer’s heart pulsated at double-time and he perspired profusely until the two trucks sped pass. I turned towards him and said, “Relax, this is only the beginning, steady yourself for the long haul!”

Then I quickly tossed to the kibitzer a forty-five and said, “Be prepared, safety off and there’s fifteen in the chamber!”

We cautiously meandered through the trees to the construction site and surveyed the area. A sizable gravel pit about four hundred yards wide extended before us, not a good place to be caught in the open. I got on my knees and cautioned the kibitzer to do the same. Looking around the perimeter and watching for shadows in the distance, a gunshot whizzed by my head.

“Hug the ground!” I shouted to the kibitzer and fired two rounds towards the direction of the gun fire.

Then I signaled for the kibitzer to stay low as I crawled to the outer edge of the pit. After several minutes of being motionless,

I remembered yelling, "OK, let's move to the center of the pit. The rest of the perpetrators must have moved on."

There was quite a large crater in the center of the blast zone and I bent down to grab for a handful of dirt and sniffed the contents.

Turning towards the kibitzer and deciding to call him by his real name I said, "You know Rick, there's a common misconception that TNT and dynamite are the same, but they are not. In fact, TNT is a specific chemical compound, whereas dynamite is an absorbent mixture soaked in nitroglycerin that is compressed into a cylindrical shape and wrapped in paper. Based on the explosive potential of nitroglycerin, dynamite is considered a high explosive which means it detonates instead of deflagrating or burn away. Now look at that crater hole."

Always the teacher to these young, unseasoned types, thank God, for the classroom was over and one slight mistake in the field meant their life!

Walking towards the edge of the crater hole and judging from its size, I said to Rick, "This looks like TNT with C-4," shaking my head as I continued, "Less than a pound of C-4 could potentially kill several people, and I'm afraid that it is the primary weapon of most terrorist's arsenals. And what we have here is allot more than a pound of the stuff, judging from the size of that crater."

Turning back and walking towards our vehicle, Rick stopped and surmised the situation as he asked me, "What the hell are they up to?"

It's the years of experience that made me knowledgeable, with the years of scars that go along with learning some things the hard way. I began to like this inexperienced pup, kibitzer, which probably made me more talkative on the way back as I reminisced about the good-old-days. Then I pulled out a small bottle of Jack Daniels from my jacket's pocket and took a swig before offering the bottle to him as I said, "At least those bastards haven't graduated to Semtex or HMX, yet!"

Grabbing for the bottle to take another swig before saying, "You know, I was stationed here in 1967 at our embassy during the Biafran War. That was a hell of a blood bath and it was an excuse for many of the native tribes to kill each other, especially between the Yoruba and Ibo tribes."

I took another two swigs before saying, "Because of the different factions, tribal hatreds led to revolts by army officials, and there were political assassinations and the killing of thousands of Ibo tribesmen. There is still much bitterness over that civil war and Lagos is still a bad port for contraband!"

I took another swig before throwing the bottle away as Rick chided, "Hey, I wanted another swig myself."

Smiling and being amused by this young pup, I just pulled out another bottle from my other jacket pocket and said, "I always travel with two!"

Then I continued this one-sided conversation by commenting, "there is no rhyme or reason for terrorism but without any formal governments, there is no law and order, hence, chaos abounds!"

Then I went on reminiscing about my time at the Iranian Embassy and the people's Mujahedin terrorist organization. Old warriors, as we age never die; we just talk you to death.

Before dropping him off at the shipyard, I gave him a stern warning, "Watch your back, there are eyes everywhere including on your ship!"

Then I told him, "Time is of the essence, we need to find out their plan, and pronto!"

As I sped off to some hole in the wall place where I stayed, Rick felt some relief that we would be working together. He realized then that Jackson McKenna was the mentor needed in order to stay alive.

The wanton criminal mind knows no boundaries; respects no laws and will do whatever it needs to accomplish its end. Hence, the necessity of a National Security Agency, NSA responsible for global monitoring, collection and processing of information for counterintelligence purposes. Unlike the Defense Intelligence Agency, DIA and the Central Intelligence Agency, CIA, both of which specialize in foreign human espionage, the NSA does not conduct human source gathering. And that is where the CIA program of kibitzers come into the picture; for wire taping and satellites can only gather half of the pieces to the puzzle, the other half is by espionage and kibitzers.

Long-Range Tracking and Identification known as LRIT, is an international tracking and identification system incorporated by the IMO, International Maritime Organization under its SOLAS convention to ensure a thorough tracking system for ships throughout the world. But rogue ships don't register and there was enough intelligence gathering that four rogue ships originated from Novorossiysk, Russia, their main port on the Black Sea.

Hence, new orders came forthright for McKenna and the new kibitzer, as both were bound on a merchant ship for Istanbul.

Five days at sea gave us time for better acquaintances. For Rick to get romped in cribbage by a pro, and time for some boxing, but more importantly learning some of the idiosyncrasies of each other.

There are many perks to card playing besides the enjoyment of the game. Camaraderie, developing instincts and learning the aggressive moves of your opponent. The best of all benefits is the warm-hearted conversations.

Rick watched and learned from his mentor, McKenna, how he always sat with his back towards the bulkhead and made sure that there were two means of egress. He even got to enjoy McKenna's war stories immensely as at one-point McKenna asked Rick, "What did your dad do during the war?"

While dealing another hand, Rick explained to me that during the war, his dad had served his entire campaign in the Pacific with the marines at such death-defiant places like Guam, Guadalcanal, Bougainville, Solomon Islands and Okinawa.

Looking towards him across the table, I then said, "That explains the discipline of your upbringing, it is more than just the academy years, isn't it?"

He shook his head in the affirmative, as he continued to talk about his adolescent years of growing up in a small town of Maine.

Istanbul is a great seaport and a gateway between two continents separated by two narrow straits, the Dardanelles and the Bosporus with the Sea of Marmara between them. The most important city in Turkey, all ships sailing between Russia's Black Sea ports and the Mediterranean Sea must pass by Istanbul. Rick enjoyed the view from the ship's rail and the perspective of an ancient culture very rich in history.

Throughout ancient times, it has been seized multiple times from the Greeks in the 7th century to the Romans and the Ottoman Turks with many new names of Byzantium, Constantinople as well as Istanbul, the bridge between Europe and Asia.

Rick climbed topside as we approached our port to see the panoramic view of the city rising above the bazaars and buildings to witness three of Turkey's glorious sights, the mosques of Mahmud and Sultan Ahmet along with the massive-domed church of Sancta Sophia with their minarets all pointing towards heaven.

Major funding of terrorism comes from the drug trade and Turkey sits at the center of a drug-smuggling crossroads. Synthetic drugs transit from West to East, while opiates move in the opposite direction. According to the British Foreign Office, as much as 80% of all heroin used in Britain has come through Turkey. A cohort of Russia, Iran sponsors many terrorism activities and our troubles were just beginning as the two countries funneled drugs, money and their acts of coercion through Turkey.

The ship docked and as the gangway was lowered, a tall, lean fellow climbed aboard. Jackson recognized the individual as he yelled to him, "I guess they allow all sorts of degenerates aboard!"

The tall, lean fellow looked up towards the upper deck and once he spied Jackson gave a mighty laugh and replied, "Looks like the degenerates are already on board."

The two men met on the lower deck and Jackson beckoned me to come forward and introduced his old-time associate and friend, Altan Tiryaki which in Turkish means crimson sunrise.

Then Jackson introduced me as agent 274.

They both laughed as Altan said, "Just call me "AT" for I don't get into that James Bond baloney!"

He further continued by saying, "In this business two things are important, watch your back and true friendships; and friendships mean real names."

Rick took a liking to AT immediately as he said, "My real name is Rick!"

After a firm handshake, we proceeded to the Thrills & Spills of Babylon, a lounge in the Beyoglu district patronize by every drug lord in Istanbul. Known for its middle eastern style food, harem-like design and belly-dancing-shows along with the great Bosphorus view, AT revealed what he learned about the rogue ships.

"I'm not sure of the number of Russian ships involved in the whole operation but here is what I do know. There are four rogue ships to smuggle drugs, chemicals and supplies to support covert operations all based out of Novorossiysk, Russia. The Kiev, Nikolai and Vladivostok are in port now in Novorossiysk. The Raevsky II which you observed in Lagos makes regular runs with chemicals and sometimes drugs. There are other ships but I haven't learned their names or whereabouts."

AT stopped long enough to enjoy his drink and the view of exotic dancers before saying, "Now, tomorrow we will travel to Hopa by truck and board a fishing trawler that goes out for mullet, herring and anchovies. We will head up the coast to Novorossiysk and see what we can learn about these ships."

Jackson asked, "Any problems along the coast?"

AT smiled and said, "Just those damn Russian destroyers! They have fired upon two trawlers in the past month and sank one this past week."

Then AT turned to me and asked with a deep laugh, "Are you a good swimmer?"

I replied, "Pochemu konechno!" which meant, why of course, in Russian.

And he replied, "Cok iyi." Which meant, very good in Turkish.

The overland trail was pleasant, if you like potholes every three feet, but it turned out to be a beautiful, sunny day as we arrived in Hopa. Boarding a fishing trawler reminded Rick of his youth days when he went lobstering off the coast of Maine. Everything was fine until he popped open the bait barrel and got a whiff of that foul smell. It just clung to his nostrils. Well, all fish have that same odor, but fortunate for all, this time he didn't barf over the wrong side of the boat.

The plan was simple, travel by day under the guise of fishing, and do the excursion at night into Russian waters to the port of Novorossiysk. God willing, it will go well!

AT had scuba gear aboard and asked Rick if he did any scuba diving?

His response was short and simple that he was in the scuba club at the academy. AT just smiled and said, "You will be my assistant!"

It was fortunate for us that the Russian destroyers were patrolling off to the west as we steadily made our way along the coast to Novorossiysk. Overcast skies meant no visible moon which made our boat a shadow upon the waters as we quietly proceeded into the port. AT said, "Time to put on our scuba gear."

The waters were cold, dark and murky as we descended below. AT ignited an underwater flare to see two attached DPV units under the bottom of the boat. Diver propulsion vehicles were strapped to the bottom of the stern to avoid detection if searched. AT lead the way and I followed in pursuit to the docked ships.

All international ships of more than 300 tons are mandated to carry a transponder that broadcasts their position, course and speed as a collision avoidance system. The automatic identification system known as AIS, is data transmitted through very high frequency, VHF radio waves. A ship's captain can switch the device off to avoid being detected, hence the purpose for our escapade to attach magnetic transmitters to the ship's propeller.

Before the dawn of a new day, transmitters were attached to the Kiev, Nikolai and the Vladivostok. Each ship had their own black box and could be detected by either satellite or submarine. The signals from the transmitters were clear even with the cavitation caused by the props.

Now, all we had to do is get out of there undetected. Then the cat and mouse game of wait and see where each ship was bound for. The trip back to Hopa should have been uneventful as a Russian guided missile destroyer, the Smetlivyy, was spotted off the port side of our boat.

The Kashin-class destroyers were built for the Soviet Navy in the 1960's and 70's and their Soviet designation is Project 61. Admiral Viktor Sergeyevich Sysoyev is in-charge of the Black Sea Fleet, a fleet of enormous historical and political importance for Russia. But to understand the belligerent, punitive attitude of Russia, one must have a thorough understanding of Russian history.

The homeland of Russia has been inhabited by people for thousands of years and its first modern state was founded in 862 A.D. by King Rurik, ruler of Novgorod.

Comparatively speaking a fascinating history when one considers that our first colony that survived at Plymouth Rock was in 1620 and the United States Constitution established in 1776.

Throughout the centuries, the Slavic peoples lived under the authority of kings, tsars, multiple wars and brutal revolutions. Revolutions were ignited in present times by the fuse of Karl Marx with his Manifesto. The foundation for brutality was laid by such harsh leaders as Lenin and Stalin and further infused within their society by such dastardly leaders like Khrushchev, Brezhnev and Kosygin.

This is before the era of a Mikhail Gorbachev, a leader that tried to bring about positive change of freedom of speech and openness of government, "Glasnost", and a restructuring of the economy, "Perestroika." The Russian people have become throughout the centuries callous in their attitude, beliefs and perception due to heartless leaders, countless wars and endless revolutions. Trust therefore within the people is lost and without trust, truth never abounds.

The fishing trawler was only a mile out from Novorossiysk as the Russian destroyer illuminated our boat with searchlights and fired across our bow. Our skipper stopped the engines so that the Russians could exercise their right to board our fishing trawler. The entire purlieu around the Black Sea is considered part of the Russian homeland despite the fact that Turkey joined NATO in 1952.

Jackson McKenna winked at Rick and gestured with his hand as if to zip his lip. He understood the message not to speak as the Russian crew climbed aboard. AT was busy with the fishing gear as our skipper, Mahmut Yavuz, met the boarding party. The first mate, Oyku Demir stood by the helm. One of the longest series of military conflicts in European history is between Turkey and Russia known as the Ottoman-Russian wars between the 16th and 20th centuries.

The years of rift caused both men an inherent hatred for the Russians as a Lieutenant, one Chief petty officer and four leading seamen with machine guns searched the boat. Thank our lucky stars that there weren't any more transmitters aboard our trawler. They continued to search the boat for their suspicions never wavered. Nerves became agitated as the Lieutenant peered over the side of the boat and scoured the sides for any evidence of contraband. The waters were dark enough not to reflect the DPV's attached to the bottom of the stern. Once they were satisfied that there wasn't any contraband aboard, the Russian crew departed. With a sigh of relief from all, we could continue our journey.

The return trip to Istanbul was uneventful, quiet and a pleasant surprise, for Rick got to see Trevor. It is a rare occasion to mix both business and pleasure but that night friendships abounded as we sipped our raki, a local Turkish drink known as "Lions Milk," made of twice-distilled grapes and aniseed. The camaraderie was great and the Turkish belly dancers were intriguing as inhibitions were lost and the night became wild, loose and fun.

Hormones have a way to arouse and excite the most tempered shyness. Jackson was amused at the kibitzer's attentiveness with the naked Turkish belly dancer. She only wore earrings but her naked body accented them very well! The following morning, feeling the affects of the raki and a pleasurable evening, Rick jumped into the showers. He remembered the words of the infamous song, "Eight beautiful belly dancers in a Turkish bathtub," even though it was the first time that he ever heard the song. His voice was off key but loud!

> "Eight beautiful belly dancers in a Turkish ba-th-tub, washing my body for me.
>
> Washing my body for me, hip-hip hooray, hip-hip hooray, washing my body for me.
>
> Smiling and shampooing my hair and beard, singing and laughing with me.
>
> Singing and laughing with me, hip-hip hooray, hip-hip hooray, singing and laughing with me.
>
> Scrubbing my hairy chest and sturdy back, while whistling a tune with me.
>
> While whistling a tune with me, hip-hip hooray, hip-hip hooray, whistling a tune with me.
>
> Washing my belly with a mighty cheer, how many beers to fill me.
>
> How many beers to fill me, hip-hip hooray, how many beers to fill me.
>
> Scrubbing and rubbing my derriere, giggling and more giggling with me.
>
> Giggling and more giggling with me, hip-hip hooray, giggling with me.
>
> Washing my five toes & three legs, willy-dilly I'm as happy as anyone can be.
>
> Willy-dilly, I'm as happy as anyone can be.
>
> I show my full appre-cia-tion, nine happy people are we.
>
> Nine happy people are we, hip-hip hooray, hip-hip hooray, we end this terrific song on a very happy note, friendly, cheery and freeeeeee!"

Within the next two weeks all three ships had set sail and the transmitters were working fine. Satellite and submarine detection had their coordinates as the Kiev and Vladivostok were heading east but their destinations unknown. The Nikolai pulled into pier 76 in Istanbul as Jackson and I observed her docking. Observation from a distance can be misleading, for containers don't reveal the contents. Jackson winked, took out his two small bottles of Jack Daniels and handed me one as he said, "Drunken sailors out for a walk."

We both took a few swigs and splashed some of the Jack Daniels on ourselves as we proceeded to stumble our way pass the containers. And there in front of us was that symbol of:

छिद्रान्वेषी

But there were no further markings underneath the symbol.

Jackson looked towards me and said, "Whatever is to be loaded in those containers will be done here."

Two days went by and nothing exciting happened but on the third day, trucks started to appear as Jackson and I rotated watches to monitor those containers. Russian ships are heavily guarded and with difficulty we managed to observe from a distance with binoculars. This didn't help us to find out what was inside those trucks to be loaded in the containers. But once loading was completed an "N" was placed under the symbol. I turned to Jackson and asked, "What the hell does an N mean?"

Jackson smiled and said, "Think in Russian!"

Not knowing enough Russian, I was at a disadvantage as Jackson replied, "Narkotiki, narcotics."

Hence, an N instead of a D. That evening the information was passed on to AT for he knew the whereabouts of most of the drug lords in Turkey. There is no loyalty amongst thieves if the palms are greased. Most agencies whether CIA or MI6 have an unlimited supply of cash for covert operations. Grease some palms and mouths will begin to open. But one must be very careful and always watch your back!

Altan Tiryaki, just like Jackson McKenna was experienced and multifaceted in many nuances of the underworld. At one time, he was even a part of the mujahedeen, Islamic guerrilla fighters and he learned of the terrorist ways by firsthand experience.

There are two means to pay for anything in the world and I mean anything, drugs, weapons, assassinations and your own army of mercenaries. Either supply the drugs or the cash. If it is drugs, one needs an unlimited supply and between the poppies in Turkey and the heroin from Afghanistan, most cocaine and heroin goes through Turkey.

As far as the cash, there must be a laundering means and from the mafia to all sorts of crime gangs, this is accomplished through the legitimate Institutions of large banks throughout the world. Even some of your top named banks such as Bank of America, Western Union and JP Morgan are among the institutions allegedly involved. Even the Hong Kong and Shanghai Banking Corporation, HSBC, has admitted its laundering role and evaded criminal prosecution by paying a fine of almost two billion.

It seems odd that even back when Jesus appointed Judas to take care of the purse, problems arose with finances. One's heart is either true to God or manna, and it cannot be both! Through his sources, AT found out that the drugs were to be shipped to the Philippines.

Jackson's face turned a pasty white as he said, "Chemicals to Lagos, drugs to Philippines – what's next? Looks like a conspiracy to me and we don't have any answers!"

With that comment and one more excursion with my Turkish belly dancer, I was on my way back to Lagos and Jackson hopped a flight to Manilla.

CONSPIRACY & CRISIS

Thomas Paine once said, during our American Revolution in 1776, "These are the times that try men's souls. Tyranny, like hell, is not easily conquered; yet we have this consolation with us, that the harder the conflict the more glorious the triumph."

The very same thing could be said today about our conflict with terrorism. Theories are easy to surmise, but until you have all the questions answered, our sovereignty is at risk. The time is imperious for a solution to uncover what is the plan. Who will perpetrate the crime, where will it take place, when is the time for another infamy? Our federal law enforcement need all of these facts answered, especially the how and why. Until we have that, no counterinsurgency is possible.

Rick's return trip to Lagos, gave him a whole new perspective and a better appreciation for the efforts of our Justice and Security Agencies. Each had their own niche but when push comes to shove, they all worked together; contrary to the impressions of many people!

Two months have passed since returning to Lagos and the Raevsky II is still in port but why? Satellite surveillance photos uncovered three major blasts within the last three weeks. Each blast had a different magnitude which pointed to three different sized bombs. Upon confirmation of the three blasts, Rick was told to monitor the ship and let the home office know of its clandestine operations.

A hiccup in surveillance happens when the unexpected occurs. The Raevsky II departs on the morning of his third day back in Lagos. Within two days of observations, ten units with the symbol of the Devil's Advocate were loaded on the Raevsky II, but the question remained, how many units were loaded before his return?

Then to his surprise, the Nave de Caos, ship of mayhem from Colombia appears and docks at the same pier of the Raevsky II. Over the next four days 2600 containers were loaded on the Nave de Caos with forty of these containers labeled with the Devil's Advocate symbol, prior to her departure. This information was relayed through Sparks, his radioman, to our contacts. It was paramount for satellite surveillance to keep track of the two ships for their port of calls.

Sunrise peeks over the horizon as a new day dawns on the Philippines and Manila begins to come alive in her streets. Police officers are already investigating 22 deaths of various officials and two journalists who had the audacity to speak out against the Sputnik gang, the largest and most notorious cut-throats in the Philippines. It is difficult to fathom how a predominantly Catholic nation can harbor such delinquent gangs and crimes of death squads. But to understand the milieu of a culture, one must know its history of development from the very beginning to trace the lines of discontent.

Through the sovereignty of successive foreign rulers, first the Malay aristocracy with its ruler's equivalent to kings as they were addressed as panginuan, lords, to the Indonesian Hindu empire of Majapahit, stringent rules were enforced. Then under the control of Spain in the 1500's, to the occupation and rule of Great Britain, shifting back to Spain again before the Spanish-American War gave the United States control of the island, many stringent changes were made.

Then after World War II as the Philippines achieved its independence, many of the flagrant rulers adopted death squads to achieve control of its citizens. The heinous actions of their rulers caused many to acquire callous attitudes, harden their hearts, loose their faith and survive within gangs who preyed upon the innocent.

Historically, these death squads conducted extrajudicial killings, forced disappearances and genocide. Their reputation became renown around the world as they sold their services to the highest bidder and were known as the "CAFGU" or citizen armed force geographical unit. Between the CAFGU and the Sputnik gang, assassins became available on the open market.

Vadik Vasyutin, a henchman for Leonid Brezhnev of the Union of Soviet Socialist Republics became an established customer of their services as he met with Exequiel Bautista, leader of the Sputniks.

Jackson McKenna was also in Manila observing the drug laden ships of the Kiev and Vladivostok. McKenna's hair stiffened on his arms as he spied Vadik board the Kiev with a group of Exequiel Bautista's gang. He thought to himself, "drugs, a renown henchman with the Sputniks, and bombs being manufactured in Lagos; now some of the pieces of a conspiracy were coming together."

All the drugs were a down payment for services to be rendered but when, where and who were still questions that needed to be answered. The next few days were hectic as McKenna monitored the ships unloading their cargo of drugs and followed the trail from the island of Luzon to the island of Panay where an indiscriminate few were trained in the art of assassination. There are many ways to liquidate a foe and the proper education of poisons, weapons, bombs and venomous creatures gave a range of options to expedite the deed.

Under the guise of a fishing trawler, Jackson once again went on a fishing expedition. The Philippines is entirely in the northern tropics with more than 7,000 islands. The largest island is Luzon where the main city of Manila and chief sea port is located. As Turkey transpired into the major crossroads for drug distribution, Manila is one of the major highways and buy-ways for all drugs. In an increasingly borderless world, international drug trafficking is expanding inexorably around the world. It has become the new commodity replacing cash to purchase weapons or services worldwide.

There is no way McKenna would have found the training base for the Sputniks without the aid of two local natives of the Malaysian stock. His two compadres known as Masakal and Saksak which in Filipino meant, “strangle and stab,” knew every island well. They also knew every devious gang and most unscrupulous individuals on the islands. In the southern end of the Panay Island there is a village known as Moroboro where caves abound. One cave known as “Lapuz-Lapuz” is where the training camp of the Sputniks existed.

Throughout the centuries, the various natives of the Pacific Islands from the natives of Borneo, the tall, dark skinned natives of Indonesia as well as the local natives used the cave for sacrificial ceremonies. Skulls mounted on fence post lined the pathway to the cave could be seen as the two compadres led McKenna cautiously to the opposite end of the cave.

The name of “Lapuz-Lapuz” originated from the two entrances at either end of the caves. Known as the “den ni satanas,” the devil’s den, revealed perverted horrors of torture and the art of killing. Even McKenna’s skin tightens and a chill went down his spine as he witnessed live demonstrations of mutilation and massacre of life. Many kidnapped individuals from around the world were brought here for ransom. If the concerned parties could not furnish the ransom, then the poor souls were tortured to death in the rituals of bloodletting, evisceration and other means of butchery. The torture, the deafening screams and agonizing perversion sickened McKenna. The three unknown perpetrators made their clandestine way out of the cave.

It was a relief to McKenna when they made it back to the trawler, but now there is a definitive urgency to uncover the missing pieces to the puzzle. He will not rest easy until he finds the key to the meeting between Vadik Vasyutin and Exequiel Bautista.

There was one old native on the island that McKenna took a special liking to for he had a sense of humor along with a good disposition. He had served during WW II on the American side against the Japanese. His favorite expression was "tuktok ng umaga," which meant top of the morning, in Filipino. And to the delight of McKenna he introduced him to a favorite native drink of Lambanog, which is like a coconut vodka. It tastes like hell, but after the fourth one, "WOW", packs a wallop! McKenna could now live up to the Filipino words, "Ako ay dumating, nakita ko at ako drank," which means I came, I saw and I drank! Then McKenna had to wash it down with Jack Daniels.

Well, the twosome became one and the old guy who was a fisherman now, kept an eye on the Sputniks for McKenna and even made two trips to the caves to reconnoiter the area. Tala was his name and he understood the old tongue of the Tagalog language.

Under the cover of night, Tala would travel to the island. He spent three days on the island to sneak into the cave and just sit in the darkness and listen to the Sputniks. Tala closed his eyes and concentrated to catch key words and one night he overheard several times, "pataksil na pagpatay USA" which meant, assassination in USA.

It took another three days for Tala to get back to McKenna and report his findings. Jackson McKenna wasted no time but contacted his boss to relay the information. In-turn Jackson received orders to stay in Manila and report any new knowledge about the Sputniks as to when the hit would take place. The arduous task to remain on the islands to uncover more information from the Sputniks caused McKenna to become apprehensive and cautious to watch his back.

It's apparent that rogue ships don't have a schedule to keep for both ships were off-loaded and remained in port. McKenna was curious as to what was their new cargo and destination. Between observing the ships and watching the Sputniks, it left little time for anything else, except a local card game known as pusoy dos or Filipino poker. It was a favorite game of Tala and McKenna enjoyed the game as well with hands played by three or four people. The rudiments of the game were simple from the highest to lowest, diamonds, hearts, spades, and clubs with the two of diamonds being the highest card and the three of clubs the lowest.

Within a month, both the Kiev and the Vladivostok left the port of Manila and surveillance was maintained by satellite. The transmitters were still working as each ship returned to mother Russia. Within another month six assassins boarded a Liberian freighter, the Atlantic Mermaid bound for God knows where. McKenna furnished the name of the ship to his colleagues and it was now up to the long-range tracking to identify its whereabouts.

Tala made one more trip to the cave of Lapuz-Lapuz and the chambers of torture. Again, under the cloak of darkness, he penetrated ever so quietly into the horror chambers around midnight. The Philippines belong to the Pacific Ring of Fire where there are 53 active volcanoes. Thank God for Tala that the Lapuz-Lapuz cave was above an extinct volcano as he crawled through a lava tube to the inner side of a cavern. Exiting the lava tube, he entered a cavern with huge stalagmites rising from the floor of the cave.

Agonizing screams could be heard from the inner cave which made Tala stop dead in his tracks. He couldn't understand the purpose for all of these grotesques' tortures. This was the style of the gangs to coerce allegiance to the Sputniks. As he peered around one stalagmite, he saw three victims bound to stalactites suspended from the ceiling. There appeared to be multiple gashes on the three victim's bodies made by a Bolo knife which is similar to a machete.

There before his very eyes danced the Mangkukulam, the Filipino term for a sorcerer who practiced the art of kulamin of placing a hex on the three individuals. The curse or sumpa is part of the sacrifice to the spirits for a successful vengeance on three people. But to whom will the vengeances fall upon?

Tala tried to crawl closer to the victims so he could hear the sumpa being recited by the Mangkukulam. Once the Mangkukulam is in a trance, he sees all and hears all and became aware of Tala's presence. Not to break the spell, the Mangkukulam continued with the words, "paghihiganti sa mga pinuno ng United States." This sumpa meant, vengeance on top leaders of the United States.

Tala at once returned to Manila and reported his findings to Jackson McKenna. Unfamiliar with Filipino voodoo, Tala explained the history of kulamin to Jackson and the meaning of the curse. Now Jackson had the necessary information on whom the assassinations would be orchestrated.

McKenna enjoyed his stay in Manila, especially his new-found friend Tala, the card games, but still couldn't fathom that confounded drink, Lambanog. Times were tough on the island and jobs were scarce and during those last few nights in Manila, McKenna made sure to lose enough money to Tala to help him get by.

The return flight to Lagos was uneventful and McKenna was unaware that Sputnik learned of the old native's tricks and whereabouts. Once McKenna departed the islands, the notorious gang of Sputnik captured Tala. He was shanghaied to the island of Panay and dragged to the cave where his hands and legs were bound. Suspended from a cable and lowered into a huge snake pit of king cobras, one of the world's largest venomous snakes, Tala suffered a heinous death.

His body was later dumped on one of the main streets of Manila where the local authorities found Tala and counted better than a hundred snake bites over his entire body. The gang's warning to all in the Philippines became apparent, "don't mess with Sputnik." Many prayers were said that day for Tala. May he now rest in peace!

McKenna's inquisitive mind couldn't rest with the few clues that were uncovered. Restless, he decided to go for a walk. One of his daily enjoyments whenever he had a puzzle to solve was to hike the neighborhood, for he needed fresh air and time to ruminate over his thoughts. As he walked, his instincts, the best radar one can possess raddled his inners that he was being followed. He quickly walked down Calcutta Cres and turned on Ware House Road.

Whenever one is followed, always stay to your right and move quickly. This psychologically conditions the followers. Then find an alley with an intersection to turn either right or left. Once you reach that intersection change directions and turn left. Nine out of ten times the culprits following you will turn right. This time it worked. With a burst of energy, a very gruff Mckenna crossed a few streets to make sure he wasn't followed and went to the Apapa Club. One needs to find a large place where people congregate to blend in such as a mall or club and disappear as quickly as possible out the rear door. Then find a place to wait it out.

He found a sidewalk café where he could watch the approach from both ends of the street. Any shady character will retrace their footsteps and McKenna wanted to make sure that the culprits didn't find him. His job definitely got to him at times. The proof in life that the struggle between good and evil is ongoing.

The second thing McKenna enjoyed were his drinks. A top of the morning with a Drambuie, a top of the afternoon with a Glenlivet and a top of the evening with a Jack Daniels. Then most evenings, a mighty good night with a Sambuca. But for now, until he definitely knew that there was no one following him, he just ordered coffee.

The news about Tala's death devastated McKenna and made his resolve to solve the code intensify tenfold. With a sweep of his hand, he sent bottles and glasses flying off the coffee table in his room. He became adamant that those bastards would pay! He reached for a pad of paper and with pen in hand scribbled in large capital letters the word, "SZESTU."

Underneath the coded word, he wrote pataksil na pagpatay USA and explained to Rick what part of the acronym stood for, assassination in USA. Now, McKenna asked, "Where does this fit into the puzzle of the acronym?"

"In Russian, assassination is translated into the word, "ubiystvo!" Now we're both looking at the acronym and see that the last letter "U" is for assassination in USA.

McKenna getting a little anxious exclaims, "The rest of those damn letters explain the how and when. We already know the culprits behind the scheme! The Russians are supplying the drugs to pay for the bombs being made in Lagos and the hitmen from the Philippines. But what on earth is the rest of the coded acronym?"

Within a week, confirmation from satellite surveillance put the Raevsky II and the Nave de Caos in Colombia. No confirmation on the whereabouts of the Liberian freighter, Atlantic Mermaid, had surfaced.

Jackson contacted Trevor in Istanbul to stay vigilant for the Kiev and Vladivostok and observe their actions from a distance. And cautiously advised him once again to watch his back. Good advice that went unheeded as Trevor made his way across the border and up the coast to Novorossiysk, Russia.

No one can ever traverse the border into Russia without continually being observed and followed. The first day he observed the two ships being loaded in port and as he tried covertly to get closer to the containers to look for any distinguishing symbols, he was nabbed by the KGB.

The disappearance of Trevor was like a piercing dagger into McKenna's body as he remembered the old days of clandestine cat and mouse games with that State Security. He knew all too well that Trevor must be retrieved within 48 hours or be lost forever.

The adversities in life were too insurmountable for McKenna to bear. How could he have lasted so long to avoid capture and successfully traverse the walls of espionage? McKenna blamed himself for Trevor's misfortunes.

There was an old adversary of McKenna's who had served well in the KGB but found himself at odds with the Kremlin and ended up as a double agent. He now lives in London and McKenna was aware how to contact him. The two old adversaries had become good friends because old warriors either disappear, die or learn to survive with each other. His name was Karpichkov, now known as Carl and quickly put McKenna in touch with another double agent from Belarus.

Mstislav Alexandra, as his fate would evolve was the only son of a cousin to Tsarina Alexandra, the wife of Tsar Nicholas II. History revealed that the whole family of the Romanovs were executed in 1918 in the wake of the Russian revolution. The gunshot-bayonet murders took place in a cellar in the city of Ekaterinburg, Russia. Some old warriors neither die or desist but strive to get even. Mstislav, whose name means, vengeance and glory, was such a person. He learned to work right under the establishment's noses and tirelessly worked to undermine their causes.

Every country has underground routes to allow passage for covert operations unbeknown to the authorities. Established throughout the centuries and safeguarded for the cause of freedom, these clandestine freedom fighters aren't loyal to any one nation. To them the cause is more important than any nation!

Mstislav, upon receiving word from Carl, began his search to find the whereabouts of Trevor. Time was of the essence and the clock kept ticking as Trevor was hauled off to the Volgograd Oblast Prison.

Volgograd, Russia was about a nineteen-hour drive from Hopa, Turkey. Prisons in Russia can be categorized as four types of facilities.

- Pre-trial institutions
- Juvenile labor colonies
- Corrective labor colonies
- Prisons

A favorite game of Mother Russia is known as "prison roulette," where any apprehended suspect is whisked off to one of their detention centers and processed into the prison system within the first twelve hours. Then forwarded to another prison for indoctrination where the suspect will be tattooed with the location number of the penal colony of their destination. This finally becomes their permanent residence or place to be shot.

Mstislav, once a prisoner of one of the 146 penal colonies of Mother Russia, knew the system all too well. Some of the prisoners were transferred multiple times and their paper work lost, so that no one, not even Mother Russia could find the culprit. The search led Mstislav to the Black Dolphin Prison in Orenburg, Russia where the trail went stone cold.

Trevor was placed in an eight by six-foot, cement-wall cell. There were no windows, so one could not tell the time of day and in due time without the sun or moon to guide you, time of day is lost. No clothes, no shoes just his skivvies and t-shirt. There was a cot, a hole in the floor for a toilet and a sink with no running water. Bleak, cold, dismal and a day without time can cause a person to deteriorate into insanity.

Meals were bread, water, some broth and sometimes some beans or rice and bits of meat. At least that is what he was told, and he wasn't sure if the meat was dog, rat or fowl. Once a day he was allowed in a fifty foot by one-hundred-foot courtyard. Sometimes by himself, other times with a handful of prisoners from other cells. Most spoke Russian, a few spoke English but without hope most people choose not to speak at all.

As time progressed the interrogations became less and less, showers were allowed one a month, the eyes became dull and a muted stare became the norm. Trevor was now a prisoner to his cell and to his thoughts and wondered if there really is a God. How could my life become a piece of driftwood weathered and scarred? The tattoo on his body read penal colony number 96.

Mstislav personally contacted McKenna and few words were exchanged for both men knew all too well that hope exist anywhere in the world except for in the prisons of Mother Russia.

The news of Trevor disheartened the both of them, but throughout the years, both men had learned to cope and survive through such infamy. Whereas the news of his friend affected Rick to become disillusioned. This was no way for anyone's life to end.

McKenna looked at Rick with empathy and said, "The hollow moments in life are the worst and there are worst things in life then death, for in death we believers begin our spiritual life. But as for Trevor, he is neither living or dying but is stuck in purgatory and it sucks! But we can achieve a victory for Trevor by stopping this damn conspiracy and it will be a win for all of us."

The bitter discontents in life can be overwhelming, especially if one is to lose faith and the will to persevere, for apathy moves in subtly at first and then overpowers you to a slow death.

Jackson then pulled out a bottle of Jack Daniels and we both took a swig. He reassured me that Mstislav would keep trying to locate Trevor, but for now the trail was cold.

During this time-period, there was another young pup studying law at the Leningrad State University and he became an apprentice of the KGB. He was about my age and would eventually graduate from law school and join the KGB full time. His name was Vladimir Vladimirovich Putin and as his destiny evolved would someday test the resolve of the United States.

This man understood the adversities of life all so well. The youngest of three children his birth was preceded by the death of two brothers, Viktor and Albert. Albert died in infancy and Viktor died of diphtheria during the siege of Leningrad.

Putin's mother was a factory worker and his father a conscript in the Soviet Navy, serving in the submarine fleet. His grandmother was killed by the German occupiers of Tver region and his uncles disappeared at the war front.

There was still unfinished business regarding the Kiev and Vladivostok, but since the transmitters were still working, McKenna decided to wait for confirmation on their next destination. Satellite confirmation showed the Raevsky II transferring cargo to a Liberian freighter, the Wandering Star, in the middle of the Atlantic Ocean. This skillful deception known as sleight of hand to change cargo, supposedly throws off the authorities to apprehend the contraband.

The other known Liberian freighter, the Atlantic Mermaid docked at a port in Altamira, Mexico a known port for drug smugglers and terrorist. This is an easy port of call to smuggle contraband into the United States through either Brownsville or the Reynosa-McAllen border in Texas. There are no safe areas in the state of Tamaulipas, Mexico due to crime and violence related to the activities of the Transnational Criminal Organizations. There is much on-going turf war between rival factions of the Gulf Cartel TCO's.

Jackson McKenna's plane had landed at a remote air strip of the McAllen Airport where he met Wade Andrew Washington from the Department of Justice as he shook Jackson's hand and said, "Call me WW, I'm in charge of this lynch mob!"

He turned and introduced Jackson to the others as they proceeded to their vehicles. "This is Samuel Phillips of the United States Marshall Service and over there is Corey Bennett, FBI and watch out for that guy who is hot tempered Johnny Fletcher of the ATF and finally this is Frank S. Douglas of the DEA.

Jackson McKenna turned to Frank and asked, "What does the "S" stand for?"

Frank quickly replied, "Shotgun!"

They all proceeded to a hanger where WW quickly summed up the low-down and the plan. "You CIA boys gave us quite a conundrum!"

"All departments have been working your code, trying to break it down and this is what we've got so far! That damn acronym, SZESTU, puzzled us at first but when you came up with the last letter meaning assassination in Russian, well it didn't take long to put most of it together."

Then Corey Bennett broke in with, "NSA has been flooded with scuttlebutt about blackouts!"

A perturbed WW resumed the lead with, "Yea, as I was saying, and in Russian blackouts is setka zatemneniye, and then the rest of the puzzle came together creditably with SZESTU stands for "setka zatemneniye elektricheskiy svyaz transport ubiystvo."

"Grid blackout-electrical-communication-transportation-assassination", now we know the what but need to determine the when and where!"

Stopping long enough to light-up a cigar WW continued, "Thanks to you we also know the who and surmised that they are our top three leaders."

Just then hot-tempered Johnny Fletcher spoke up, "We are not sure how many bombs have been shipped but know it's a substantial number and we don't know the targets!"

Now a perturbed WW said, "That's why we have all the agencies on this and are ready to do a full court blitz."

WW continued, "And gentlemen, we need to get this right because there will be no second chance!" And then he added, "This is too big to SCREW-UP!"

There was a table in the center of the floor of the hanger with a large map of the United States. The map showed the electrical grid complex with local electricity grids interconnected to form larger networks for commercial purposes. At the highest level, the U.S. power system in the lower 48 states is made up of three main interconnections, which operate independently from each other.

- The Eastern Interconnection encompasses the area east of the Rocky Mts.
- The Western Interconnection, the area from Rockies west.
- The ERCOT covers most of Texas
- Both Eastern & Western Interconnections are linked with the Canadian Grid

The network structure of interconnections helps maintain the reliability of the electrical grid by providing multiple routes for power to flow.

A disturbed WW said, "Now these damn buggers of terrorist want to blowup as many of them as they can. And to top it all off, most of the forms of communications today require grid support and so to destroy the electrical grid, will also destroy our communications, sort of like killing two birds with one stone or a very big bomb. Now what is left is the transportation grid of roads, bridges and railway." He stopped long enough to take some of his blood pressure medicine before continuing. "I don't know which will kill me first, this cigar or these damn pills to help this overworked heart!"

Again, he stops long enough to take a couple of puffs on the cigar and then says, "The drugs and arms were shipped into Mexico for payment to the Cartel for their protection to transport the bombs to various airports where several light aircraft were available. From satellite surveillance, it was ascertained that six airports are deemed as suspicious activity:

- General Servando Canales International Airport
- General Lucio Blanco International Airport
- Agualeguas Old Airport
- LaEncarnacion Airport
- Rancho San Salvador Northeast Airport
- Rancho Guadalupe South Airport

"Presently each airport is under heavy surveillance on the ground and we are ready to move in once the bombs are on the premises."

Wade further said to McKenna, "Your assigned to Johnny Fletcher's group. We need to intercept the bombs on the ground; we cannot afford what will happen if those bombs get air borne. But if necessary our backup is from four air bases on alert from:

- Laughlin Air Force Base in Del Rio, Texas
- Holloman Air Base in New Mexico
- Luke Air Base in Arizona
- Edwards Air Base in California

"We have backup C-130's with Army Rangers if necessary. Now it's that damn waiting game which drives me nuts!"

Wade Andrew Washington took in a deep breath before he said to McKenna, "You know, our air force is one of the largest and most technologically advanced in the world, with better than 5,500 manned aircraft, but all it takes is one rogue terrorist with a damn Cessna to cause allot of havoc, and God help us if many casualties. Most people don't realize the kerfuffle that this causes in time, money and resources to protect our country. It takes a great deal to preserve the home of the brave and land of the free!"

There was much eager anticipation with surveillance in place from satellites above and six covert crews to watch each of the airports. Johnny Fletcher's crew were at a business park of Small Parts Inc. near the General Lucio Blanco Airport of Reynosa, just off the main drag of the Celle Palma Senegal road behind the airport. The waiting game had begun.

Surveillance had detected the other ships with bombs and the Sputnik assassins bound for New Orleans. It seems our assassins from the Philippines made a switch in Colombia. Within a blink of an eye and the signature still wet on a new set of orders, I found myself on a flight to Naval Support Activity in New Orleans. The switch from merchant marine to naval reserve officer was a good cover and the CIA felt something that the terrorist wouldn't suspect. And since the assassins knew McKenna, it was better to send me to reconnoiter the territory. And to my surprise see Danny with a beaming smile from ear to ear as he said, "You're going to be stationed here?"

"Right on," I replied.

Danny was up to speed on the drugs, bombs and assassins but the process was slow to identify how many and who the assassins were. The NSA picked up chatter about six unidentified assassins and bits and pieces filtered in from both agencies of CIA and MI6 but what I found intriguing were the six names confiscated by Mossad and the ISI of Pakistan.

These two agencies had taken years to infiltrate terrorist organizations throughout the world and like magic, could retrieve necessary information out of the air. Each one of these sadistic terrorists were responsible for massive bombings throughout the world and assassinations but neither had a dossier or recognizable picture to go with their name. The names transmitted to the CIA were:

- Dakila Flores
- Flordeliza Castillo
- Isagani Salazar
- Marichu Mendoza
- Reynante Bautista
- Sinagtala Torres

ISI is Pakistan's most important intel agency and worked feverishly to identify each assassin. The organization is so powerful that it practically runs the country. Throughout the years, the ISI became the backbone of the Pakistan government achieving one of its greatest victories by defeating the Russian soldiers in Afghanistan. They had a personal interest in defeating the Russians then, and a personal interest in defeating their plot now.

Getting settled-in at the officer's quarters seemed odd, but it did feel great being back in the states even though no contact was to be made with family or friends.

PLOT OF EVIL

Our forefathers were certainly guided from above as they endeavored to create our constitution. There has always been controversy when it comes to politics, religion and journalism. But when it comes to our Bill of Rights, especially that first amendment; It is a blessing! Thank God for that First Amendment of freedom of religion, speech, press and the right to assemble and to petition. Boy, did they get it right! But sometimes to form a more perfect Union, establish justice, insure domestic tranquility, provide for the common defense to promote welfare and secure liberty, we must go through extreme measures that our forefathers had no conception of.

Our six feathered assassins somehow flew the coup and were not in New Orleans as expected. The concern by all is that a blitzkrieg was about to take place and we had no idea on where or when but had some concept on who! The only ace that we were holding is the knowledge that the blackout grid had to occur first. In the early seventies, the United States was easily accessible to terrorist and the smuggling of contraband into our country and simply disappear without any trail to follow.

Wade Andrew Washington pounded his fist against the table and yelled at Corey Bennett, "How the friggin hell can six people disappear, I thought you FBI boys were good at your jobs?"

A flustered Bennett replied, "A BOLO is put out for suspicious activity at gun shops, target ranges, stolen vehicles et cetera with anyone of Filipino descent in all states!"

WW looked at Bennett and his only reply was, "Big Friggin Deal!"

WW continued his ranting and raving episode with, "Assassins loose in our country, God only knows how many bombs, which airports harbor the bombs and when the hits will be consummated?"

A perturbed WW turned to Johnny Fletcher and Jackson McKenna and asked, "Anything else we don't know?"

Jackson pulled out his bottle of Jack Daniels and took a swig before saying, "This has not been a Top of the Morning!"

Turning a deep bluish-red in the face, WW just turned and stormed out of the hanger.

Meanwhile surveillance at each of the airports was maintained as apprehension intensified about the assassins.

Danny and Rick managed to find the Liberian Freighter, the Wandering Star, docked at pier 77 in New Orleans and now they started thinking like a Jackson McKenna.

Rick snapped his fingers, looked at Danny and said, "What if those damn assassins were on the Wandering Star and not the Atlantic Mermaid, where would they go?"

Danny quickly replied, "Get out of town so not to be noticed and leave no trail."

No matter how diligently the assassins try to be inconspicuous, one cannot escape all means of surveillance. Request through the CIA and FBI for satellite surveillance of the Wandering Star revealed six people climbing into a Suburban and leaving pier 77 from New Orleans.

The demographics of Filipino Americans show that there are better than three million Filipino's in the United States with a large contingency residing in Bay Minette, Alabama, a short drive on route 10 from New Orleans. With plenty of cash in their possession, the six subversive assassins made their way to Bay Minette.

Nestled in the pine forests of North Baldwin County, Bay Minette is conveniently located near Mobile, Alabama. This beautiful southern hamlet is home to a thriving timber industry and the surrounding forests are the playground for the southern sportsman and water enthusiast for the nearby Tensaw River Delta and warm waters of the Gulf of Mexico. But Bay Minette is a hamlet that also attracts clouds of the mystique and bizarre that envelops the town. Many stories of mischief, mayhem and murder surface when one looks closer at the history.

History shows that the devious inhabitants of Bay Minette wanted to remove the county seat from Daphne to Bay Minette. To accomplish such a deed, the town leaders connived a scheme to lure the sheriff and his deputy out of Daphne with a false story about a murder. While the law enforcement was pursuing the fictitious killer, the townsmen stole the Baldwin County Courthouse records and delivered them to the new courthouse in Bay Minette. Upon learning about the connived deed, the sheriff of Daphne investigated the case and in turn disappeared. The said mayor back then of Bay Minette was a guy by the name of I. P. Dailey. He was the proprietor of a two headed crocodile. And as the name states, he relieved himself and of the town of Daphne their sheriff. The sheriff was never seen or heard of ever again.

There was also a gunsmith shop in Bay Minette that for the right price, one could purchase any weapon on the black market. Known as the "Coalition Freedom Fighters Gun Shop," nicknamed, "Shoot them Dead," just the nickname alone makes the hair on your arms stand up, along with a remote private target range to test your purchase and practice your aim. This was a sniper's paradise located in the middle of nowhere at the junction of State 59, seven-mile road and T. J. Peale Rd, which stood for Tank Junior Peale, commander of the local Ku Klux Klan back in the late 1800's.

There was no time for dickering as a ward of cash was placed on the counter for three M1A1 Bazookas and three Mossberg MVP long range rifles. The rocket launchers along with the ammo and no paper-work for a meager $10,000.00 was worth the price. They loaded the suburban and got directions to the target range.

All six insurgents were x-military and knew the weaponry well. Castillo, Mendoza and Bautista would handle the rocket launchers and Flores, Salazar and Torres stood guard with their Mossberg's. The sick bastards joked about striking like a cobra and killing instantly. Two days at the target range honed their skills, reaffirmed their commitment and prepared them for their plot.

And the two nights were spent at the Baby-doll Virgin Gentleman's Club in Mobile on Hustle Ave. This extra-curricular activity calmed their nerves, satisfied their hormones and intensified their zest to commit the unthinkable. Especially on their last night of amorous flirtations, all six of the flippant bastards invited one of the baby-dolls on a picnic of what they thought would be a sheer delight. Instead, the poor souls the following day were taken to the firing range.

Upon their arrival the girls objected to this crappy place for a picnic. They were dragged from the cars and tied to stakes positioned two hundred feet within the gravel pit. The first three girls were the targets for the Mossberg's as they were shot dead with deadly accuracy. Then the next three girls, screaming of their nightmare to the top of their lungs, were fastened to trees as Castillo, Mendoza and Bautista adjusted their sights on their rocket launchers and when ready, blasted their human targets to smithereens. Bay Minette will never be the same as the local gazette read the following day, "Blasted Body Parts Burst Asunder."

The culprits searched for two extra used vehicles for sale in Bay Minette, paid cash and exited in three different directions. Danny and I arrived on the day that the culprits left town with no traceable evidence. The FBI quickly got sketch artists to speak with the patrons at the Bay Minette Inn where the insurgents stayed. They very meticulously wiped-down everything within their rooms. But as usual, only one of the culprits always handled the cash to keep a low profile on the other five.

A fairly good description was given to the authorities on the one individual who paid the bills with cash. From those descriptions, a concise sketch was made and distributed to all authorities. Both local authorities along with the FBI were sickened by the dastardly sight at the firing range and it is a sad epitaph for humanity whenever any unconscionable atrocities take place.

Meanwhile back in Texas, a flabbergasted WW barked out, "We cannot afford any slipups and allow planes to leave the ground with bombs aboard!"

When tensions arose above a boiling point, Corey Bennett of the FBI remained calm and collective because he understood the necessity of rational thinking during insidious times. Having been involved with many think tanks to negotiate effective solutions he asked WW and the others, "What essential meetings this past year have global consequences?"

WW was the first to respond with, "Four things come to mind!"

- SALT II-Summit talks with Russia
- Roadmap to peaceful relations with China
- Middle East Peace Process
- End Vietnam War

Reflecting out loud as Corey Bennett said, "Now understanding that the Russians instigated this conspiracy, what meetings affect Russia the most?"

WW replied, "The SALT II meetings." The "what if" scenarios elucidated the dilemma and pointed the way!

"Yes, and the Middle East Peace Process," interrupted Samuel Phillips, "especially since giving Israel missiles to defend themselves from an aggressive attack!"

WW then added, "So, let's concentrate on those two meetings."

WW took out his pipe, packed it well with tobacco and before he lit it said, "Now when Nixon took office, he intended to secure control over foreign policy in the White House and the way I understand it, he kept Secretary of State William Rogers and Secretary of Defense Melvin Laird out of the affairs of foreign policy. He utilized his national security guy, this Henry Kissinger, from what I understand. Those two fanatics became known as "Nixinger" and concentrated the power within themselves."

WW stopped talking long enough to light his pipe and take a few puffs before continuing, "As Nixon got distracted by Watergate, Kissinger took charge of all national security policies. And then the United States got into a big quagmire, what a damn mess!"

WW while shaking his head, looks at Corey and the others before saying, "I don't mean to lecture a history lesson, but the damn politicians create the havoc and it's up to our agencies to get them out of it!"

WW curses and then adds, "We think that all the problems in the world come from cold hearted dictators, but politicians that are callous, ruthless and power-hungry mongers who want total control are just as bad. Just look at the mess in Chile!"

WW stops long enough to catch his breath, before turning to Jackson McKenna and hands him a directive from the president that reads, "Needed in Chile ASAP!"

Wade Washington sees and understands the frustration that McKenna is going through right now. He sympathizes with him and tries to ease the pain by saying, "Thanks to you and the CIA Boys, we are on top of this subversive attack but there is more brewing in the wind and right now Chile is ready to blow!"

Internal matters are always handled by the Federal boys and foreign excursions by the CIA.

Nixon was up to his neck with Watergate and a second round of SALT negotiations began in late 1972, since SALT I failed to limit deployment of ICBM's on both sides. Russia was threatening unilateral action and the Middle East is a complete political debacle.

Now in Chile, opposition to the democratically elected president, socialist Salvador Allende, helped pave the way for a military coup of death and despotism in his country. Nixon authorized the CIA to infiltrate Chile, hence the need for Jackson McKenna to stop Allende's Presidency. The situation intensified and escalated our forces worldwide to DefCon three.

Jackson's arrival in Santiago always intrigued him, for the people are warm, fun-loving and friendly. A country so long and narrow that it's head is burning with the tropical sun while it's feet are freezing with the winter's snow. This country has some of the most magnificent mountain scenery; the highest in the Andes.

There are two island possessions off Chile far out in the Pacific, the Easter Islands with the colossal stone statues and the Juan Fernandez group islands which inspired Daniel Defoe to write his Robinson Crusoe tales more than three centuries ago.

Chile comes alive with her beautiful scenery, friendly people and many legends that help explain her natural phenomena, teach us some of life's lessons and are just plain good stories. One of McKenna's favorite myths was the Laguna del Inca. Legend has it that an Inca man fell in love with a beautiful Inca princess whose eyes shone like emeralds. They were married on a mountain top and the bride slipped and fell to her death. Heartbroken, the man wanted to give her a special burial in a tomb and buried her in the nearby lake. As the entombed princess sank to the bottom of the lake, the waters turned the same color as the princess's eyes.

Whenever Jackson could break away from his covert activities, Chile was his favorite vacation destination. But this was no vacation, it was a hot spot ready to explode and more than just a thorn in the side of the United States; this is a missed opportunity for diplomacy.

Exiting the aircraft, Jackson climbed down the stairway where he met the assigned CIA agent, Rene' Vieaux and another kibitzer, Sinclair. Rene' Vieaux's reputation preceded him as Jackson firmly shook his hand. Never formerly introduced, Rene' was part of the largest paramilitary operations ever undertaken by the CIA in the small Southeast Asian Kingdom of Laos. For more than 13 years, the agency directed native forces that fought major North Vietnamese units to a standstill. It was Director Richard Helms that later observed, "it took specially qualified manpower; it was dangerous; it was difficult." "The CIA did a superb job!"

Sinclair was assigned to the port city of Valparaiso just due north of Santiago to monitor the ships for covert contraband activity. Guess what two ships made runs with weapons to Chile? Our two adversaries, the Kiev and Vladivostok.

Sinclair brought Jackson up to date by saying, "Between the two ships better than 5000 containers of weapons with the familiar mark of, छिद्रान्वेषी on each container with a "A" underneath each symbol have been unloaded."

Sinclair added, "Other ships have come in with Cuban mercenaries! And most of those arms are in their hands.

Jackson shook his head and said, "Smells like a coup to me."

Then as Jackson gathered his luggage, he asked Sinclair, "Do you have any idea where the arms and mercenaries are stationed?"

"Negative," responded Sinclair.

"We will need to do some reconnaissance and find out," said Jackson.

Rene' showed satellite pictures to Jackson showing tank buildups surrounding Santiago as he responded, "It looks like we are too late to intervene!"

Jackson McKenna, the CIA's savant of sleuths, understood the urgency of expedient actions and instigated what became known as Track II. An all out attempt to incite a military coup and crisis across the country. Nothing ever goes right when two oppossing coups take place, one by the Chilean Army and one perpetrated by the CIA.

A composed McKenna asked Rene', "Are all contingencies in place and ready to go?"

"Absolutely!" replied Rene."

False flag operatives made up of mercenaries, Chilean renergades and some senior Chilean military officers were ready to stage a coup of their own after being informed that the U.S. would actively support a coup, but would revoke all military aid if such a coup did not happen.

With U.S. encouragement, McKenna contacted right-wing Argentine military officials to kidnap Chilean army chief of staff, General Renee Schneider.

With the plot in place, the three CIA comrades headed to the Santiago Blue Lounge which was in close proximity to the presidential palace to meet with a couple of insurgents to futher plan a time for the coup. The coup d' etat would strike from three seperate areas simultaneously to force Allende out of office.

Renegade soldiers from Argentina were already amassed in Concepcion and would join forces with the local insurgents in Rancagua to attack the presidential palace from the south and east sides. The mercenaries would attack the naval port of Valparaiso and seize control of the naval vessels rendering no support from the Chilian Navy for Allende. Some of the top military staff with the third brigade of the Chilean army would attack the palace from the north side and exercise a military vise to squeese a surrender from the president and his supporters.

Synchronizing their watches that the attack would begin within 24-hours, all hell broke lose as the buildings began to shake, a thunderous roar of cannon fire lit up the sky and the rumblings of army tanks lined the streets to the presidential palace.

General Augusto Pinochet, Army Commander and Defense Minister of Chile got wind of an organized coup attempt by the CIA and decided to strike first with his own takeover. He had designs to be president himself and as the army struck a blow at the palace, the Chilean Navy seized control of all ships in Valparaiso.

The Chilian Airforce lend support by dropping bombs on the palace and surrounding area, hitting the cafe where McKenna and the others were having their meeting. Machine-gun fire erupted wounding many innocent by-standers as the Chilean Army attacked the palace and surrounding buildings.

McKenna was severely hit as a tank crashed through the front wall with soldiers surrounding the perpetrators. A number of the patrons were arrested including Rene' and Sinclair. They were handcuffed, loaded on a truck and hauled off to Santiago's National Stadium. McKenna who was bleeding profusely lying on the floor, was left for dead.

Allende made his final plea to the good people of Chile that he would not resign the presidency and tried to rally in vain supporters with the cry, "Long live Chile! Long live the people! Long live the workers!"

After the address, Allende joined in defending the palace along with his loyal followers but this was a fatal act as the army stormed the gates. Many were killed and Pinochet's coup a success.

Allende supporters were rounded up and detained in Santiago's National Stadium as Pinochet's soldiers rampaged the city throughout the shops and taverns, arresting any suspicious suspects. There were better than a thousand-people arrested, including one American.

Pinochet's troops were standing guard within the area, as the people were off-loaded from the trucks and ushered into the stadium. Victims with hands tied and their eyes blindfolded were escorted by soldiers. A swift rifle butt for the slow ones, convinced them to move faster. A thousand thoughts raced through Sinclair's mind, his blood surged through his veins, his heart throbbing harder with each rhythmic beat and wondering why, while he was led by a soldier to his final resting place? Reciting the Lord's Prayer on his lips, "Our Father, who art in heaven, why me O Lord, hallowed be thy name," as he trips and falls to the ground, all the while still reciting the Lord's Prayer.

"Thy kingdom come; thy will be done on earth as it is in heaven."

A solder kicks Sinclair and forces him to get up and proceed to his death-bed.

He continues his prayer, too afraid to stop, "Give us this day our daily bread; and forgive us our trespasses as we forgive those who trespass against us," and before he could finish praying, his ears burst in pain from numerous machine guns firing, echoing throughout the stadium. Numerous bodies fell lifeless to the ground resonating with a hollow thud. Within one day, all were summarily executed and buried in a mass grave site.

The body of Jackson McKenna disappeared without a trace and his death unconfirmed. Some say close friends hijacked his body and he was nursed back to health.

There was another legend that McKenna enjoyed, known as Rapa Nui, Easter Island, the beginning of the world, where a couple met, fell in love and found the world is beautiful. Perhaps now, McKenna found his Rapa Nui.

On September 13, Pinochet was named President of Chile. The takeover of the government ended a 46-year history of democratic rule and the CIA in Chile.

The news was not received well back in America from all sides, our government, the CIA and family members of those slain. This isn't the first time that our government has supported wrong choices and may God help us, probably not the last.

The news about McKenna and Sinclair devastated Rick, right to the center of his heart. The anguish left him empty for he liked the old guy and learned to appreciate his instincts. His thoughts about Sinclair, even though he hadn't known him for too long, left him guilt-ridden because he died so young. Death is not bias for it takes all ages and strikes when least expected. This becomes one of those reality checks in life where one is not sure where to turn. Moments like these are the crossroads in our life!

Rick returned to New Orleans and waited for his next set of orders. Whenever he was troubled and needed a reality check, he turned to his faith and went to the military chaplain and began with the customary, "Bless me Father, for I have sinned and opened-up to him a trail of iniquity, trials and death of his colleagues and close friends. They talked for better than an hour as the chaplain said, "You need a little more than what the penance of confession can give you, for in soul searching, spiritual guidance is needed to keep you on the right path. May I suggest a retreat house that can help you on your way?"

The retreat house that Rick patronized was a Benedictine Monastery which opened a whole new perspective on spirituality. The daily horarium of prayer, worship and contemplation led him down the pathway to search deep inside his heart. The search for true meaning in life and the pathway to peace only comes through continual perseverance of prayer, knocking on heaven's door and spiritually listening. A spiritual awakening was in store for Rick but where would it take him, only God knows.

THE PLOT THICKENS

The trail of the assassins went stone cold and the nerves of the agents were at a boiling point to find any clue as to their whereabouts. The United States department of Justice were rattling their sabers and wanted answers from any and all individuals suspected in the collusion. The Latin motto, "Qui Pro Domina Justitia Sequitur," appearing on the Department of Justice Seal meant not only words to live by but also words to die by! Who prosecutes on behalf of justice? Life has seen too many injustices!

Presently the United States utilized a color-coded terrorism threat advisory scale. Inspired by the success of the forest fire color code, it was duplicated but the specific government actions triggered by the different threat levels were not always communicated to the public. The five-color threat ranged from the minimal risk level showing green color and progressed with the rainbow colors to blue for general risk, yellow for significant risk, orange for high-risk and red at the top of the totem pole for severe risk.

Even though the assassins were in the United States, the risk level for the federal agencies were set at orange of high-risk to intensify security at government buildings, public facilities and airports. But the public threat level was only set at blue for general risk so not to panic the public. Once assassins and location threats are identified, then both levels would be raised for extra security measures.

Collaborated efforts from all agencies for surveillance from above and observation on the ground monitored the terrorist's activity. There is an old game that terrorist like to deceive authorities with which is fashioned after a child's game known as leap frog; except this game is called leap truck where multiple trucks are lined up but not all are loaded with cargo from the ships. Once they all disperse and head in different directions, it is anyone's guess as to which trucks have the contraband.

One of the conundrums for any law enforcement agency is that evil exist in individuals and not in any nationality, religion or nation. We must learn not to harbor prejudices towards our neighbors but look for the evidence of iniquity committed. It is not all carte blanche!

Wade Andrew Washington was losing sleep over this specific conspiracy, for it was too big and all to encompassing with devastating consequences for our country and the entire world, if it succeeded. All agencies were stretched to the snapping point and hopefully all the bases were covered to apprehend these dastardly culprits. Wade had seen too much evil in his lifetime and understood the intricacies of evil and how it devoured the heart first, then the mind and lastly the soul so that only the devil can gain ownership of the body. For once the heart is hardened and empty, one can commit any atrocity and without the mind there is no conscience and without a soul one must wander forever, wailing and gnashing your teeth in the eternal, un-consuming fire pits of hell. The clock is ticking and there are still too many unanswered questions.

All contingencies are ostensibly set in place and the DOJ, the department of justice, has the lead to coordinate all other agencies to form a dragnet and apprehend these insurgents and bust this conspiracy wide open. A special meeting was called by the director of the CIA, Richard McGarrah Helms, at Fort Hood the largest active duty armored post in the US Army with the 504th Military Intelligence Brigade to meet with WW of the

DOJ and all assisting agencies by the order of Henry Kissinger to, **"Get off your ass & get ahead of this problem!"**

Since the CIA debacle in Chile, the CIA has been on the hot seat to reprieve its mission and accomplishments. Helms looks at WW and says, "OK Wade, bring me up to speed on this conspiracy!"

Wade very meticulously goes over the details beginning with the transport of weapons and drugs from Russia to Lagos, Nigeria for the manufacture of bombs. Then he proceeds to the assassins from the Philippines infiltrating into the United States through the port of New Orleans.

Helms belligerently interrupts Wade, "Who are the assassin's targets?"

Wade sheepishly replies, "We're not sure but believe our top leaders."

Wade continues by explaining the offloading of multiple bombs in both Mexico and New Orleans. The shipments to Mexico are to be loaded onto planes and the shipment of bombs in New Orleans are to be offloaded into trailer trucks. Then he tries to explain the meaning of the intercepted clue on "SZESTU."

Helms gets even more impatient as he asks, "What are the target areas for the bombs?"

Wade sweating profusely replies, "The planes will hit our electrical and communications grid network. The trucks we surmise to blow-up bridges and railroad crossings to disrupt our transportation network."

Now a heated Helms is standing and yelling, **"WHEN?"**

Wade replies meekly, "We don't know!"

Helms stands-up agitated as hell, flushed in the face and with a sweep of his hand, clears off the top of the table sending papers flying in every direction as he barks at Wade, **"GOD DAMN WADE, this is too big, not to have answers!"**

Madder than a bull dog showing his teeth, Helms orders for his private phone and ask to be connected to Wes Armstrong, Major General of Black Ops. As he is waiting to be connected he mutters, "Wish to hell Jackson McKenna was still around!"

Helms scratching his head and thinking to himself about McKenna's last confirmation that informed his agency about the assassins from the Philippines. If the information is correct then this Bautista, leader of the Sputniks, should know the plan in full detail.

Just then Major General Armstrong answers his call.

"Major General Armstrong here!"

"Wes, Dick Helms, I got a problem!"

"How can I help Director?" replied Wes.

An adamant Helms tells Wes, "Critical code Red, two men that I need you to locate, kidnap and take to the farm!"

Helms explains the details about the two men, Vadik Vasyutin, henchman for Brezhnev and Bautista, leader of the Sputniks in the Philippines.

Wes replies, "Director, fax me the dossiers on both men and give me 48 to 72 hours to apprehend and deliver those culprits to the farm! The C-130's are revving their engines as we speak!" and hung-up.

The Special Activities Division, known as SAD, is a division of the United States Intelligence Agency responsible for covert operations and within SAD there are two separate groups; SAD/SOG for tactical paramilitary operations and SAD/PAG for covert political action, such as what took place in Chile.

Now as far as reference to the farm, this is a covert interrogation outpost along the Bayou Teche River somewhere in Louisiana. It is not on the map!

The farm is for reptilian breeding of alligators and crocodiles. Coming face to face with a crocodile or an alligator, one would see a mouth full of serrated teeth that would likely scare the bejeezus out of you. Alligators have wider, U-shaped snouts, while crocodile's front ends are more pointed and V-shaped. When their snouts are shut, crocodiles look like a toothy grin because the fourth tooth on each side of the lower jaw sticks up over the upper lip. For alligators, the upper jaw is wider than the lower jaw, and so when they close their mouths, all their teeth are hidden. Both species can grow from 12 to 14 feet in length but with good breeding, one can produce the mother of all reptiles and reach a length of 20 to 25 feet of bone chomping meanness'.

The Trahan brothers ran the farm and were paid handsomely as cleaners for the CIA. Guillaume and Boudreaux Trahan were big boys and wrestled anything that moved, crocs, alligators, boas and people. Informants, criminals and terrorist were sent to the farm and the reptiles cleaned them up!

Helms concluded the meeting pounding the top of the table and shouting to the top of his lungs that he wanted a full-court press, find these subversives and no screw-ups!

Corey Bennett of the FBI and Samuel Phillips of the United States Marshall Service oversaw finding the trail of the assassins. Before the day concluded, Danny and Rick were back in Bay Minette explaining to Mr. Bennett what they knew. Sam Phillips listened attentively to what each had to say and then taught those young guys the art of tracking, "You know tracking a suspect is no different than tracking an animal." Then he asked the question to see how clever we were to figure the answers, "How do you track an animal?"

As youngsters, they both went hunting with their grandfathers and responded by saying, "Examine the footprints on the ground!"

"Fine," He responded and then Sam asked, "what if there are no footprints?"

Both Danny and Rick were scratching their heads as Danny replied, "Find a trail of something left behind or something lying ahead like broken branches."

"Good, now you're thinking." Sam stopped long enough to ask, "what things are needed on every trip?"

Sam decided to answer the question before we could respond. "They are food, gas and a place to stay. Whether they use cash or credit, they leave a trail. Tracking is the same whether beast or human, either circle the woods or circle the towns until you find a trail and connect the dots to follow their direction."

He gave them a moment to let that settle in before saying, "Most people use credit cards but we will check within a small circle of stores, gas stations and motels for their cash receipts and find a trail in what direction the culprits are heading or in this case three trails."

Now Corey Bennett intervened by saying, "To make our job a little easier since we know the culprits were here in Bay Minette, an APB, all-points bulletin will be issued along with sketches and models of the three vehicles to all authorities as well as stores, gas stations etc. in the surrounding states to help identify these bastards."

Within a day, information started coming in that made one of the trails quite evident as the search continued for all three parties.

Corey Bennett pointed to Rick and said, "WW wants you back in New Orleans, pronto!" He handed him a brief case of papers while saying, "Danny will work with Sam Phillips on the trail of the assassins, while you catch a C-130 back to Lagos, Nigeria."

He quickly snapped back, "Why Lagos?"

"It's all in the brief case, son, now get moving for it is now 1400 hours and your flight with Major General Wes Armstrong takes off at 1900 hours this evening."

Checking his watch and knowing that he had a three-and-a-half-hour drive back to New Orleans, he drove like a bat out of hell to make his flight. The C-130 had its engines revving with Wes Armstrong and his crew already onboard. Barely enough time for strapping himself in, the rear door was closed and the plane took off as Major General Armstrong ordered him to open the briefcase. Rick followed orders as he opened the briefcase to go over the papers and study the photographs. Since he knew the layout of Lagos and Jackson McKenna wasn't available, he would become the snare to trap Vadik Vasyutin, the henchman for Brezhnev. Apparently, there was a meeting to take place between Lagos Logistics Inc. and Vasyutin with a 24-hour window to capture the henchman. Information that Wes obtained from the SAS, Special Air Service, a special forces unit of the British Army similar to our Navy Seals.

The unit undertakes a number of roles including covert reconnaissance, counter-terrorism and hostage rescue.

Especially in many of the colonies under the British Crown with colonial Nigeria being one of them. The colonial period proper in Nigeria lasted through most of the nineteen hundred until 1960 when the country gained its independence. But the SAS still maintained documents on such subversive groups such as the Lagos Logistics Company. Collaborative efforts from various intelligent agencies from around the world is key for many of the successful missions.

Another C-130 from the U.S. 7th Fleet in the Pacific was en-route to the Philippines. The C-130 is a four-engine turboprop military transport aircraft with six integral wing tanks carry 6700 gallons of fuel that can cruise at 374 mph. A second Black Ops team were prepared to apprehend Bautista and strike at the head of the Sputniks. Any special operations group responsible for covert operations normally do not carry any objects or wear any military uniform that would associate them with the United States.

Both C-130's are in the air en-route to their destinations as hot-tempered Johnny Fletcher and his crew of ATF agents monitored the planes being loaded in Mexico. At the same time trucks were leaving terminals from New Orleans and heading North on route 55. Terrorist are rampant in our country, bombs are ticking and assassins are on the move. WW's blood pressure is at 180 and climbing.

Shotgun, Frank Douglas is concerned for the total count appears to be up to 35 trucks and supposedly all loaded with bombs. The DEA would observe the trucks by air as helicopters were dispatched and vans of agents pursued the suspected trucks loaded with bombs. Emergency calls by the DOJ were put out to the state police of each state along the Mississippi River. Road blocks were set up and time is not on the authorities' side to stop the perpetrators from blowing up, what can only be surmised at this point, as bridges and God knows what else?

Shotgun, who was known for his persistence, on the radio with his agents as he asked, "How many trucks are leaving the terminal?"

One agent replying, "Hell Frank there are literally hundreds of trucks entering and leaving the terminal within the last four hours, how are we to keep track of each truck?"

Frank Douglas in his concern calls WW and ask for more help to stop all of the trucks. A perturbed WW firing back with, "From what I understand there are supposedly only thirty-five trucks loaded with the bombs!"

Frank in his desperation repeats the words, "Lost track of carriers, lost track of carriers!"

WW issues an all-out alert to the various state police in the surrounding states to stop and search any truck along US highways. He then adds the disclaimer; possible targets are bridges and major railroad crossings.

The game of leap truck has begun as trucks with known bombs traveled along route 10 East and West, some along route 55 North and only guessing on any detours to be taken. The first road blocks were in Louisiana and Mississippi States checking all trailer trucks. One truck slipped pass a major road block by exiting on highway 61 to Vicksburg. Within three and a half hours our fears were realized as the first bomb went off on the Vicksburg Bridge along Highway 20. The nightmare has begun as an emergency status of the National Guard within Louisiana and Mississippi are called to action to stop all trailer trucks from crossing the borders.

The second fiasco occurred within the hour just outside the city limits of Batesville, Mississippi, as one trailer truck approached a National Guard roadblock. The orders were simple and direct from the DOJ to all State Governors and State Police, "Code 10-45," which from the APCO codes mean bomb threat and stop at all cost!

Sargent Troy Fenton is celebrating his 30th wedding anniversary and 25 years with the State Police. He kissed his wife goodbye this morning anticipating a phenomenal day.

His orders were clear for the day. Set-up a roadblock on highway 55. All trailer rigs stopped and searched. Roadblocks were set to prevent access into Memphis to avert any catastrophic damage of major bridges. Ten state troopers and ten national guard personnel were activated and stood their post with barriers to stop and search all trucks. What should have been a smooth, normal day turned into a chaotic nightmare.

One trailer-rig approached slowly and once the driver noticed the road block ahead of him, accelerated his rig, passing all other vehicles in the outer lane. Sargent Troy yelled to the other guardsmen, "spread out the magnum spikes and then get out of the way."

Precautions were taken for run-away trucks with magnum spikes for tire deflation as the guardsman hurriedly laid out the spikes fifty feet behind the barrier.

The driver of the rig easily smashed through the barrier and once his tires blew out over the spikes activated the timer to set off the explosives. The timer was set for four minutes.

The trailer truck came to a screeching halt as the State Police and Guardsmen approached the vehicle with their weapons drawn and ready. The first minute has already expired.

Sargent Troy Fenton instructs the driver to step out of the vehicle with his hands up. The driver slowly steps out as two officers step forward to frisk the suspect and have him show some positive ID.

Now Sargent Troy has the suspect walk to the rear of the vehicle to unlock and open the doors. Two more minutes have expired as the driver slowly unlocks and open the rear doors.

Two State Troopers, along with Sargent Troy climbed into the trailer to inspect the cargo.

A catastrophic blast burst asunder and could be heard throughout Memphis and all the way into Little Rock. Thirty-four people were within the blast zone and thirty-four people died.

Sargent Troy Fenton never made his anniversary party and thirty-three others never made it home to their families.

This action triggered the surveillance crews at each of the Mexican airports stand ready to search and seize all planes. In lieu of the explosion from the trailer truck, God only knows how much devastation would be caused by the planes.

WW beckons the Secretary of State to call the Mexican government for joint cooperation to stop this conspiracy. That phone call caused a quagmire since the Mexican Cartel had their hands in the government's pockets. Permission was denied and slamming his fist against the desk, Henry Kissinger instructs the president of Mexico that the United States is prepared to do whatever it takes to defend our borders. That insinuation got both the Mexican military and cartel involved to protect their assets and a gunfight ensued at each of the airports.

Secretary of State Kissinger in turn authorized our air force at high alert, "Don't allow any planes from Mexico to cross our air space."

A frustrated Kissinger slammed down the phone and crossed the hallway to the oval office to break the news to the president.

Nixon could be heard yelling to the top of his lungs, "**Watergate, war with Mexico, bridges blowing up in Louisiana, bombs going off, what the hell else can go wrong!**"

Before any answer could be given to those questions, the Mexican military arrived first at the General Servando Canales and then at the General Lucio Blanco International Airports and battles erupted. Hot tempered Johnny Fletcher was severely wounded, and the ATF were both outmanned and out maneuvered. As action enraged at these two airports, the drug cartel had their forces arrive at the other four airports killing many of the ATF agents and a diplomatic war erupted between the United States and Mexico.

Back at the Whitehouse a perturbed Nixon told Henry that you cost us Chile, but you will not cause a fiasco with Mexico, that you either get us out of this mess or resign.

Many of the innuendos about Nixon are true, but one of his famous nicknames of "Tricky Dick" was well earned. As Watergate will come to prove, passing the blame was one of his greatest attributes.

Three small Cessna's took off from the Rancho San Salvador Northeast Airport and Laughlin Air Force Base scrambled jets to take to the skies. Once the Cessna pilots noticed the US Air Force jets, two of the planes turned back while the third plane made a run straight north. Failing to turn back the third Cessna was short down, crashed and burst into flames. When one is caught between a rock and a hard place and your facing the devil and the deep blue sea, there is no turning back! As the saying goes, "damn those torpedoes, full speed ahead!"

Nixon is now on the phone with the President of Mexico, Luis Echeverria, "Mr. President Echeverria, President Richard Nixon speaking, and I will cut right to the chase! The United States is in the middle of a conspiracy of bombs, black outs and assassination attempts! If it wasn't serious, then I would not be on the phone with you. Many of the bombs are coming through your country. I need your assistance and cooperation to stop this conspiracy or we can go to "**war**!"

Raising his voice to accent the inevitable. "Now I ask you Mr. President, do we have friendship between our countries, or do we burn asunder?"

Sometimes, to cut through all the red tape, it is better to have leaders fight over a cause then troops skirmish on the ground!

President Luis Echeverria chose friendship and within the hour had the Mexican Military at each of the airports to give assistance to the ATF. At least for now there was a reprieve on any black outs within the United States.

Two rogue trucks were heading Northeast on highway 79 through Arkansas loaded with enough explosives to take out the bridge between Memphis and Arkansas along route 40.

WW scanning over a map of the southern portion of the United States and asking Frank Douglas, "If you were a terrorist, what would be your next target?"

Frank scrutinizing the map, then says, "Not enough hours to make it to Chicago and road blocks should prevent anything north of Memphis, so I would say Memphis bridge."

WW puts out an APB on all back roads as well as major highways and is also concerned about the bridge at St. Louis as he wipes his sweaty brow and adds, "I don't want any more explosions!"

War is hell! But terrorist's acts of violence are harbingers of doom!

In the quiet of the night a Grumman G-111 Albatross amphibious aircraft takes off the deck of the Kitty Hawk somewhere in the Pacific. Unclassified destination for the Pasig River, Manilla, Philippines near the National Oil Corporation. Combined intelligence from the CIA and MI6 has confirmed a meeting between Bautista and weapons manufacturers at the Chevron Pandacan Terminal. A number of Black Ops are already on the ground waiting for the suspects and the aircraft that will transport the Sputnik leader to the farm.

Like clockwork at exactly nine PM, Bautista and his entourage arrive in four vans and meet with Russian emissaries at the terminal. The left end of the terminal is a warehouse where a truckload of weapons arrives to be inspected and hopefully a deal to be made. Bautista has his sixteen bodyguards and the Russians have their henchman. Six of the body guards stand watch outside of the warehouse not realizing that this is their last night on earth as tactical knives slash their throats. Black Ops stealthily move in with silencers on their weapons killing all except for the horrified Bautista, who thought he had adequate protection.

A specially made clamp known as the "BOC," Black Ops Clamp was fastened around Bautista. This clamp is made for such occasions with a medium size clamp attached around Bautista's neck. A second larger clamp goes around his waist with a bar straddling his back between the two clamps. Both of his hands are handcuffed to the bar and his feet are shackled. Bent over and led by two Black Ops by the bar, Bautista is dragged to the river's edge as the Albatross lands on the river. The Albatross maneuvers in close to shore and Bautista is hastily hauled aboard. Without missing a beat, the pilot of the Albatross revs up its four engines and takes off. It is now 9:55 PM and the Albatross heads for the Kitty Hawk.

Bautista dazed, baffled and clueless as to what just happened, looks around the plane and wonders if he will live long enough to see the sunrise. Men that neither feel or show any compassion towards others have no remorse. Two hours later landing on the deck of the Kitty Hawk, Bautista is hauled off the Albatross and reloaded on a C-130 bound for Louisiana. There are no pit-stops and the Black Ops are eager to deliver the package to its destination.

There are refueling maneuvers in mid-air to make the final destination and touchdown will be within twenty-six hours. The man in charge, Colonel Jeffreys just stares at the monster responsible for so many atrocities throughout the world. He knows what treats are in store for Bautista at the Farm. Words aren't enough to describe the mayhem, grief and brutal deaths caused by this bastard. Bautista rubbernecks around the aircraft feeling very uncomfortable in the clamps and just looks at each of the Black Ops on board.

In a quiet field on the outskirts of Lagos, Nigeria another C-130 lands with a Black Ops force commanded by Major General Wes Armstrong.

Major General Armstrong looks at Rick and says, "Listen up, I will only say this once. Just received confirmation that we got our man in the Philippines! Now, I want this joker, Vadik Vasyutin, just as bad! Our people on the ground confirm that he will be at the Galleria Dream for mixed business and pleasure. You know this place?"

"Yes Sir," Rick replied.

"Alright, we have no time for any play rehearsals and besides they can spot a phony! Play it straight, you're an agent for the CIA and want to know about your friend Trevor. They may ask you some questions, answer them truthfully and play it by ear. You will be on your own inside for ten minutes, so it is up to you to stay alive. But within ten minutes all hell will break loose, so stay low to the floor once the action explodes. You know what Vasyutin looks like from the pictures. His body guards will search you, so no weapons and no wire. Just remember you have some information for his ears only, and that will get you an audience with him."

Wes eyes him over and ask, "Are you nervous?"

"Hell yes!" was his reply.

"Good, then you'll do alright." Wes replies as he gives a broad smile.

He looks at his watch and yells out for all to hear, "synchronize watches at nineteen hundred and ten minutes."

Then he looks at all of his men as he states, "It's a twenty-minute drive to the club and so forty minutes roundtrip plus the execution and capture. Liftoff with our package will be within one hour!"

Agents that were on the ground had vans for us at a remote spot. One learns to clear your mind and not dwindle on anything as to be able, willing and ready for the ordeal to be successful. There are five vans and as we approach the Galleria Dream, two vans drive to the east side of the club while two proceed to the back.

Rick drives his van to the front entrance and parks by a large baobab tree. For this time of year there was a cool tropical breeze coming off the ocean which relaxed his impulses and calmed his nerves. He entered the club which triggered the ten minutes. It took a minute to look around the club and noticed Vadik sitting in an alcove with two other men from Lagos Logistics and five body guards. Two young lovelies were dancing on his table. Rick waited another minute before crossing the floor and now had eight minutes to pull off the planned shenanigan. As he approached Vadik's table, two body guards pushed him back and asked in Russian what he wanted.

He responded by asking, "Do you speak English?"

It is amazing that most people in our world do speak English, whether good or bad. One of the advantages of being a world power and a place that most would like to live.

They replied by saying, "yes," and he explained that he had some valuable information for a Mr. Vadik Vasyutin. He was surreptitiously brought to a corner of the club and then frisked for weapons and his shirt ripped opened to check for a wire. He now had about six minutes left. The body guards led him to Vadik as he stood and asked his guards, "What is the meaning of this?"

Rick very calmly explained to him that he was a CIA Kibitzer and had some essential information for him. He laughed and asked in very good English, "What the hell is a Kibitzer?" He turned to his body guards and laughed, "It sounds like a cookie to me!"

Then Vasyutin turned and scrutinized his countenance for he could always tell when someone is lying. He then pushed him back and said, "What is this?" Always suspicious and not liking the young lad's looks, he didn't even hesitate for his information but told his body guards to take him outside and kill him. As they escorted Rick to the side doors, Wes and his Black Ops crashed the party shooting anyone standing as Rick plunged to the floor.

Multiple gunshots ricochet throughout the establishment, killing most of the body guards. Wes who is six-foot-eight, weighs close to 290 lbs. and wears a 15-inch boot, kicked Vasyutin in the groin so hard that he collapsed to the floor.

Wes then looked at me and yelled, "Are you coming!"

The impact of that kick caused me to grimace as I cupped my nuts and replied, "Yes Sir!"

The C-130 was originally designed as a troop military transport aircraft capable of using unprepared runways for takeoffs and landings. It is now the main tactical air lifter for many military forces worldwide. With our cargo onboard, we were bound for the states.

The flight time gave all of us a chance to reflect and gather our thoughts, calm our nerves and catch some shut-eye. One doesn't really sleep in such situations but cat naps and is prepared for the unexpected.

THE FARM

Many popular conceptions throughout the centuries have tried to describe the visions of hell in lucid, vivid terms beginning with the Renaissance poet Dante Alighieri with his visions in the Inferno, or Paradise Lost by John Milton and even the Place of the Damned by Jonathan Swift, but words are not enough to describe the unending pain that one will feel in the un-consuming fire of Hell.

The "Farm" is such a place of extremes, extreme fear, pain and anguish. Vadik Vasyutin and Bautista are on their way to hell. Rendezvous' were made at some remote spot in Costa Rica. Just one of the many CIA bases around the world. A world power has to be prepared for any contingency to intervene and prevent any faux pas. Transfers were made of the two suspects to one C-130 bound for the farm.

Their chains from their handcuffs are attached to the floor as both men are seated apart from each other. No chances to confer their stories for an alibi. It's a three hour and twenty-minute flight to the farm with no stewardess or rest room. No window views as both men are hunched over by their chains. They can only stare at each other from thirty feet apart. Their eyes meet and if only thoughts could be heard what infamous tales would they tell? One just has to look at each of the men and see their apprehensive consciences working overtime. Their eyes revealing fear as they should for hell is extreme, excruciating pain beyond all comprehension. They stare and look around and then down upon the deck for the reality of the end is as apparent as the final eschaton.

In the middle of the night the C-130 landed, for only night landings can keep the anonymity of the Farm. No roads lead to the Farm, one approaches this place by either air or water. No salutations, no fan-fair as the two thugs are dragged in shackles to the barn and tossed down on the rough floor planks. A winch lowers a hook which is connected to the shackles of Bautista, unaware that he is the bait to break Vasyutin into submission and spill his guts out. The winch is operated by Guillaume who picks up Bautista feet first. Then another hook is lowered for Vasyutin and he too swings high overhead to see a large trap-door in the floor below. The crocodiles and alligators haven't been fed for two weeks and are hungry for anything with flesh and bones.

Boudreaux laggardly walks over to the opening and lifts the trap-door slowly while starring into the fearful eyes of his two captives. He smiles and shows his missing teeth as he takes a bucket of animal guts to throw down the hole. What appears to be calm waters below, suddenly comes alive with thrashing, snapping reptiles twenty to twenty-five feet in length. As Guillaume lowers the first victim, Bautista yells an agonizing scream and I'm not sure which occurs first the screams or the excrement of the body for they seem to happen simultaneously.

There is nothing that Bautista can say to save his life for he is to be the impetus to cause Vasyutin to talk. One is not aware of anything as he is lowered inch by inch, but a hungry crocodile can leap ten feet out of the water and into the air with those snapping jaws of death ready to shred you to pieces. As the body of Bautista is slowly lowered, the body of Vasyutin swings high overhead watching with dreadful eyes bulging from their sockets, blood rushing to his pulsating head. Who can perceive what is going through their minds. Living a nightmare, the fear explodes first in his mind, then his heart causing his blood to gush throughout his body, pounding harder and harder and harder.

Guillaume stops the winch with Bautista's body dangling fifteen feet above the water. One croc lunges out of the water towards the body of Bautista as he closes his eyes and jerks his body like a contortionist smelling the foul breath of the croc and feeling his snapping jaws against his forehead.

Five minutes pass which seems like an eternity and then Guillaume lowers the cable another eight feet. Simultaneously, two crocs lunge with their jaws wide open and tear the body off the hook and splash below in a frenzy with all the crocs and alligators joining in the feast of flesh, bones and guts.

The blood, curdling screams from Vasyutin could be heard in Russian all the way into Canada. Even if one did not know Russian, one understood what he said from the smell of fear permeating from his body and the anguish uttered from his mouth. He is now begging for his life, begging for mercy from a man that never showed any to his multiple victims and wants to tell them whatever they want to know. Major General Wes Armstrong shakes his head in the affirmative for this is exactly what is needed, and signals with his hand five more minutes of torture to Guillaume.

After five excruciating minutes for Vasyutin just hanging there, Wes Armstrong signals with a thumbs-down to lower him slowly. Vasyutin throws-up and gives a gut-wrenching yell which tells Wes this man is definitely ready to give a full confession. Wes signals to Guillaume to allow Vasyutin to wallow in his barf on the barn floor.

Boudreaux walks over to Vadik Vasyutin and unshackles him, while picking him up off the floor with one arm. Weighing in at close to 380lbs and being used to wrestling alligators, Boudreaux had no problem handling this henchman. He was taken to the cabin and allowed a shower to get cleaned up, dressed and given a decent meal. Once he finished his meal and given a shot of vodka, then Wes, Wade Washington and a lawyer from the DOJ came into the room to listen attentively to what Vasyutin had to say.

Wes offered him a cigarette and as he accepted, took out his lighter to light the cigarette with a complete change of etiquette. Once Vasyutin accepted the consequences and became a compliant confessor to give a complete truthful account, the hostilities ceased. A pad of paper is laid on the table to write down his confession while a tape recorder is turned on as Wes states his full name and rank for the recording.

"On this date of our Lord and Wes states the time and date, Major General Wes Armstrong interviews," and asks Vasyutin, "state your full name, title and who you work for."

And then as he gives his full name, title and who he works for, Leonid Llyich Brezhnev, the General Secretary of the Soviet Union since 1964, an elaborate plan unfolded before their very ears that caused their spine to twinge and heart to pound a little harder. The plan was much more devious then any of them could ever conceive. He wrote down his words slowly in English asking how to spell many of the words for English is the most difficult language to learn from his native tongue. Wes helped him with the words as he carefully proofread what Vasyutin had written and WW listened intently as he spoke the horrifying words of World War III.

The United States' perceptible conclusion of Russian coercion was fully confirmed by Vadik Vasyutin's confession. First would come the disruption of the electrical power grid and our communications grid followed by bombs to disrupt major transportation throughout the United States. Then the blatant audacity of Russian leaders orchestrating the assassinations of three of our top leaders. Pandemonium would follow as Russia declared war upon us and hoped for total annihilation.

A sensation of shock hit all three of the men as the devious plan unraveled before their very ears. WW being extremely enraged at the putrid bastard as he walked around the table. He stood directly behind Vasyutin and then grabbed his head with both of his hands and smashed it against the table.

Wes stood up unexpectantly and asked WW, "Was that as good for you as it was for me," as he chuckled and said, "Good Show WW!"

The words still echoed in his ears of, "Assassinations would follow of the President of the United States, Richard Nixon, the Vice President who was now Gerald Ford and the Speaker of the House, Carl B Albert to create pandemonium so that the ultimate threat of World War III would render Russia an all-out victory."

WW is now pacing back and forth and still can't believe the whole plot.

The hollow, insidious news was too momentous to keep under wraps as WW took a flight direct to Washington DC to break the news to the President of the United States. A special meeting was called of the JCS, Joint Chiefs of Staff and Congress because now with the full plan revealed and all questions answered the conspiracy became a real threat as the President sets the DEFCON threat for the first time in the history of the United States to DEFCON 1, nuclear war is imminent. NORAD had only gone to DEFCON 2 during the Cuban Missile Crisis as maximum readiness for all branches of our arm services is alerted.

It is imperative that we send a unanimous, urgent message from the United States to warn Russia that we know of their plan and are prepared to go the whole way to defend and uphold our way of life. DEFCON ONE means all missile silo hatches are open, all submarines with nuclear Polaris missiles armed and ready; all carrier groups on station ready to launch planes and missiles and all long-range B-52 Stratofortress bombers are ready to launch. The keys are inserted and the access codes are set; once the button is pushed, there is no turning back! It will be a sad epitaph for all humankind, if we ever must use such divisiveness!

A new set of shackles was placed on Vasyutin and loaded on a C-130 by Wes Armstrong as he wanted to accommodate him to his final resting place at Guantanamo Bay, GTMO, pronounced Gitmo. Built in 1898 by the United States when first seized in the Spanish-American War; established a naval base and was used for special covert detentions, long before its infamous reputation.

A side trip would be made to drop me off at the Algiers Naval Support Base in New Orleans, rich in history with the importation of African slaves in the 18th century, this area was used as a holding area for the Cajuns who survived the Great Upheaval when the British expelled them from Nova Scotia.

I sat quietly wondering what God thought of all this; how we humans utilized His beautiful creation? He created a beautiful world, life and all that could have been glorious but what He created; humankind has continually desecrated. Watching Wes and seeing the strain and scars on his face told a story of infamy that he has seen and the courage to persevere to fight for what is right. But the scars symbolized the burning question are we humans following the path of truth? Then I studied the countenance of Vasyutin and wondered if this is the face of true evil? Another tyrant who had become a deadly statistic of wrong choices? Too many humans lose their way, forfeit their faith and cause many to pay for their wrong choices. More questions arose and I found it necessary for another talk with the military chaplain.

Now that the entire plot has been revealed, it wasn't necessary to follow a cold trail to find the assassins. Knowing the outcome of the scheme, it was a game of wait and capture. I was reassigned to Corey Bennett's team and oh, what a tangled web, devious minds can conceive! The Russian leaders thought they could cause absolute chaos to force us to lose WW III. The truth of the matter is, there is no such thing as winning such a catastrophe; all humankind would be losers! The absolute necessity is to prevent it from ever happening.

A critical piece of information that Wes managed to coerce out of Vasyutin is the key date of February 23rd for the assassinations. Known in Russia as "Defense of the Fatherland Day," honors those in Russia who are currently serving in the Armed Services now and within the past of the Fatherland. It is now January 30th and we have exactly 24 days to find the culprits.

A heated debate at the Whitehouse whether to go public with this information goes well into the night. These are troubled times and stress is peaking at maximum overdrive with Watergate, Spiro Agnew under investigation for accepting bribes and income tax evasion, the House Judiciary Committee begins hearings on Ford's nomination as Vice President and Soviet Premier Leonid Brezhnev is coming to the United States for the Summit II talks.

Nixon yelling to the top of his lungs, "Imagine that two-faced bastard coming here in the guise of peace and sanctions a hit on me, that putrid, two-faced bastard! The Japanese tried the same thing with their innocent meeting before bombing Pearl Harbor!"

Nixon stands up and pounds his fist on his desk before saying, "Find those assassins and let's end this conspiracy and for the Love of God, put a stop to this horrific idea of WW III. Two World Wars have left enough sadness and scars on the earth, our world can't afford another one!"

A strategy meeting was held between the FBI, the Secret Service and the United States Marshall Service to drop a dragnet over the assassins and haul them in before the unthinkable happens. With our top three diplomats on the hit list, the itineraries of all three men were scrutinized and the cat and mouse game of apprehending the assassins began. One of Nixon's staff members suggested that an imposter that looks like the president should make the public speeches in lieu of the discerning information on hand. Once again, the president slammed his fist on the desk top and said, "Balderdash! People can spot a phony a mile away!"

Trying to regain his composure, he then said to Henry, "I'm in enough of a conundrum with Watergate! What kind of a ruckus would explode with imposters?"

Conferring with his top advisers, President Nixon looked around the Oval Office and said, "Such dire faces, well, what do you think John?" as he looked at John Ehrlichman?

"An assassination would get you out of a hell of a lot of trouble!"

Henry cleared his throat and interjected, "One hell of a comment John!"

Laughter erupted and the tension for the first time eased up.

Nixon then said, "Gentlemen, I thank you for your service, but I need some time alone with Henry," as he ushered his advisers out of the room.

As Haldeman, Ehrlichman and Charles Colson set their drinks down, Gordon Strachan turned to Haldeman and said, "Where's the CIA when we need them to clean up this mess?"

All exited the oval office and as the door closed behind them, Nixon looked at Henry and said, "Well my old friend, Viet Nam, Russia, Chile, Watergate and now assassinations, what are we to do?"

Henry stood up, muttered a few phrases and exclaimed, "Declare war on Russia!"

And then added, "There are no safety nets on this one, the illegal we do immediately. The unconstitutional takes a little longer!"

Nixon nodded his head and conceded that this just might be the end! As the president climbed the stairs to his living quarters, he could hear a familiar sound from outside the White House of chants of protestors on Pennsylvania Avenue. The cacophony of shouts echoed not about the Vietnam War but instead shouted, "Jail to the Chief!"

The dragnet was pulled tighter and tighter as the DOJ's intelligence gathered information on the assassins. Like bloodhounds, the Marshalls and FBI agents closed in and uncovered three trails. One of the trails led the FBI to Stone Mountain, Georgia. Dakila Flores and Flordeliza Castillo showed up at an out of the way motel in Stone Mountain and paid cash for the room which sent an alert to the FBI. All overnight establishments from bed & breakfast to fancy hotels were issued an APB, to be on the lookout for two suspicious characters of foreign extract that are cash-paying customers.

A special conference by the Georgia Chapter of the APCO, Association of Public-Safety Communications Officials on meeting emergency response obligations in today's world would be given in two days at one of the conference centers at Stone Mountain Park. Their main guess speaker would be, Carl B.

Albert, Speaker of the United States House of Representatives. The list of distinguished guests included Andrew Young voted to the U.S. Congress in 1972 as the first black congressman from Georgia since the reconstruction and Maynard Jackson, Atlanta's first black mayor in 1973.

Progressive times considering that the FBI used extensive network of informers to disrupt Klan activities in Georgia and other southern states. In the early 1970's their efforts proved effective to reduce the KKK membership substantially. Stone Mountain was once owned by the Venable Brothers, the site of the founding of the second wave of the Ku Klux Klan and Corey Bennett remembers well his active part to break their association with another faction group of the KKK in Louisiana under the leadership of a David Duke. Now as the famous Spanish philosopher George Santayana once said, "Those who cannot remember the past are condemned to repeat it."

Once the sanctioned hits are initiated, the terrorist objective is chaos, loss of our leadership and our destruction in a declared World War III by Russia. It was imperative to apprehend these desperado terrorists to expose this conspiracy to the world.

Agents were positioned at both the main and west entrance gates at Stone Mountain Park, an impressive beautiful park with the dome of the mountain extending skyward formed as part of the Blue Ridge Mountains some 300 million years ago. City garbage trucks with front loaders and local cement trucks were strategically positioned throughout the park to box in the culprits once they gained access to the park.

Corey Bennett's undercover FBI team were positioned at the main entrance while Samuel Phillips' US Marshalls team remained stationed at the west entrance. It was a beautiful sunny day in the mid-fifties considering the time of year as February 5th rolled around. Eighteen days remain to foil the espionage plot that leads up to World War III. Word relayed to Bennett that another bridge was blown-up in the mid-west as one could hear the multiple expletives vehemently flow from his mouth saying, "Those friggin bastards, how did they get through our grid of road blocks?"

The next set of orders being issued by Bennett over his radio to the others were, "We need to apprehend these bastards and take them to the farm!"

One of the vehicles that fit the description of those purchased in Bay Minette approached the West Gate slowly, stopped a hundred feet back from the gate and surveyed the entrance. His inpatients weighing thin, Bennet asked over his radio, "What the hell are they waiting for?"

Once the two culprits noticed the garbage trucks parked on both sides of the entrance, suspicions arose as the vehicle did a U-turn and bolted along Highway 78. Sam Phillips radioed the others as air surveillance from the helicopters observed the car racing west on Highway 78 towards Atlanta and road blocks were set up on Highway 78 by the Cooledge Road exit. Some forethought to pen these bastards in with a second roadblock was set up behind the culprits at the Mountain Industrial Blvd. exit.

The vehicle is clocked racing at 100 mph and slams on their brakes to come to a screeching holt leaving tire marks the whole way as they notice the blockade ahead of them. Dakila Flores was driving the car with Castillo in the rear seat loading his rocket launcher. Castillo glances out the rear window and notices the flashing lights of state and federal vehicles approaching behind them.

Prepared to die for their cause, a composed Castillo adjust his loaded rocket launcher and steps out from the passenger side of the vehicle while Flores steps out from the driver's seat with his Mossberg loaded and ready to fire at will.

Aiming the rocket launcher with deadly accuracy in the center of vehicles behind them, Castillo fires the rocket and hits the first vehicle bullseye causing it to explode sending two other vehicles off the road. Castillo reloads and is prepared to shoot at the blockade in front of them as one of the helicopters armed with AGM-114 Hellfire missiles, fires upon the culprits. The explosion left a pile of dust!

Corey Bennett witnessed the direct hit from the helicopter as he was several vehicles back behind the culprits yelling to the top of his lungs over the radio, "**No, No, No**, I wanted to take those bastards to the farm for questioning!"

With two of the culprits down, that left four more to apprehend as the teams would have to intensify their search to find the others before February 23rd.

Reynante Bautista, a brother to the leader of the Sputniks, was unaware of his brother's death at the farm. Ordained to oversee the six terrorists by his brother, Reynante engineered the plot to assassinate the three diplomats of the United States. Failure is never an option for any terrorist; fight to the end and kill as many as one can, but never surrender.

The feelings that are harbored against the United States have been long in the making. Christianity, Islam and Judaism are often known as the Abrahamic religions because of their common origin through Abraham. Jews and Muslims consider his son Ishmael to be the Father of the Arabs and Isaac the Father of the Hebrews. Today, Christianity and Islam differ in their fundamental views regarding the God they worship, the nature of their religion, their beliefs about the crucifixion and resurrection of Jesus. Christians believe that Jesus is the Son of God and Muslims do not believe that he was the Son of God. And for the many Islamic followers that live in the Philippines, they harbor the same feelings. This is a conundrum that will exist until the Second Coming!

Corey Bennett who in his past youth entered the seminary to study for the priesthood some thirty-two years ago, turned to his associate and said, "It is a sad truth, that no matter which religion one follows, the ten commandments are the foundation of the three major religions, so why can't we learn to live together?"

Sam Bennett, listening attentively to Corey asked, "The big question I have is simply this, has terrorism ever achieved its aims?"

Corey looked at Sam and replied, "Since terrorism evolved and targeted most major global locations from London to Paris and New York to Melbourne, any of the terrorist groups have never and will never achieve their aims because they lack clear and concise political goals. Their only goal is violence and mayhem and that is not a permanent solution for the amelioration of all!"

The next trail that surfaced lead to the whereabouts of Marichu Mendoza and Isagani Salazar and the assassination attempt on the Vice President. Vice President Ford is traveling extensively throughout the country speaking on behalf of the administration's policies to help bolster confidence in Nixon's administration. And with all of the tensions and fiascos that were happening, this was proving to be mission impossible for the vice president.

An alert came into the FBI headquarters showing two cash paying guest checked into the Monaco Hotel in Philadelphia that fit the APB description. This is elegance above and beyond what one would expect from terrorist who want to keep a low profile. Set in the heart of Philadelphia's historic district with Independence Hall, the Liberty Bell and Benjamin Franklin's grave just a walking distance away. There is a stunning 3300-square-foot ballroom where the vice president was scheduled to give his speech utilizing the historical setting of the beautifully converted 1920's building and historic district.

As quickly as our two terrorists guest got settled into their new accommodations, the FBI, Secret Service and U.S. Marshalls descended upon the Monaco Hotel like vultures on fresh kill. There were more secret agents then guest as maids, door attendants, and the regular staff were replaced with undercover agents.

Mendoza and Salazar had a five-day advantage over the undercover agents as they went about their covert activities placing C-4 explosives with transmitter detonators in chandeliers, drinking fountains and air condition ducts above the ball room. The C-4 explosive is insensitive to heat, shock and friction as they worked for three feverish nights carefully and covertly placing the explosives. When the secret service came in the day before the Vice President's scheduled speech to check out the premises, the explosives were already in place and set.

The day before Vice President Ford arrived at the Monaco Hotel to give his speech, the two terrorists had already checked out. Surveillance cameras showed the two culprits and a trail to follow as Corey Bennett said, "They are getting more blatant and careless! We want to apprehend these two bastards alive!"

One of the trails led to the Diamonds and Gems Club for adult entertainment within close proximity to the hotel. Agents Moore and Dandy were assigned to the trail by Bennett to follow any leads. The agents walked into the club and asked to see footage of the surveillance cameras. Bona fide video showed the two culprits had spent plenty of time at the establishment to collaborate suspicions of their where-a-bouts.

The scheduled speech was to occur at 10 am that morning and as Vice President Ford ascended the stairs to appear on the set stage, he tripped, stumbled and fell to the floor causing a slight concussion where he was immediately whisked off to the local hospital. A fortuitous mishap saved his life but caused the deaths of many others as the explosives burst asunder. Chaos, panic, shouts of despair filled the air as people scattered throughout the hotel. The shakedown to scan every square inch of the establishment to uncover all of the bombs wasn't successful.

As emergency units are responding to the explosions, Corey Bennett is yelling to the top of his lungs, "All-out Blitz, I want those Bastards!" He succinctly commanded, "**Enough!**"

Helicopter surveillance managed to zero in on the terrorist vehicle traveling nonchalantly on I-95 a few miles from the 695 interchanges near Baltimore. Impenetrable roadblocks were set up with cement trucks, state police and FBI but with one slight addition, tear gas. These culprits would not pull another rocket launcher episode like Stone Mountain. WW called Richard Helms, head of the CIA and once again requested for the assistance of Major General Wes Armstrong.

Like clockwork, road blocks are set, enforcement agencies are in place and gas grenade launchers are ready as the unsuspecting terrorist approach the road block. In an instant, the terrorist vehicle comes to a screeching halt, causing chaos among other befuddled motorist and before the terrorists could react, launchers hurled gas grenades upon their vehicle. As FBI agents with gas mask approached the vehicle, a CH-47 Chinook helicopter landed nearby with Wes Armstrong and twenty of his armed Black Ops stepping lively from the Chinook. The two culprits are spread eagle on the ground rubbing their teary eyes and gasping for air to clear their lungs as the entourage of Black Ops approach them.

No time is wasted as the shackles are placed on both men and hauled recklessly to the helicopter. Within minutes, the Chinook is airborne and heading to the unknown place called the farm. It was now 7 PM and the five-hour flight would get them to the farm by mid-night. Oh, what fun is in store for our two terrorist culprits, Isagani Salazar and Marichu Mendoza with one remaining question of who will be the bait as the helicopter approaches its destination?

The insurmountable odds of peace versus coercion necessitates the readiness of special forces to go on a moment's notice anywhere in the world. This is the world that we live in! From the "Tower of Babel" to the "Tower of Terrorism," one was done for good to help humankind and the other for evil to destroy.

Once again Guillaume and Boudreaux Trahan accommodated their new guest as Wes Armstrong cautioned the brothers, that this time gaining information is more important than being feed for the crocs.

The hooks were lowered, the trap door was opened and one of the brothers controlled the crane as the other brother took the bucket of animal guts to throw into the water. Again, the waters below erupted with thrashing crocodiles hungry for flesh and bone. Guillaume hoisted both culprits into the air to dangle over the trap doors, seeing the snapping jaws of the stinking beast swirling in a frenzy for a delectable meal. It didn't take long before Salazar was screaming to the top of his lungs before the hoist was lowered slowly, closer and closer to those snapping jaws. An impervious Mendoza didn't scream but defiantly cursed Wes and the United States in Filipino by saying, "ikaw ay mamamatay infidel!" Which means, "you will die infidel!"

Wes signaled Guillaume to lower the hoist a little more and then a second signal with his hand to stop as the two culprits dangled some twelve feet above the surface of the water with crocs lunging for their new meal.

Mendoza again yells defiantly, "maruming bomba!"

That stopped Wes dead in his tracks as he heard those defiant words which meant, dirty bomb. Wes very seldom got a chill up his spine but those words sent a spasm throughout his entire body. Staff Sargent Kroner, who was fluent in Filipino confirmed what was said as he looked at Wes and shook his head before saying, "We don't have the full plot!"

Power struggles have predominated history long before Julius Caesar causing abdications, revolts and wars. With two world wars behind us, the world did not need a third. It was clear to Wes that Russia is willing to risk another world war to win this power struggle and was pulling out all the stops to get there.

Upon further interrogation of the two culprits, no new leads became available about the plot. Wes understanding the urgency of the time, requested for the C-130 Hercules to transport our two guests and once again retrieve Rick from New Orleans on their way to Gitmo. This nightmarish episode wouldn't end soon enough for everyone involved.

Located at the southeastern end of Cuba, Guantanamo Bay's U.S. Naval Base covers approximately 45 square miles and is not on anyone's destination list. Our journey was short, perplexing and imperative to retrieve information from our old nemesis, Vadik Vasyutin. Wes made it absolutely-clear that we had only one opportunity to make him reveal the plot in its entirety. This has to be a bad cop, worst cop scenario!

Upon our arrival, our two detainees were issued one of the two uniforms available. A white jumpsuit was given to Isagani Salazar who was labeled a compliant prisoner and an orange one to Marichu Mendoza for being a non-compliant one and hauled off to their cells.

Wes and I proceeded to a 10 by 10-foot interrogation room and waited for Vasyutin who appeared in an orange jumpsuit.

As Vasyutin was ushered into the room, a stern-faced Armstrong left the premises. Consulted beforehand not to smile or be friendly but direct and to the point, I began questioning Vasyutin in English.

Raising my voice, "**Vadik Vasyutin you lied!"**

He just stared at me and I continued, "**You did not reveal the entire plot to Major General Armstrong!"**

Now his face shows some expression and questions, "What?"

I point my finger towards him and said, "**You need to divulge the whole plot!"**

Playing dumb, he looks bewildered and I grab out of my briefcase a paper to show him the words which reads, 'maruming bomba,' meaning dirty bomb and the words of 'ikaw ay mamamatay infidel'.

I continue with the questioning, "**We have testimony from two of the culprits who are now detainees of Gitmo about the dirty bomb."**

He now stares at the piece of paper and is thinking.

Not to allow any time for him to concoct a story, I pressed on, **"You reveal the whole plot or .... You become crocodile food!"**

I didn't think this charade of ours would work but it did. Just the mention of becoming crocodile food changed his disposition.

At this point Major General Armstrong proceeded back into the room with two other people to witness and take down his statement.

Revelation about the dirty bomb already in the United States would heighten the panic button and keep the DEFCON level remaining at one. The name of the merchant ship and the whereabouts of the dirty bomb revealed that there are eight perpetrators in Florida and the bomb will be set to detonate at the Daytona 500 Speedway on February 17th. Wes looked at me and just gritted his teeth as he pulled that slimy bastard across the table and bashed him against the wall.

Today is February 14th the day which dissident Nobel writer Alexander Solzhenitsyn was expelled from Russia and time is running out with just three days left until the dirty bomb goes off! And only God knows when another assassination attempt on the President of the United States will take place with nine days remaining before World War III is declared. The pressure is mounting and Mount Vesuvius is ready to erupt again!

Vadik Vasyutin thought that he had bought himself more time by not revealing the entire plot for the dirty bomb. That won him a return trip to the Farm and a crocodile culinary end to Vasyutin.

The entire plot was revealed to the DOJ in conjunction with the White House as teams of the FBI and ATF descended upon Daytona with the grueling orders of locate, isolate, disarm and apprehend! Easier said than done, but our finest agents were in the field to get the job accomplished. Information was relayed to the Coast Guard to detain the Liberian Merchant Ship, the "AsMorgadana," the container ship that smuggled in the dirty bomb and eight of the terrorists to the port of Miami.

CHAPTER 7

THE RETURN OF JACKSON MCKENNA

The port of Miami, Florida is the number one containerized cargo port in the state and stands at 12th busiest port in the country employing better than 176, 000 people and contributing nearly $17 billion dollars to southern Florida's economy. Even with the most stringent surveillance, with better than 1 million containers trafficking through the seaport each year, one begins to realize the ease to move arms and weapons in and out of our country. On top of that, there are four million cruise-ship passengers passing through Miami each year. Easy entry for eight terrorists to slip into the country, especially if inside help is available.

Agents swarmed all over the Daytona International Raceway to find and disarm that dirty bomb while Danny and Rick were assigned with the Coast Guard to find any evidence that pointed to the dirty bomb. Like a deck of cards, containers can be shuffled, restacked and reused for other container ships. One container amongst a million is our new needle in a haystack!

In the chess game of life, the pieces aren't the only things that are moved. Now the boards are moved and today there are no rules, no loyalties and no honor. In this world of espionage,

God is dead. There seems to be no hearts, no conscience, just the almighty god of mammon.

The International Atomic Energy Agency, IAEA, recommends certain devices be used in tandem at country borders to prevent transfer of radioactive materials. A dirty bomb or RDD, radiological dispersal device, is a weapon of radioactive material with conventional explosives. As the Coast Guard and IAEA started scanning containers with twelve teams scattered throughout the facility, the two kibitzers showed the symbol to identify the contaminated units amongst the teams with two personnel in each team. As each hour passed, the time to detonation got closer and closer. The first six hours was to no avail as the symbol,

छिद्रान्वेषी

did not appear on any of the containers.

In the mean time the FBI and ATF teams were coming-up empty handed at the raceway to uncover any dirty bomb.

Rick radioed Johnny Fletcher, who was fully recovered from his wound, to ask a simple question of, "what if the bomb was never meant to be necessarily on the premises but in close proximity to the racetrack?"

From the other end of the radio, "Damn, we've waisted six hours, and immediately he further divided the teams to search other premises surrounding the racetrack as he asked, "Ok hotshot, any ideas where to begin?"

Hot tempered Johnny didn't like any advise from us young, inexperienced kibitzers but after working with Jackson McKenna, the lightbulb was turned on to apply the game of 'what if,' and it was beginning to pay off!

"Yea," replied Rick, "Just check the ones that the APB's didn't go out to!"

All that could be heard from his radio is, "Damn, good idea!"

There were a few local businesses and a couple of privately owned motels that weren't associated with the larger chain conglomerates. The next two hours tensions arose, as that damn clock never stops ticking!

Finally someone noticed the symbol on one of the containers and two teams swammed all over it with detection devices that picked up some radioactivity. The purpose of our efforts was to establish a trail of circumstantial evidence for proof of the alleged conspiracy that connected Russia as the main instigator. The Department of Justice is extremely interested in the holistic problem of all contingencies contributing to terrorism from the backing and strategic levels to the perpetrators at ground level committing such pernicious acts of injustice.

Meanwhile the FBI and ATF jointly found the dirty bomb of all places, in a small out of the way motel known as the Sleepy Oasis Motel. Now the tension built, as the premises and surrounding areas were evacuated and a specialized team moved in to deactivate the timer set to go off in approximately 23 hours.

Johnny Fletcher cursing under his breath, "How can we catch all the devious actions when right under our nose, a dirty bomb sits in a motel room. It should not have gotten this far!"

Corey just shaking his head muttering, "Coast Guard, FBI, ATF, US Marshals, DOJ and God only knows how many more agencies are involved and we are right down to post time! This is why the DOJ wants us to be so persnickety about gathering evidence. We've got to shut these bastards down!"

People yell about personal, private rights versus the NAS and satellite surveillence rights on everyone, but where does one draw the line when the devastating consequences affect everyone?

The bomb squad arrived on the premises and suited up, except for one individual known as 'Brucy Fingers,' Bruce Nutter was a well known explosive expert who was respected amongst his peers, and didn't want any heavy protective clothing to slow his reflexes on disarming an explosive device. He was usually a quiet, nerdy person except when disarming a bomb, then he was loquacious and talked himself through every step of the way as if giving a demonstration to all which drove everyone crazy.

His superlative manner of being cool under extreme pressure was praiseworthy but his damn loquaciousness sent many co-workers out the door.

He quietly proceeded to the bomb, laid down his toolbox and surveyed the situation. Once engaged in the disarming, then he talked non-stop, "You see that --- that is a solid pack electric blasting cap. They use a thin bridgewire and it is difficult to cut. I will trace beyond that and oh, you see that --- no, no, no, cut that wire and BOOM!"

His demolition partner jumped back two feet and tried to regain his composure as Brucy Fingers continued his job, talking all the way. "Mercury switch, that opens and closes the circuit --- one slight twitch of that and Boom!"

Most partners didn't last two years with Brucy Fingers, who has now been on the job for twenty-two years.

Speaking to his partner, "Now hand me that canister of liquid nitrogen and I will freeze the mercury switch and blasting cap and cut that bridge switch connected to the timer."

His partner cautiously hands the canister to Brucy and he meticulously sprays the liquid nitrogen instantly freezing the components. Then he tells his partner. "Once I cut that wire, you spray more liquid nitrogen on those components," as he points to them.

Once the device was deactivated and carried away in a bomb disposal container, Brucy Fingers went back to his normal, docil self. But that was not the end of the trail, for the eight terrorist were no-where to be found. Bennett was adament as he yelled, "Get all surveillance from every damn cameria in the area."

The date of February 17th passed-by without any detonation, but where are the eight culprits who set the dirty bomb? Six days remain until Russia declares World War III and somewhere in-between that time frame an assassination attempt on our President.

Corey Bennett is speaking on the phone with Wade Andrew Washington, who always looks like someone walking with hemorrhoids the size of baseballs.

"Any prospects on our assassins?"

"No Sir!"

"What about the eight perpetrators for that dirty bomb?"

"No Sir, no leads!"

WW in a frenzy and not in an eloquent voice asks, "What the hell are you waiting for, Christmas?"

Just when things seem the bleakest, every cloud does have a silver lining or as Jackson McKenna used to say, "every dog has its day!"

Jackson himself reappears and none too soon for as the bloodhound from hell, with only six days left to sniff out the trails, no stone can be left unturned. It seems the debacle in Chile left our compadre to convalesce in the shadows of Argentina. Fortuitous for Jackson that the proprietor of the Blue Lounge was a very good friend of his. Along with the aid of some friends, they hid Jackson from the authorities. The compadres expeditiously smuggled him out of the country through the Andes Mountains and into Argentina where he sought refuge. His asylum left him time to convalesce from his three wounds in San Rafael and cogitate over the debacle in Chile.

One bullet grazed his head that caused a concussion, another a gut shot that left him extremely weak and a third in his right upper leg that caused a permanent limp. The fiasco caused him to become leery about returning to the United States.

During his convalescence, he managed to get in touch with his old adversary in London, Karpichkov and learn a little more information on Trevor. It seems the double agent, Mstislav Alexandra was keeping track of the prison roulette game and our friend was at Perm-36 prison camp.

It is difficult to fathom the term 'GULAG' an acronym for the Soviet bureaucratic institution, Glavnoe Upravlenie ispravitel'no-trudovykh LAGerei that operated the Soviet system of forced labor camps from Stalin's era. Better than 14 million people were imprisoned in the Gulag labor camps and massive executions were committed.

Trevor is lost in the maze of prison camps managed by the Federal Security Service, the FSB which are the successors of the old KGB. Mstislav had an old friend in the Perm-36 prison, one of the few out of the thousands that was released after 25 years of hard labor and remembers Trevor. The inscription on the cell wall of Trevor read, '*Trevor - USA*'.

Now that Jackson was back, we slowly learned of his miraculous trek from San Rafael to the town of Castelli Ingeniero Azul on the coastline by the Bahia de Samborombon better known as the Monterey of Argentina. The weather is delightful, the ocean waters enchanting, the sunsets are beautiful accentuating the naked bodies of the women walking along the beach. Such sights gave a twinge of eroticism to Jackson McKenna and made him wonder about retirement in this hidden oasis.

Jackson particularly enjoyed the celebration of "amalgamation" where couples mingled on the beach and disappeared into the seductive, pulsating, amorous night of oblivion. But this is a town also known as the, la ciudad de la muerte, the city of death for many CIA agents sought refuge in this sanctuary along the Atlantic.

Life has a way to trigger reality checks and for Jackson, who was slowly regaining his memory back, it was his code of honor. His raison d'etre, his purpose in life that made him realize he had a job to finish. After some careful considerations, arrangements were made and he boarded a flight from Buenos Aires to Panama. There in Panama he was debriefed and recertified for back to duty.

The DOJ, FBI, ATF, Secret Service and US Marshalls are all scratching their heads for answers, when our illustrious CIA sleuth walks into the room and resumes his pugnacious position as he says, "The President is scheduled to be at the United Nations along with Henry Kissinger to give a speech on SALT II, so you should find our assassins in New York City!"

He looks around the room and ask the question, "How many agents do we have there?"

Like a lightning bolt striking, Bennett was on the phone ordering agents and swat teams to the UN building.

Then Jackson asks, "Now, is there a second dirty bomb?"

WW and Corey Bennett turn white as they both stare at Jackson with contempt for not thinking of that beforehand themselves, as Jackson continues with his questions and enjoys putting the squeeze on these political types as he says, "That is where you will find our eight terrorists."

He then continues, "Think gentlemen, think! That first dirty bomb was too easy to find and deactivate, it's a decoy dammit! The real fiasco will be caused in New York City at the United Nations!"

WW slaps his head as if a light bulb just went on and looks at Corey Bennett and says to him, "of course!"

Jackson McKenna was back in the saddle and in full control again. His hunches weren't always respected amongst his colleagues or other agencies. None the less, all learned to trust them as the focus of the hunt became Manhattan and the United Nations Headquarters.

A dragnet was setup around the perimeter of Manhattan with sharpshooters, helicopters, and blockades. The United Nations Building became ground zero. The governor was informed and a special task force formed by the police commissioner of New York City, Donald Francis Cawley and Mayor Abraham Beame for all forces and especially the SWAT teams to come under the coordination of the FBI who oversaw this circus. High-risk situations call for split second decisions and no foul-ups. There is no way anyone or group of persons can infiltrate into Manhattan without being caught on camera. The trouble is reviewing all the camera footage.

WW is conferring with the others as McKenna asks for a map of all terminal ports around New York City. Studying every detail of the container ports, McKenna asks, "which ports are the largest container ports?"

A frustrated Bennett yells at McKenna, "Hell, why not make it difficult, you got your choice of the Red Hook Terminals in Brooklyn, Port Jersey Shipping across the Hudson River, New York Container on Staten Island and the damn list goes on and on with millions of containers!"

WW understands the frustration of Corey Bennett and immediately takes control of the situation, "I want everyone's attention."

Waiting for silence he continues, "We don't need to reinvent the wheel here, with better than 34,000 uniformed officers and 76 precincts, and I may add 22 of those precincts are in Manhattan who know the streets and are out there looking for anything suspicious. The grid is already setup people! We will dissect this grid and fill in the gaps with the Coast Guard and FBI personnel looking for the dirty bomb or bombs, because I'm 99% certain that those bombs will come by container ship. Now if by chance the bombs come in by truck, the ATF will be working with the locals and DOT on all check points into the city. The FBI honchos will be working surveillance with the locals to find the assassins. SWAT and shooters are in place on roof tops, bridges etc. and we will find these bastards!"

He now steps back and takes a deep breath, sips his coffee and mulls over their next moves before saying, "New York City has better than 4.3 million people ride the subway system every day, with some 200,000 vehicles daily with some 12,000 intersections. Vigilance, does not only mean alertness or being watchful but, out-thinking the enemy. We know what these terrorists want to do, now we need to bolster the tenacity from within to stop them!"

Again, WW stops and surveys the room to see if his message is getting through before continuing, "One last thing, there is a major difference between them and us! Our Lord's prayer teaches us, Thy Kingdom come, thy will be done on earth as it is in heaven. God exist for good and not evil! Let us all call on His name to come to our assistance and fight this evil!"

One could hear a round of, 'Amen' from within the squad room.

Scheduled overtime became the norm for everyone as twelve-hour shifts is predicated until the terrorists are apprehended. Better communications between shifts is absolutely-necessary during a code one versus the miscommunications over three shifts. With 8.4 million people in New York City and some 10,000 cameras, the daunting task of surveillance intensified with Corey Bennett reminding everyone that London has some 500,000 security cameras. The governor called-up the National

Guard to help guard and patrol access to the nine different subterranean levels throughout New York City.

Our duty to serve and protect our people and keep America safe is not fully encapsulated in our constitution or our combating criminality to the extremism of terrorism. The brilliance of our forefathers who framed our constitution could not foresee the nefarious wrongs of today. This is where suspect tactics, perimeter control and Marshal law comes into fruition. To reestablish law, order and justice for our beautiful way of life, extreme actions are required in extreme circumstances.

WW understood this so well as he coordinated the collaboration between agencies. Simultaneous events had to occur instantaneously from the menial task such as welding manhole covers shut, removal of trash bins, to securing control of all cameras, scrutinizing all modes of transportation, coordinate intelligence network of all agencies and implementing the nauseating military control; for the only defense against terrorism is offense!

Contingencies were in place to shut down public transit if necessary. Helicopters were in the air with FLIR, forward looking infrared sensors to spot heat signatures. This is not the normal police foot chase and search. This manhunt is for an absolute takedown! Just watching that sixth sense survival mode on the various faces showed the tension. This is the last play of the last quarter and we are behind by four points. A touchdown is needed! This is the adrenalin pumping, caffeine gulping time with no slip-ups.

Huge explosions rocked Manhattan simultaneously from three different locations. Emergency crews rushed upon the scenes as hazmat, police, fire trucks and rescue squads received word from the Office of Emergency Management to proceed with caution.

The apprehension of the police commissioner and the FBI were paramount. With 472 subway stations and 27 subway lines the major concern was, "How many more bombs are imminent?"

Any major bomb blast disrupts life, communications and a sense of stability. But multiple, coordinated blast causes mayhem, panic and paranoia. The message is sent out by radios that shelters are in place, evacuation is implemented and medical aid along with rescue is en route.

Subways are immediately shut-down and the massive headache of transit buses to transport the many stranded commuters is en acted. The imminent explosions occurred at Penn Station, Grand Central and Midtown East causing transit disruptions and chaos.

Emergency BOLO's went out and the urgent request for all agencies to find any more pending bombs.

Jackson, Danny and Rick were on their way to Battery Park where helicopters were waiting to take each of them to the various shipyards. An all-out blitz to find those bombs is issued, along with the Coast Guard, New York's finest in blue and the ATF.

Within each of the precincts, camera footage was scrutinized and pertinent snap shots of suspects for the assassins were forwarded to the newly built One Police Plaza in the heart of Manhattan. WW was talking to Corey Bennett as one snap shot came in showing two individuals going into the Ambassador Grill that looked like our perpetrators, which is near the United Nations Building. Plain cloths detectives visited the establishment to find a lead to the assassin's trail.

They are definitely casing the premises and there is only one pertinent question. "Location, location, location, from what location to take a shot?" asked WW to Corey Bennett.

Police Commissioner Cawley spoke up saying, "The Church Center for the United Nations is my best bet! It's a twelve-story building directly across from the United Nations headquarters with a bird's eye view of the entrance."

SR stood for two things in New York City, Shea Reid, one hell of a fine detective, and Scotch on the rocks. Both were synonymous with Shea. He circulated the most recent pictures of Reynante Bautista and Sinagtala Torres to the proprietors of the Ambassador Grill and then like a bloodhound on a fresh trail, pieced together their daily itinerary. He was a beat cop for twenty-years and been a detective these last fifteen. One doesn't last thirty-five years without learning a few tricks about survival and getting the perpetrators.

Born and raised in New York City, he ate, worked and loved this city, especially Shea Stadium and the Mets capturing the franchise's first World Series title over the Baltimore Orioles in 1969 and the Jets advance to Super Bowl III. Now, he of all people did not want to see anything heinous happen in his beloved city. Having been a beat cop, he learned of expediency to your destination and started walking and timing his progress from the Ambassador Grill to the UN. It was a comfortable two-minute walk. Now he retraced his footsteps back to the Grill. Thinking to himself, 'these bastards have to be close,' he started looking for places to hide out. Once a positive ID was established by the workers at the Ambassador Grill, extra personnel were called in to case the block and surrounding buildings. One by one pictures were circulated at hotels within walking distance to the United Nations.

Shea put a few assumptions together, "inconspicuous places, low cost and within walking distance to the UN," and started narrowing the search. Then like a bloodhound on a fresh scent he walked up 44th Street and turned onto 2nd Ave. and just surveyed the surroundings.

Thinking to himself, "if I were a terrorist where would I go," walking ever so slowly, again studying his surroundings, suddenly stopping, looking and wondering, "where to hide in plain sight?"

He then proceeds onto 2nd Ave and then crosses 45th and then 46th Streets and turns up on 47th Street. He walks a few steps gazing up at the Vanderbilt YMCA building and wonders to himself, "who indeed would hide out here?"

Proceeding inside the building, Shea walks over to the front desk and discreetly shows the picture of the suspects.

"Yes Sir," The front desk manager said, "They were here but checked out early this morning."

Detective Shea quickly responds, "Have those rooms been cleaned by maid service and if not, I would like to see those rooms?"

The manager checked with housekeeping and the rooms were just as the perpetrators had left them and Shea quickly called in for extra officers to case the rooms for fingerprints and any evidence that would be helpful.

The front desk had no registration of a vehicle indicating that the perpetrators must have ditched the car before checking in. Thinking to himself, "where the hell are they?" Shea had New York's finest in blue, check local cabs for cash paying customers. The trail went stone cold, but one cannot go very far with weaponry without being noticed.

Frustration abounded as the various teams were shuttled by helicopter to the shipyards. Thank God for Jackson McKenna's bloodhound nose for sniffing out the trail for it seems he could find clues in the dark as he radioed back to headquarters to ask the question, "Any shipboard supplies bound for the United Nations?"

Checking the supply roster of inbound ships one agent noticed, "artistic artifacts" bound for the Church Center for the United Nations. The ship was the, "Nigerian Star" bound from Lagos, Nigeria to New York City and was scheduled to dock at the South Brooklyn Marine Terminal.

Jackson impatiently ask, "Which is the most likely way to truck the artifacts to the church center?"

The agent quickly responds, "Two possibilities are the Hugh L. Carey Tunnel but that is a toll road and the Brooklyn Bridge."

Jackson quickly fires a short burst of superlatives and then tells Corey to get his thumbs out of his ass and set-up road blocks into Manhattan from the Brooklyn Bridge.

The tension is building and the urgent request for the president to cancel his appearance at the UN is denied. The President himself had choice words about the chicken advise as he exclaimed, "I will not run with my tail between my legs! The entire world must know how important this SALT II Treaty is and my speech at the United Nations will break the ice on cold war diplomacy!"

A perturbed Jackson McKenna replies to WW, "Tell Mr. President that SALT II won't do us any good if World War III erupts!"

Roadblocks and checkpoints are setup at both the Brooklyn Bridge and the Hugh Carey Tunnel as precautions.

The second helicopter team landed at the South Brooklyn Marine Terminal and boarded the Nigerian Star. ALL containers were already off-loaded as they raced through the registry to account for their destinations. A description of the symbol on the side of the container was faxed to all authorities and roadblocks were quickly put in place.

The helicopter with Jackson and Danny landed at the New York Container facility on Staten Island and started their thorough search. Tempers can fly when work progress is impeded by search warrants but the tedious task of searching literally thousands of containers is essential to find the dirty bombs. Scrutinizing the cargo registries, Danny noticed any containers off-loaded from either Nigerian or Liberian freighters were placed in bays 92 to 102. Each bay contained 10 rows by 10 columns stacked five high, so each bay housed 500 containers. The monotony at hand of finding that one critical container required patience and due diligence but time was not on our side. Racing down the rows looking at all the symbols on the side of the containers, Danny was unaware of the terrorists as he stumbled upon one container that was breached.

We were trained to be kibitzers, agents to observe, scrutinize, retain and report but not engage. At this point Danny should have gotten back-up, but anxious to prove himself, he proceeded to further investigate as one terrorist stood guard with a razor sharp 18-inch blade of hell. Danny turned the corner, unaware of his foe as the 18-inch blade slit his throat and a gunshot to his head rang out alerting the others. Within the horror of the moment, there is an instantaneous cognizance that transitions the mind in a flash from the shock, through the pain, to an awareness of the end, and finally to a sublime peacefulness of eternity.

The other agents cautiously moved in as they heard the single gunshot and a battle ensued as Jackson moved in returning gunfire. Within minutes better than twenty agents were upon the scene as four of the culprits were killed. Not knowing if these four terrorists were part of the original group that left Florida or if there are any more terrorist present; a sense of trepidation gripped all of law enforcement. Scrutinizing the dirty bomb, Jackson felt some relief that the dirty bomb hadn't been activated. The bomb squad came upon the scene to properly dispose of it. Jackson radioed to Bennett, "one agent down, one bomb deactivated, and four terrorists killed."

He made the request to Bennett that he wanted to be the one to break the news to other agents when the time became available.

The roadblocks were in place at the Brooklyn Bridge and the tedious checks had begun. All trailer trucks were stopped and checked. Another three hours had passed and no dirty bomb had been discovered. Questions are being asked if there is another dirty bomb and where the hell is the original load that left the terminal. Tracking the shipments, there is one truck that cannot be accounted for with the destination for the Church Center for the United Nations.

Jackson McKenna arrives upon the scene and nods for Rick to come over to his vehicle. As the security guards continue to check all types of trailer trucks, Jackson takes out his flask of Jack Daniels and hands it to him.

He responded by shaking his head and saying, "Too early in the morning for a drink!"

McKenna encourages him to take a swig and then breaks the unwelcomed news about Danny. There is never any good way to break the bad news except with being straight forward and having some compassion. Rick couldn't digest the news or believe his ears as he repeated the words, "Danny is dead!"

Flashbacks zoomed through his head of nostalgic times. One cannot control those flashbacks as they instantaneously rush through your brain. Happy times of roommate days at the academy, sailing, having a beer together, enjoying those mixers and of friendships.

Out of the original four compadres, Rick was the only one left. Life appears to be too short for too many. He remembered their days together at the maritime academy, the good times, the fun times and then graduation and the choices they both made to serve.

The Brooklyn Bridge roadblocks never uncovered another dirty bomb and we wondered if there was indeed another bomb or not. A trace was put on the lost truck and the search continued.

CLANDESTINE RESCUE

The Russian word for fate is, "Sud'ba," and there is an old Russian legend that confirms that death may be evaded but that the result might not be desirable. Whether it was fate or faith, the death of Danny affected the both of us, especially McKenna who now felt remorseful for losing all three victims on his watch. The thoughts haunted him that he should have never allowed Trevor, a neophyte agent, on the trail of the Russian ships, or Sinclair involved with Track II in Chile and now the loss of Danny to a cut-throat terrorist. McKenna boarded an unscheduled C-130 flight for Helsinki.

There was a KGB major, an Anatoliy Mikhaylovich Golitsyn, whom defected to the United States from Helsinki in December of 1961. He divulged sensitive information about the KGB network of espionage. Especially details concerning the Cuban missile bases and the heinous threat of World War III, which in his mind would be a futile war. A mutual respect and friendship developed between Anatoliy and the agent that helped him come to America, who just happened to be Jackson McKenna.

Determined to find answers, McKenna solicits his old friend's aid to help locate Trevor within the Russian penal colony. In his later years Anatoliy became an American citizen and author of two books about the long-term deception strategy of the KGB leadership.

His vital connections with the, compatriot "boyeviki," fighters, within his underground circle of friends smuggled out information to Anatoliy for his books to further their cause of freedom. Jackson hoped that now their connections could help locate Trevor.

McKenna lived for the action. The thrill of espionage made him feel alive for the game to outfox the enemy kept him sharp and alert at every corner. But the two things he hated most were these long plane rides for it made him face those things he couldn't control. The second most dreaded item he couldn't fathom was death of compadre. Unexpected death is a jolt in life! Each person handles death differently, and for Rick it was regrets, regrettably his choice about the CIA. For McKenna, his resolve to save Trevor just intensified tenfold.

The C-130 landed in the middle of the night on a remote air strip in the Suomenlinna district of Helsinki, Finland which consists of eight islands. Five of the islands which has the greatest concentrations of fortifications are connected by bridges. The area is no longer a vital military base and Anatoliy thought a good place for their covert meeting. Instead of the normal Finnish postal addressing scheme of street name and house number, the addresses consist of letter code for the island and then a house number. An excellent location for safe houses for agents and defectors.

A nostalgic reunion between Anatoliy and Jackson took place in house C-82 with a warm embrace and a couple shots of vodka for their mutual admiration for each other went beyond all boundaries. As the night progressed, the lightheartedness changed to a soberness due to the grave consequences of the trip.

There is an old proverb for covert agents of, "Perpetuus Motus," Latin for never ending movement if one wants to stay alive. A map laid out on the table showing a zig-zag trail of alternate routes to follow in finding the location of Trevor, never staying longer than one day in any location.

The conversation goes back and forth like a badminton game first enjoyable laughter about fond memories and then turning dire because of the intense circumstances.

"I understand that there are some 490 prison camps throughout Russia?" Jackson ask Anatoliy.

Anatoliy smiles at his friend and to reassure their friendship puts his hand on Jackson's shoulder to console him as he says, "Only Russian newspapers are good for that propaganda, for the real truth is appalling. There are better than 30,000 Gulag labor camps."

Jackson is discombobulated with such facts, as a frown comes over his face and he sits down to digest what was just revealed.

"You know," Anatoliy continues, "I could write books on what is left out of the Russian newspapers! For the record there are better than 36 million prisoners versus the 2.5 million that are published. And there are camps with 25 to 30 thousand prisoners instead of the 500 to some 1000 prisoners that the establishment boast."

Jackson looks up and ask, "Will this be a mission impossible?"

Anatoliy responds, "I would not have come to help my old friend if that was true!"

He then gets the bottle of vodka and pours Jackson another shot before continuing, "Usually in the ploy of prison roulette, it takes five to ten years to lose a prisoner. Now, there are far fewer detention processing centers and as this Trevor is continually being processed, there will be a paper trail. And the networks of underground fighters are many. We will find him!"

The last confirmation from Mstislav Alexandra had located Trevor at Perm-36 prison camp and so the underground route begins with our two compadres leaving Helsinki by boat to dock at a wayside Inn in Tallinn, Estonia. The Finnish Security Intelligence Service known as, "Supo" monitors all border crossings at key checkpoints and has close connections with the CIA for covert backdoor entrances into Mother Russia. Finland is located in a precarious strategic position between the cold war blocks as the cat and mouse games play out between the superpowers.

Tallinn's old town is one of the best preserved medieval cities in Europe. Ever since the German Knights of the Sword first built a stone fortress here in 1227, every foreign empire that ruled Estonia used the castle as its base and is appropriately now home to Estonia's Parliament. Often dubbed the Silicon Valley of Europe, it has the highest number of startups per person in Europe and will be our first meeting place to begin our excursion into Russia.

In a wayside café at the base of Toompea Castle a meeting took place between Anatoliy, Jackson and our illustrious double agent, Mstislav Alexandra, who acquired new information about our lost kibitzer, Trevor. After some greetings with a handshake and a shot of vodka, it was down to risky business for Trevor or detainee A-649, was transferred to penal colony No. 2 OIK-2 OUKHD, popularly known as White Swan Prison in Solikamsk.

McKenna first asked, "Why is the prison named White Swan?"

Mstislav smiles at McKenna and then shrugs his shoulders as he says, "There are two theories, the first, named so for the white buildings and secondly, the way the detainees are moved across the prison grounds, bent over almost 90 degrees with their hands thrown behind their back in handcuffs, appearing like a swan."

Just then Anatoliy breaks into the conversation to explain to Jackson what he and Mstislav already know, "This is one of the worst prisons with the main task of total isolation and closure to any means of communication with the outside world."

"During White Swan's entire existence, there have been no confirmed escapes!" Mstislav explained.

Then Anatoliy leans over the table to lend some comfort to Jackson as he says, "One of the tenets of our faith is hope, but in the Russian penal colony hope gives way to doubt and eventually lack of trust. It doesn't take long to break down the human spirit where hope doesn't exist."

Mstislav quickly adds, "if there is any hope to rescue Trevor, we must do it quickly!"

Jackson then asked, "how long before Trevor is moved to another prison camp?"

Mstislav just smiles again and responds, "a day, a week, months or years, who knows, there are no whys, when or where in Mother Russia."

One of the underground compatriots walks into the café and Mstislav recognizes him. He stands and signals for him to come over to his table. The meeting is cordial but abrupt for he has fake passports for two of us and an itinerary map to the White Swan prison. Anatoliy will not venture any further but return to America due to his fear of the Russian regime.

The name of the compatriot is Dmitry Kuznetsova. He becomes our driver from Estonia to Moscow where crossing the border will be the first test for our newly fabricated passports. Our first meeting place in Russia will be at the church of the Epiphany in Yaroslavl.

There is much skepticism to risk using our newly acquired passports, as we avoid the checkpoints at airport and train stations. Traveling by car is slower but much safer. The first checkpoint crossing of the border into Russia is through Luhamaa.

It is cold, bitter cold and a busted car heater didn't help our journey for it is a twelve-hour drive from Estonia to Moscow. The Volga backfired twice and Jackson wondered if the damn old thing would make it. Dmitry spoke pretty good broken English and between the cold and his constant questions about America, he kept the two men awake. Relieved that the border crossing was successful, a relaxed atmosphere dominated the ride until we picked up a tail.

Dmitry cursed as he looked into the rearview mirror, "Damn KGB, all drive a Moskvitch!"

Jackson asked, "Can you lose them, Dmitry?"

Dmitry laughed as he said, "One doesn't lose the KGB, you have to out-lisa them!"

Dmitry's broken English wasn't too bad to understand, but there were certain words he couldn't translate as Jackson turned to Mstislav for some help.

Mstislav replied, “lisa is a Russian word for fox, you have to out-fox them.”

Mstislav conversed with Dmitry in Russian about the KGB. Then he told me the plan as he said, “We are six hours away from the city of Zubtsov where we cross the Volga River. There is a café where we can get something to eat, refresh ourselves and make a clandestine switch of cars to outfox the bastards.”

Mstislav asked a few more questions of Dmitry in Russian and then turned to me and said, “Try to get some shut-eye before arriving there and I’ll wake you!”

Mstislav nudged me awake as we approached our destination. A light snow is falling on the ground on a chilly, overcast day as Dmitry pulled up to the café Uyut. He made sure to park on the street in front of the café to avoid any suspicions from the KGB who were still following us.

Inside the café, Dmitry got a table by the front window so that the KGB could keep a tab on us. He ordered three chebureks, a pastry stuffed sandwich with mince meats and spices and some drinks. While we ate our lunch, Dmitry drew a diagram for the both of us. The drawing showed a grocery store across the adjacent street and directed us to sneak out the back door by the rest room.

He spoke to Mstislav in Russian once again saying, “Cross the street and walk to the alley on the far right of the store. There will be another Volga parked in the alley-way and the driver’s name is Oleg.”

Mstislav asked, “Can we trust our new driver?”

Dmitry smiled and said, “You better, he is my brother, Oleg Kuznetsova.”

Mstislav smiled at me and said, “We are in good company!”

We finished our sandwiches, used the facilities and snuck out the back door. The KGB were none the wiser as Dmitry sat there enjoying his food with some shots of vodka for the next hour. This gave Oleg plenty of time to drive us out of Zubtsov and back on the road heading towards Moscow. The trip was pleasant for the heater worked and Oleg asked many questions about America.

The drive to Moscow along M-9 took three hours with another three hours just getting through the congested traffic in the city nicknamed “the Forty Forties. Then Oleg proceeded north to Yaroslavl where Mstislav explained that two compatriot fighters will meet us at the Church of the Epiphany. Both of them are from the town of Nerekhta, a place I used to visit as a boy to see relatives. A place of fond memories playing with my cousins.

“Russian roads are made worst by Russian drivers,” Jackson thought to himself.

A road trip around Russia’s Golden Ring is a circuit of about a dozen ancient towns of northeast Moscow, each with its own set of glittering onion-domed churches, medieval fortresses and walled monasteries. Clogged intersections, clusters of potholes, what locals call “hens’ nests,” giant trucks on narrow roads; big-bellied Russian traffic-police trolling for offenders, bring the flow of traffic to a stand-still. “This is driving Hell!” But the view of Moscow, such a wide city, with its thousands of golden domed churches was well named Forty Forties, for there are better than 1600 churches in this city.

One astonishing fact that Jackson learned from Oleg, that years ago backed by the Muscovite princes, there was an extraordinary missionary movement which became a key force for unification of Russia. Seeking salvation in nature, some 150 monasteries were built within a span of 100 years. But the time from 1964 to the present 1970’s became known as the “Brezhnev Era,” where the Soviet Union achieved nuclear parity with the United States.

Finally, our arrival into Yaroslavl at the Church of the Epiphany. A car was parked in front of the church and as the driver got out of the vehicle, Mstislav relaxed with a sigh of relief for he recognized him. Taras was an old friend as well as one of the compatriot underground fighters. After a warm greeting and an introduction to Jackson, Mstislav had Oleg follow Taras with the vehicle to a dacha, Russian for seasonal home in the exurbs of Yaroslavl.

One always had to be careful about covert meetings for as the legend forewarns, "the ears of Mother Russia hears all, knows all, controls all." The continual brainwashing by propaganda infuriates the spirited heart. Our Creator has endowed us with a mind, heart and soul. Then a will to perceive, believe and resist those ideologies contrary to our very being.

Vadim, another compatriot fighter, was inside the dacha along with four others. A scrumptious meal was prepared for our guest and it was a welcome site.

After a fine meal of soup, roasted meat, potatoes and some golubtsy which is stuffed cabbage leaf's; we had a typical drink of kompot. Then it was down to business. Vadim had surveyed the prison and fully apprised each of us of the pending situation at White Swan prison.

One of the guards is a member of the compatriot fighters, a countryman that believes in justice for all and that Russia must rid itself of their Neanderthal practices of the gulag prisons. Vadim smuggles out information about the prisoners to their families. In turn, he conveys messages and supplies of personal mementos to the prisoners, a bible, cross, or a picture. If caught, he would be shot.

Trevor is still at the White Swan prison where a wake-up call by cannon fire starts their day. Each morning the time for their wake-up call is different. Anywhere between 4 to 6 am. This is followed by a roll call which is taken three times a day. Exercise in the courtyard followed by breakfast and then forced labor of brick laying, hauling timber or digging grave sites. Due to the deplorable living conditions, there are many weekly deaths. Tuberculosis is rampart throughout the prison and spreads from person to person including the guards. No one is safe for all can be infected by aerosol transmission through sneezing, coughing or even talking to each other.

The daily work on most days last until 7 pm and then dinner. It was rare to have any time for yourself. After dinner there is a short time to clean oneself with cold water and then doing cleaning stations became the norm throughout the prison. The prison guards are on a 2-hour shift change to break-up their monotony.

Vadim wouldn't provide the guards name for security reasons but concluded the briefing by saying, "Russian prisons are essentially torture chambers with continual beatings, forced labor, lack of sleep, fights and the prisoner's roommates are dysentery and TB.

Jackson sat there numb, words are useless to express his inner feelings. His resolve to get Trevor out of there, has become his vendetta!

Now he stands and explains the conceived mission to Mstislav on how to free Trevor. Mstislav interprets in Russian the plan to the others while Jackson pulls out of his pocket what looks like a cigarette lighter. Then he explains to Mstislav, "this is a "TTL," the defense department calls it tagging, tracking and locating device."

Mstislav is intrigued with the device as he looks it over and ask, "how does it work?"

Jackson opens the lighter, pops it out of its case and reveals a chip that he can activate for GPS tracking. Now he says to Mstislav, "see this devise here," and points to a pin switch. Removing a needle from his shirt collar, he shows Mstislav how to activate the switch.

"This signal is good for one hundred miles and I need one of your people to place it in a discrete field nearby for an air-drop of supplies."

Mstislav looks confused as he says, "Air drop from where?"

Jackson tells him, "Trust me old friend, I cannot say, but I need your people to retrieve the supplies quickly when it is dropped."

Jackson then tells him, "Have your compatriot fighters take this beacon now to a field and activate it. Within twelve hours they will need to retrieve the package once air-dropped."

Unbeknown to most people, the USS Saratoga CV-60 has a long and illustrious naval history serving in the Mediterranean. The aircraft carrier's past campaigns include in the waters off Guantanamo Bay during the Cuban Missile crisis, off the coast of Lebanon during the Israeli six-day war and off the shores of Vietnam. Now once again cruising the Med conducting covert operations for the CIA.

The CIA made arrangements for Jackson before leaving for Helsinki. Stealth jet fighters fly covertly along the Ural Mountains within Russia to test their capabilities of avoiding detection. Two beacon devices are to be utilized by Jackson. The first device, the cigarette lighter beacon is to be activated for receiving supplies of the Fulton surface-to-air recovery system known as, "STARS." This is the common type of gear to retrieve covert agents in the field for the CIA. Recovery kits are designed for one and two-man retrievals. A second beacon is to be attached to the recovery kit which will be used to retrieve both Jackson and Trevor when the time comes.

Jackson looks at Mstislav sternly as he says, "My friend, time is pressing, how much further to the White Swan prison?"

Mstislav replies, "It's about a nineteen-hour drive."

"Once we get the package, then we leave for White Swan!" said Jackson.

Now Mstislav gestures for Vadim to explain the plan to get Trevor out of the prison.

Vadim explains the best he can in both broken English, but mostly in Russian the details. Mstislav must translate to Jackson most of the details as he says, "Two of the guards inside, our compatriot fighters will assign Trevor to the hauling wood detail for two days."

Jackson shakes his head in the affirmative and says to Mstislav, "Within two days, I will take Trevor home!"

The herculean task required insidious planning right down to the last detail. The travail showed in the tension on McKenna's face. There is no turning back, it is either success or death. There are no second chances!

The forests were plentiful by the Urals which were an hours' drive from the White Swan prison. Jackson contemplated the plan and waited for the package. He couldn't rest until he had the package safely home.

Flyovers by stealth jet fighters made rendezvous with the beacon signal and successfully jettison the package for the drop. Now it was a nineteen-hour drive to the prison. Oleg returned home, as Mstislav, Jackson, Taras and Vadim piled into a 1960 jalopy, a Ladas car that was no Mercedes, but it got them there in one piece. Taras and Vadim took turns driving. Mstislav and McKenna alternated keeping watch for any tails and getting some shut eye.

The only stops along the way were made for gas, pit stops and to stretch our legs. McKenna kept going over the plan in his head for all possible contingencies and played his favorite game of, "What if's." This is what made him so good at his job. His leadership to handle any situation in the field and his passionate zeal to win is unprecedented.

Our entourage arrived near the prison none too soon, as prisoners were escorted to a dump truck and climbed onboard. Taras with binoculars identified Trevor climbing onto the truck and then checked out who were the guards.

A sigh of relief came over his face as he said, "Okhranniki-nashi sootechestvenniki, vse v poryadke."

Mstislav translated to me, "The guards are our compatriots, it's ok!"

As Taras further surveyed the scene, he noticed a second vehicle with four more security guards to trail the truckload of prisoners. With a frown on his face, he said to Mstislav, "Beda, bol'she okhrannikov." Which meant, trouble, more guards.

There is only one way that leads to the forest, as Vadim shifted the Ladas into gear and revved up the engine. He wanted to get ahead of them and raced down the winding road.

Taras yelled, "Proklyatyye dorogi!" which meant damn logging roads!

Vadim seem to hit every pot hole and rut in the road as I yelled, "Chert poberi!"

It was clear to everyone that I knew a little Russian even though my accent was off, as all laughed at my exclamation of, "God dammit," in Russian.

Vadim raced the Ladas three hundred kilometers beyond the logging area and parked the car to let Taras and myself out to reconnoiter the area. We had but one chance to retrieve Trevor. Then Vadim shifted the vehicle and drove a mile down the road to setup the recovery system. It didn't take long to unpack the retrieval system and once set they activated the beacon. Now we had to synchronize our time; two hours between reconnaissance flights picking up the signal and radioing it to the USS Saratoga. The remaining waiting time would be for the C-130E to rendezvous with us for the pickup.

Waiting for the right moment to strike can be nerve-racking for most, but I was an old dog at this and enjoyed the hunt. The stalking was the best part of the job. No jitters, just calm nerves and the tenacity to strike for the kill if necessary. Taras and I laid low in a group of trees with much shrubbery to hide behind. The trees buffeted the cold winds and we shared one canteen of water and a sandwich.

Two hours have gone by and the recovery system is set-up. Mstislav and Vadim have rejoined us while we keep an eye on Trevor from a distance. The work for the prisoners is tedious cutting the logs, hauling the six-foot lengths to the truck and heaving them into the bed of the dumpster. At least the work will keep them warm.

Mstislav looks at me and says, "Damn cold for my weary bones!"

I shook my head in the affirmative and just smiled. What could I say to relieve the cold, all of us were shivering and had another two hours to go.

Lt. Cmdr. Ritter got the signal as the five-man crew prepared to take off the deck of the USS Saratoga. C-130's initially did take-offs and landings without the use of catapults and tail hooks. Co-pilot Tillerson monitored the controls while flight engineer Becker monitored the engine controls. Veteran flyers from the Vietnam era, wild horses couldn't pull these guys apart. They knew each other's moves and watched everyone's back.

Engines are revved for the short take off and the C-130 climbs into the wind to achieve lift. Climbing high into the sky and banking to the starboard side setting a course towards the Ural Mountains. The navigator is plotting the course of the last signal reported by the stealth jet fighters to locate the beacon as the navigator yells, "Speak to me Scotty!"

A low altitude flight through the Ural Mountains to avoid radar detection is demanding but necessary. It has to be in your blood to do this job. The pilot asks the navigator for an update on their ETA for entering hostile air space. The navigator replies, "Kiss the Blarney Stone for we are already there!"

The hands are numb due to the cold and the aching pain in my bones is from the arthritis, as Jackson rubs his hands to keep his blood circulating. He looks at his watch multiple times within the pass couple of hours and signals to Mstislav that time is right to make the move. Dusk is beginning as Mstislav tells Vadim to contact the guard that will help Trevor escape. The prearranged signal with the guard is simple; if and only if, Vadim is a good stone thrower. There are six guards positioned around the perimeter of fifteen prisoners. Two of the guards are underground compatriots, while the four others are regular militia. Vadim must throw a stone to signal our man without alerting the others.

Jackson contemplated killing all four of the militia guards, but at all cost must avert an international incident, especially concerning the diplomatic circles since we are not supposed to be there. He watches Vadim throw the stone and is ready to do the unthinkable if necessary.

"Good shot," Jackson thought to himself as the stone hits our man in the leg. The other guards are oblivious to our actions, as the guard signals for a pit-break. The prisoners walk towards the trees to relieve themselves. Trevor steps into the fringes of the forest, as Jackson is ready with Mstislav to guide Trevor to the car 300 km away. Trevor shows no emotion as he is startled to see McKenna. They moved jauntily through the woods with Jackson always looking back towards the other guards. His troublesome leg giving him a bit of pain to keep up.

Trevor trips and falls to the ground as both Mstislav and McKenna help him back up onto his feet. The terrain is rough, cold and hard as Trevor tries to regain his balance. Both men help steady Trevor to his feet and guide him to the vehicle.

Once all of them were in the vehicle, Vadim starts the Ladas which backfires and stalls alerting the other guards. Taras jumps out of the vehicle to shoot any perpetrators that come through the woods. Vadim turns over the vehicle again as gun fire erupts from the forest. Bullets are whizzing by with stray bullets killing Taras and hitting the back of our vehicle.

The jalopy finally starts and Vadim races like a bat out of hell to the spot where the retrieval system is set-up.

The car comes to a screeching halt as Vadim slams on the brakes. Once there, I jumped out of the vehicle and turned to retrieve Trevor, who is slumped over in the back seat. He was bleeding profusely from two gun-shot wounds in his back. Mstislav quickly takes off his shirt and wraps it around him as a tourniquet to slow the bleeding and says to McKenna, “I can’t do any more for him now!”

The two of them carry Trevor over to the retrieval system and strap him in. Then Mckenna quickly straps himself in the harness and can hear the C-130 in the distance.

Mstislav, a bit shaken roughly grabs for my hand and yells, “Goodbye my friend, I hope the both of you make it!”

McKenna yelled back over the noise of the C-130’s engines as it approached closer, “What about you and Vadim?”

“Don’t worry about us, we will disappear into the mountain villages of the Urals!”

The C-130 glides out from the shadows of the mountains and retrieves the two men, as the hook connects with the retrieval system catapulting the both of them into the sky.

Trevor gulped and yelled in anguish and all I could do is hold on to him, looking back at Mstislav waving his hand.

The retraction device hauled us onboard like a fish on a line out of water. The loadmaster on the plane helped us aboard and then closed the rear cargo door. Trevor is freed! He looks around and can't believe his eyes as he begins to cry and asks, "No more prison?"

McKenna just wrapped his arm around Trevor and replied, "No more prison, you're going home!"

The first aid kit was gathered and the flight engineer and loadmaster strapped Trevor down. His life was in their capable hands now as they extracted the two bullets and poured plenty of anti-septic on his wounds. I watched in horror to see all of the gash marks on Trevor's back. He had been unmercifully tortured for there had to be better than thirty deep lacerations on his back. They bandaged him the best they could and we all said a prayer on our breath. God willing, he will make it to sickbay. There were some mighty fine doctors on the USS Saratoga.

Totally exhausted, McKenna passed out for the remainder of the flight.

Hours later, awoken by the thump of landing on the deck of the aircraft carrier, McKenna looked over towards Trevor who motioned for him to come closer.

His words were shallow, blood was oozing from his mouth as he whispered to McKenna. His words weren't audible as McKenna kneeled and leaned forward to hear his last words, "Bury me at sea and tell my parents that I love them!"

I wiped the blood from his mouth and then he expired with his last breath before the medics could remove him from the C-130. I wasn't prepared for this, sometimes even the best plans run amuck. The hollow moments in life makes us gasp for air, pray to Him and experience an apathy of life. And yet, some hope, because he will now hopefully start his new eternal life.

I reported to the Captain about my mission, conveyed Trevor's last wishes to him and then retired to a ward room.

Burial at sea by aircraft carriers in the present time are usually done only with cremated remains. That evening Trevor's remains were given their final resting place amongst the waves of the sea. The Captain gave a short eulogy and the piercing sound of taps were played.

"Day is done, Gone the sun,
From the lake, From the hill,
From the sky.
All is well, safely rest,
God is nigh.

The following morning at dawn, I caught a C-130 flight back to the states. Life can be riveting at times and as I gazed out my plane window, sunrise peeked over the horizon. Dawns early light is a daily reminder of God's special light and as His Son tells us, "I am the light of the world. Whoever follows me will not walk in darkness but will have the light of life."

Sometimes the heinous events in our life dulls our senses and blinds us to see His light. Extremely exhausted, I slept a good part of the return trip home while the C-130 refueled in mid-air.

TWO DAYS

Two days remain until the President of the United States addresses the United Nations. What is America's destiny and does God still bless America?

The search continued for the assassins and a dirty bomb in New York City while Jackson's flight hit turbulence which awoke him and he contemplated about the visit to Trevor's parents. How does one console and give some comfort to the family who has just lost a son? How could home of the brave and land of the free come to this? Since WW II there have been too many wars, too many deaths and way too many covert actions.

In another private ceremony, a slain CIA officer, Danny, was buried at Arlington National Cemetery. A plain coffin which was borne by six Marines and draped in an American flag was laid to rest. Each of the first 78 agents has a star on the wall in the lobby of the agency's main building in Virginia. It isn't simply enough to dream of a better, safer world but with God's guidance, build it!

Ralph Waldo Emerson once said, "From within or from behind, light shines through us upon things, and makes us aware that we are nothing, but the light is all." With God's light, we learn that we can, and with His guidance, we will persevere!

Now there are many sleuths on the trail of the terrorist from different agencies but the one sleuth in New York City that made an uncanny difference to uncover the slightest detail is Shea Reid. Like a bloodhound on the scent, he walks the trail, sniffs, walks some more and finds the slightest details that most detectives would fail to catch. Like a sixth sense, he feels the perpetrator's presence and now ponders right or left.

He then proceeds down East 43rd Street to where it crosses 2nd Avenue and goes into the Dunkin Donuts shop to get a cup of coffee. Looks around and wonders where are those bastards? He pays for the coffee and decides that he needs something a little stronger. Proceeding down 2nd Avenue to Calico Jack's Cantina, he hesitates and is aware of the perpetrators presence and enters the cantina to order a scotch on the rocks. Now this is better, he thinks while looking around the establishment. There in the corner at an inconspicuous table sit Reynante Bautista and Sinagtala Torres vehemently talking together. Shea wishes he could be a fly on the wall to listen-in on his suspects.

He gulps his scotch and then asks the bartender for another scotch and a phone. The bartender reaches under the counter and brings out a phone and places it on top of the bar. As the bartender makes another scotch, Shea makes a call to his old compadre and undercover cop, Billy Frump known on the streets as Pickpocket. The only thing Shea tells his compadre on the phone is, "Got a job, meet at Calico Jack's Cantina, pronto!"

Dressed like a street bum, Pickpocket stays on the street just outside Calico Jack's. Even a simple dress-code wouldn't allow him into the establishment, but he leans against the front of the building and just waits. A long-time associate of Shea Reid, the two have worked together now for some ten years and know each other's idiosyncrasies' like the back of their hand. In a blink of an eye, Pickpocket could snatch a client's wallet or watch, but more importantly he can pick trade secrets and be on his way.

Shea sips his scotch now, and nonchalantly watches his suspects. The two are drawing something on a piece of paper and are working on their plan of attack. Shea thinks better with at least three scotches and so orders another scotch on the rocks but tells the bartender to water it down. He watches his suspects and wonders where the hell are they hiding out? The two suspects get up to leave the Cantina as Shea pays his tab and then follows his suspects out the door. Once outside Shea stretches, looks up towards the sun and then looks over to Pickpocket and gives him a nod. From now on Pickpocket will be on their trail.

The two suspects meander towards East 43rd Street and then towards the United Nations Headquarters. Pickpocket crosses the street to the opposite side and ever so slowly stumbles down the street. The two unsuspecting souls walk and turn onto a street that leads them to 45 Tudor Place. Whistling to himself, Pickpocket can't believe his eyes for this place had class and a one room studio went for $350,000. This place is no skid row nor any terrorist typical overnight accommodation. Once he established their residency, he then called Shea Reid who alerted headquarters and the FBI.

Random calls to 911 were sporadically coming in about a trailer truck that was torched near Central Park. The fire and police departments were dispatched to the scene. Fire trucks arrived first at the location and the local authorities set up road blocks to avert traffic. Once the scorching fire was contained, the abandoned truck and license fit the description of the terrorist vehicle from the shipyard. The FBI arrived on the scene and the bomb squad scanned the remains for radioactivity. Low-level amounts of radiation were detected to prove that this is the trailer truck to transport a dirty bomb but where is the bomb?

The CDC was alerted, a federal agency for the center for disease control which supports public health preparedness and prevention.

WW is on the phone with Corey Bennett demanding, "Find that damn bomb!"

Bennett slams down the phone and looks agitated as he says to his associate, "don't they think we are trying to find that damn bomb!"

The main danger from a dirty bomb is from the explosion, which can cause serious injuries, but the radioactive materials used in a dirty bomb would probably not be an imminent threat or cause serious illness except to those near. The local police chief points to Central Park and tells Bennett, "This is the 65th Street Transverse in an 843-acre park. Good place to hide a bomb!"

Bennett shaking his head, "Great, just friggin great!"

Trying to pacify Bennett, the Police Chief tells Bennett, "Look, we are prepared for this contingency and I'll divide teams to close down Central Park and evacuate all people. There are some twenty gates and 58 miles of paths with 21 playgrounds and 36 bridges. We will isolate, dissect and cover every inch of this park!"

And that is just what was done with great propensity, numerous personnel, dogs sniffing every pathway, building, bridge underpass and Geiger counters galore combed every inch of the 843-acre park.

The police chief understood all too well the pressure that the FBI chief was underneath and told Bennett, "We are in this together!"

Just then another radio call comes for Bennett informing him about the suspected terrorist at the Tudor Place.

He immediately responds, "I'll be there in twelve minutes!"

Forty-Five Tudor Place is a 26-story apartment complex directly across from the United Nations building and an excellent location from which to make an assassination hit. These bastards have done their homework and up to this point we have been one step behind them. Bennett decides, 'time to change the tactics,' and calls WW to solicit the help of Major General Armstrong one more time. Once Bennett arrives, New York's Cities finest in blue are there along with SWAT teams, FBI and that sleuth team of Shea Reid and Pickpocket.

Reid quickly introduces Bennett to their illustrious city vagrant and undercover cop, Billy Frump.

Bennett barely gets out of the car before asking, "Are you sure these are our terrorists?"

Reid replies, "One hundred percent!"

A map of the city and a blueprint of the complex is laid out on the hood of the car as Billy explains the logistics, "They have a room on the 20th floor on the Northeast corner."

Bennett shakes his head and says, "I'm in the wrong business, where the hell did they get the money to afford a place like this?"

The United Nations which has 39-floors is in perfect view from the terrorist's room. Most dignitaries' including the President of the United States usually enter from the 43rd street entrance and is directly adjacent to the Tudor Apartments.

Bennett adamantly says, "We take those bastards out today and I would like them alive to learn as much as possible about this coordinated assassination hit. Major General Armstrong will have a C-130 waiting at LaGuardia and SWAT has a helicopter ready to take the suspects into custody to the C-130!"

The police chief in charge of his unit asks Corey Bennett, "We have time to evacuate the hotel?"

"Are you crazy, and alert those bastards? No-way, two teams approach from each end of the corridor, elevators are shut down before we move in and the FBI has the lead! Do I make myself clear?"

All teams respond, "Affirmative!"

"All right, let's move in!"

Four SWAT teams will move in with two setting a breach and hold the perimeter while the other two lead-teams move in from opposite ends of the corridor for a dynamic entry.

One could hear talking and laughter coming from the room as one of the terrorist says in Filipino, "Praise Allah, when I die I will have 21 virgins!"

As the two teams approach the suspects, one of the terrorist leaves the room and notices the tactical teams coming down the hallway and quickly turns to warn Bautista in Filipino, "Pulis, Si Allah ay Dakila," which means, "police, Allah is great!"

Reynante Bautista is cleaning and checking his 60-mm rocket launcher and quickly loads his weapon while Torres pulls out a 45 and fires upon the approaching SWAT team.

Return gun fire can be heard from both sides of the hallway as the SWAT teams return fire killing Torres. Bautista quickly aims his rocket launcher towards the door and awaits until the SWAT Teams approach the room. He then fires a blast that could be heard throughout the complex, knocking out the wall, door and killing five members of the SWAT team along with one FBI agent.

Tear gas is thrown into the room and two masked agents quickly apprehend Bautista. With handcuffs on his hands and shackles around his ankles, the SWAT Team drag the suspect out to an awaiting helicopter. Before loading him onboard, Bennett yells, "Hold up," and walks over to Bautista to eye him man to man. He looks him over and says, "You may not understand what I'm about to say, but our first President George Washington once said that 'perseverance and spirit have done wonders in all ages.' And I'm telling you something that you may never understand. Through perseverance, America has become a land of the free and home of the brave. We never give up and we will persevere to remain one Nation under God!"

Bennett just stares at Bautista and smiles before saying, "That means we build liberty for all lives and the only thing that you terrorist know, is to lose hope and tear down life."

He stares at him one last time and says, "Through perseverance, you terrorists will fail!"

He then signals to the others with a wave of his hand to continue the boarding. It was a short flight to LaGuardia and then a longer flight on a C-130 to the Farm.

The temptation to give up is common among everyone but failure is not something many of us can endure gracefully; and with courage to persevere, success will become our destiny as we have proven in two world wars.

Personnel may be costly but what is the cost of one human life? Now increase that by 100-fold, 1000-fold or even more! Forty-two teams of personnel scoured Central Park path by path, rock by rock, tree by tree and building by building and no dirty bomb was to be found.

Reservist were called in and intensified the search to uncover that dirty bomb. The park remained closed and would not reopen until the safety of all could be guaranteed. Between the local authorities, the FBI and the DOJ, the perplexity of the problem caused major concern as WW said, "I don't know which is worst, finding the bomb and then worry about deactivating it, or not finding the bomb and wondering in fear?"

Jackson McKenna returned from a very special side-trip to see Trevor's parents. A condolence visit is not one that you enjoy but an obligation one does out of honor and respect. He conveyed their son's last dying wish of his love for them and country. Then he presented to them the burial flag of their son, hugged Trevor's tearful mother and shook a proud dad's hand.

It is times like these that life's tender moments make us the strongest because of our inner strength to call on God to bolster others and pray. In times of need His strength lifts us up, if we turn to Him. McKenna was concerned about what to say to Trevor's mother but as if there was an angel on his shoulder, the words just seem to flow. Trevor's mother asked in a tearful voice while grabbing for McKenna's hands to hold her steady, "These hands touched my son?"

"Yes ma'am," replied McKenna, "It was an honor to serve with your son!"

He continued to say to her, "He was brave right up to the end!" Then they sat down together as McKenna consoled Trevor's parents by just being there.

Now back in New York City, the urgency of work snapped Jackson out of his somber mood, as he is brought up to speed on the present conditions. Receiving instructions once again to put his nose to the trail of those elusive terrorists. And as usual, the sleuth started asking questions, "Can this be a decoy to throw us off their trail?"

WW turned towards Jackson and asked, "What do you mean?"

"Well," Jackson started to say, "Why torch a truck?"

Now everyone is looking bewildered as Jackson continues, "They wanted us to find the truck and jump to conclusions that the bomb was taken to Central Park."

Looking at the police chief, Jackson asked, "You must have plenty of surveillance cameras around here that would give us some clue as to where this damn bomb was taken!"

Again, the tedious task of searching through all the surveillance footage was at hand. The best detectives are on the case of the missing bomb and none of them are raw recruits or untrained, but you can't become a good enough sleuth by simply watching. But you can become a great one by observing and learning what is missing and applying your sixth sense as to which trails to follow.

Within the hour, bingo, the surveillance shows another trailer truck pulls-up and a transfer of the dirty bomb was made with the markings of Averitt International on the sides of the trailer. Jackson and the FBI were on the terrorist's trail once again. Photos of the truck were taken along with a warrant to apprehend all involved with this conspiracy to Averitt International. The meeting between Averitt International management and the FBI on these allegations went from outrage, to becoming compliant once the photos were revealed.

The trail begins with a Filipino supervisor who is helping the terrorist and their devious, intricate scheme begins to unravel. The truck, crew and destination become known and the switch at Central Park foiled. A delivery of humanitarian aid is to be made at the United Nations building to display to all nations the cause of freedom and hands across the sea to help and give comfort.

One of the purposes of the United Nations, as stated in their Charter, is "to achieve international co-operation in solving international problems of an economic, social, cultural and humanitarian character." The Organization is now relied upon by the international community to coordinate humanitarian relief operations due to natural and manmade disasters around the world. One of the coordinators of the aid is UNICEF and their building is right across the street from the United Nations. A mad scramble takes place to locate that trailer truck.

Pieces of the puzzle are coming together as more information from Interpol comes across the desk of Corey Bennett. As a condition of membership, the United States maintains a National Central Bureau, NCB, in Washington, D.C., which serves to maintain liaison with the Organization's General Secretariat in Lyon, France along with the National Central Bureaus of INTERPOL's 189 other member countries.

Julien-Yves Bubois who was brusque in his manners and blunt in his speech annoyed everyone he encountered including Corey Bennett. Mr. Bubois felt that the French should still rule the world as they once did, that the French Resistance won World War II and French should be the national language. He went so far as to say in his snobbish attitude that the Americans have no couth and have never learned proper etiquette.

Jackson McKenna who was standing behind Mr. Bubois took out his bottle of Jack Daniels, took a swig and then proceeded to take out his revolver to shoot Mr. Bubois. But Corey Bennett being the total bureaucrat and patriot that he is intervened by welcoming Mr. Bubois and his important service by embracing Mr. Bubois and signaling for Jackson to put that damn gun away.

Graciously accepting the welcome, he said, "My friends call me JY, but you may call me Mr. Bubois."

Information came into the hands from Interpol that the French freighter, the SS Marseille was approached in Abidjan, Cote d'Ivoire to transport assassins to the United States as immigrants. Upon refusing such a request, the terrorist turned to the Liberians and succeeded. That upon further investigation Interpol uncovered that Russia has a mole in the FBI and that the United States has a traitor in the NSA and that is how information is slipping into the hands of the Russians.

Jackson McKenna having served during World War II in France with the army knew something firsthand about the French Resistance. Patiently waiting for Mr. Bubois to finish, he then spoke up to say, "I remember that during World War II, Lyon was the center of the French Resistance. That with all the French etiquette, there was a Klaus Barbie who tortured prisoners of the occupying German forces and became known as the "Butcher of Lyon."

Mr. Bubois graciously bowed to Jackson's knowledge of French history but corrected him by saying, "We simply talked to the Germans with whips, knives and branding irons." Then he said, "Vive la France!" and left the room.

Corey Bennett is shaking his head as he says, "As if we don't have enough problems, now we have a mole and a traitor!"

Jackson quickly replied as he spits on the floor and took another swig of Jack, "We have no couth, Ha! The JY stands for 'jumbo yuk.' Let us catch these traitors and send them to the Farm too!"

Corey Bennett looks at Jackson philosophically and tells him that they're aware of the traitor in the NSA, for he leaks information every time it rains. He has been branded with the code name of, "rainfall."

Now Corey turns and walks around his desk as he says, "But the mole in the FBI, I wasn't sure until now." Shuffling some paperwork, "I'll instigate an investigation and catch this bastard!" Then he just looks at Jackson and says, "You know all you sleuth's, you, Reid and even Mr. Bubois all come from the same casting mold, just varying degrees."

Jackson upon hearing those words is insulted for the comparison with a Julien-Yves Bubois and just shakes his head in disgust. Then he takes another swig from his Jack Daniels and says, "Vive la America!"

The Secret Service is expeditiously dispatched to the United Nations building for a full security search to prepare for the presidential address within two days. FBI respond to the UNICEF building looking for both assassins and a dirty bomb. And the police were searching for the Averitt International transport truck, while a radio dispatch came into FBI headquarters.

"Assistance is needed at the Baltimore/Washington International Airport. Apparently, an attempt by a Samuel Byck to hijack a commercial airliner and force the pilots to crash into the White House is underway.

After a short scuffle and a shooting of both pilots, an officer shot Byck through the plane's door window wounding him. He survived long enough to kill himself.

Bennett looks at McKenna and says, "It must be a full moon, for all the nuts have come out of the woodwork!" Bennett tells McKenna, "I'll catch up with you at One Police Plaza once I finish some paperwork. You know, it's days like this that I think of retirement! Sunny beaches, Long Island ice tea and no worries about bombs, terrorist or assassins!"

Jackson McKenna smiles and replies, "I know the feeling!"

McKenna nods, turns and walks out the door. Between the abattoir at the airport and the Tudor Place there have been nine killings. Jackson McKenna shakes his head and isn't ready for anymore briefings as he turns into One Police Plaza.

He notices Rick, whom had just finished a tactical search at one of the ship yards for bombs and peeps his car horn to grab his attention. Rolling down his car window he yells, "I need a drink before going inside and my flask is empty. How about you?"

Rick acknowledged in the affirmative and Jackson considered if this was as good of a time to break the news about Trevor.

Finnegan's Headless Pub was around the corner and that is just where the two of them wound up. A couple of Drambuie's and then a Glenlivet Scotch and then the conversation got somber. "I haven't slept good for so long," groaned McKenna.

"Yea, with all that has been going on, my head hits the pillow at night but I don't sleep," Rick said.

"Sometimes I think we are in the wrong business, but this is all I know, and this is where I'll either stay or die," McKenna continued.

Then he pauses for a minute before saying, "I've been on a covert mission to find Trevor."

Rick looks at his dire expression and senses the pending bad news.

Jackson begins slowly and unravels the trip, the plan and the consequences.

Rick doesn't respond but listens attentively.

Then Jackson reveals the burial at sea on the Saratoga and the side trip to see Trevor's parents.

Rick asked the somber question, "How did that go?"

McKenna looking melancholy replied, “One of the hardest things that I’ve had to do because facing Trevor’s parents reveals why we do this job.”

Rick looking a little puzzled asked, “What do you mean?”

McKenna sternly replied, “If we allow terrorists or any bad guys to get the upper hand, then the true meaning of life is for nothing. Courage and resolve go out the window!”

Rick replied, “Amen!”

McKenna just smiled and took a long gulp of his drink as he said, “No more work tonight, there is always tomorrow to fight crime!”

Rick agreed and gave a salute with his drink before taking another sip.

It wasn’t long before the magic question popped up as Jackson asked, “Why are you in the CIA?”

His reply was, “He didn’t know any better!”

At that, they both laughed. Then to my surprise McKenna got very philosophical as he said, “If all we see does not expose the truth, then what lies in the shadows?”

Waiting for my reply, he further continued, “Our job is to uncover what lies in the shadows.”

Rick agreed but replied, “A person needs more of the truth and less of the shadows!”

At that comment, McKenna just sat back and finished his drink. As they both leave the establishment, McKenna looks up towards the Empire State Building and says, “Clear skies, good night for a walk.”

Rick bids him a good night and goes back to his hotel as McKenna takes a jaunt to Battery Park Place and just stares across the bay at the Stature of Liberty.

RETRIBUTION BEFORE GROUND ZERO

An emergency meeting is called by "WW," of the Department of Justice. The impromptu meeting is short, direct and perilous as three people meet at Battery Park. Dick Helms of the CIA and Corey Bennett of the FBI are the only ones there as WW informs them, "Our Statue of Liberty is all about enlightenment to the whole world!"

Looking across the bay at the Statue of Liberty, he then continues to say, "We have a mole in the FBI and a snitch in the NSA. Traitors, Bastards to their country, traitors should be shot! But with all of our liberal lawyers, no one deserves the death penalty. If our God sees fit to send the dastardly offenders to hell, then by God we should execute traitors by firing squad."

He impatiently walks back and forth before continuing, "assassins in our country, multiple bombs and the threat of WW III."

Now WW is fuming with anger and frothing at the mouth, "These two dastardly bastards have disappeared!"

He gives the names of these two individuals who are responsible for the information leaks and the suspected couriers who work for the Russian Embassy.

WW just stares at the Statue of Liberty and cogitates over what he is about to say, "The necessary paperwork is being processed as we speak to deport the delegates from the Russian Embassy."

Then he turns to Dick Helms and Corey Bennett and very definitively points to the Statue of Liberty as he says, "Traitors are not to be tolerated; search, find and liquidate."

The French have a beautiful expression to describe a notorious traitor as, "mal fame' traitre." And one has the extreme urge to want to "cracher and vomir!" That is spit and vomit when one thinks of such a person.

The Mafia has its vendettas and the CIA its requisitions, which causes the church to have many requiems. Prayer is the most powerful tool that any human being has but only if it comes from a sincere heart, mind and soul of the individual praying.

Greg O'Neal who worked for the FBI for close to twenty years and Fred Webster who worked for NSA some five years are both on the run. Having drained their bank accounts, a major warning is given to law enforcement of both guilty parties that skedaddled to Mexico.

The port city of Ensenada is a coastal city of Mexico on the Baja peninsula. Home to both cruise and merchant ships, this is one of the world-wide destinations of the underground to disappear to other countries. Whether one travels by boat, drives or flies to get here, this is the place. No questions asked, fake passport furnished to countries with no extradition treaties with the United States for the undisclosed amount of $10,000 dollars.

Greg O'Neal booked passage on the Liberian container ship, the Gato, bound for the Marshall Islands. Sweating profusely, he knew his chances of escape were narrow at best. Any major foul-ups in the FBI or CIA is a death sentence and being a traitor is at the top of the list for major blunders. So why did he do it. In Greg's case after twenty years of being passed over for promotion, he wanted revenge, "tout fini!"

Fred Webster enjoyed fast cars, fast women and betting on the race horses. For him it is money, and a bribery for information was a quick and easy way for his squanderlust. He had top clearances at the NSA and acquiesced to do the unthinkable, steal information. At least that is what he first thought, as he booked passage with a humdinger of an escort who was hot, scrumptious and delightful 24/7 on the Norwegian cruise ship bound for the Samoa Islands.

It was a sunny, balmy day when both men left their domicile in America for the paradise of the Pacific Islands.

Dick Helms wasted no time but through his channels of contacts initiated the "Super Vacuum Cleaner," a group of Black Ops whose sole purpose is to clean filth or literally, suck them off the face of the earth. No questions asked if no bodies are found!

There are no names, no credentials, no place of known residence. The coded contact of SVC is 011-506-SVC-KILL. Once the package disappears, a sum of $600,000 dollars is wired to a Swiss account.

Corey Bennett of the FBI and Director Lt. Gen. Lew Allen of the NSA were reassured that the packages would be proficiently handled. National Security of any country is vital but world powers have a fastidious duty to uphold, protect and defend from all threats, domestic and foreign.

A trace to uncover each scoundrel is sequestered only for black ops intervention. Depending on which foreign agency is interviewed, the collective consensus reports some 11 underground levels, 33,000 gangs in the United States and an estimated 55,000 gangs worldwide. Based on these estimates, geospatial maps are prepared and updated to visually display the reporting jurisdictions. Another map is prepared that shows major crimes committed such as murders, robberies and espionage. This multi-agency fusion center integrates all this information from the alphabet soup of acronyms of all agencies to foil further criminal acts.

Today there is no place to hide and the world sees all, especially on CNN.

Fred Webster nonchalantly boarded the Norwegian cruise ship thinking to himself, "what a beautiful day."

The steward took his luggage and led Mr. Webster to what he thought would be his ward room and that luscious escort. Her name is Jumpsie and pleasure is her gain as previously planned to meet in Ensenada. Walking along the promenade deck, Mr. Webster asked the steward, "Which deck level are we on?"

The steward, who is actually a Black-Ops agent turns towards Mr. Webster and smiles but never answers him as he continues his way down the promenade deck. Coming to a doorway, the steward stops and opens a door, then gestures with his hand to Mr. Webster to step forward. He turns to ask the steward another question when the steward smashes Mr. Webster over the head with a billy club. Between the smashing hit with a billy club and tumbling down a flight of stairs, Fred Webster passes out.

Another Black-Ops agent stationed below in the engine room, places a hood over Mr. Webster's head. Together, the stewards lift Mr. Webster by his hands and feet and haul him off to the engine room.

The Norwegian cruise ship has four boilers, constructed by Chantiers de l'Atlantique in France. One of the boilers had a tube leak in one of the many tubes that circulated water between the steam and mud drums. Having plugged the tube from each end to prevent any more leakage, the repair crew stopped for lunch.

The Black Ops bound Webster's hands and feet with duct tape. Then removing the hood, gagged him and placed the hood back over his head. Then one of the Black Ops climbed inside the mud drum through the oval manhole and pulled Webster's body to the center of the twenty-foot-long mud drum. Climbing out of the hole ever so carefully, both of the men closed and batten down the door.

Once the engineering crew returns from lunch, the boilers will be buttoned-up and begin the filling process with water. The dimensions of each boiler are about thirty feet high by twenty-five feet across the front, by twenty feet on a side. The operating pressure of each boiler is 900 psi supplying superheated steam to the turbines for ship propulsion. A most gruesome way to die and disappear from sight. This becomes the end of the story for our Mr. Fred Webster who was boiled and scalded to death with all remains, bones and all turned to sludge.

Meanwhile, WW back at the Department of Justice instigated the paperwork to uncover the trail of leaks from both the NSA and FBI. Most crucial leaks are not done over the phone or computer but smuggled by courier to their final destination. It was paramount to find the leaks and plug them up permanently.

An adamant Wade Washington looks at Corey Bennett and Says, "Long before I ever entered this job with the DOJ, I had considered entering the seminary. I am Lutheran and have a deep reverence for God. But as Judas was a thorn in the side of Christ, these traitors are thorns in my side. We need to eliminate them. They should be brought to justice!"

Corey Bennett looks at WW and shakes his head before saying, "Collecting the proof is difficult!"

WW stands and walks over to the wall where there is a picture of the signers of the Declaration of Independence and tells Bennett, "These men had ideals and a true belief in justice, faith and freedom!"

WW impatiently walks back and forth, all the while saying, "The dilemma is substantial proof and getting the lawyers to see the light of day!"

Then WW stops long enough and slams his fist against his desk before saying, "This damn conspiracy of multiple governments, assassins, embassy's and traitors is too colossal to wrap the arms of justice around it to contain."

He then walks to the cabinet and pours himself a glass of bourbon as he turns and gestures one for Corey.

Corey acknowledges with a nod of his head as WW pours another glass and tells Corey, "As magnanimous as the ideals of the Bill of Rights are, there are times when either war has to be declared or counter espionage has to take precedence!"

Then Corey stands to accept his drink and says to WW, "For the protection of the republic or the people, when it comes to war vs counter espionage, then I choose counter espionage, period!"

After some more contemplation Corey continues by saying, "I personally believe that our forefathers didn't have the foresight to deal with all contingencies of today in our constitution.

Then they both sat down and mulled over their next steps as they enjoyed their drink.

Our illustrious Mr. Greg O'Neal is in for a rude awakening as he parks his vehicle and retrieves his luggage. He looks across the way towards the containership, the Gato. Smiling and thinking to himself, "Once onboard, I'm safe!"

Suddenly, a black van pulls up with no markings and no license plates but stops directly behind Greg O'Neal's car. Two Black Ops jump out and quickly sedate, bind and gag our Mr. O'Neal. He is expeditiously taken to a small airport on the outskirts of Ensenada. Loaded onto a C-130 cargo plane with the markings, "Hawaiian Express," that was the last time anyone saw our illustrious traitor.

There are currently three active volcanoes in Hawaii. Kilauea is the most violent and has been continuously erupting for some time. It is an eight-and-a-half-hour flight to their destination as the pilots check the weather conditions and wind speed. The sedation should last about six hours before Greg O'Neal wakes up for his last time.

There is very little danger of flying over a volcano as long as there is no eruption. Hence, upon arrival the C-130 will descend to within one hundred feet above the opening of Kilauea and drop our Mr. O'Neal into the volcano. The lava's hot temperature reaches better than 2000 degrees Fahrenheit. The two Black Op agents were taking bets on whether he would burst into flames before hitting the lava or asphyxiate and char his lungs due to the hot gases. A bet that neither one could financially collect since there is no way to validate the outcome.

The back door is opened and our Mr. O'Neal is dragged from his seat and positioned for the drop zone. With one mighty push and no parachute, the exit was swift.

There's a multitude of activity within the Department of Justice as WW wrestles with traitors, espionage and jurisdiction on embassy sovereignty. The Attorney General is up to his armpits with legal mumble-jumble to combat diplomatic immunity. The best place for the legal team to find answers on diplomatic relations are the Articles of the Vienna Convention, especially Articles 21-25.

Richardson is arguing with WW as he states, "the premises of any Embassy shall be immune from search, requisition, attachment or execution. The archives and documents of the embassy shall be inviolable at any time and wherever they may be."

WW getting red in the face yells, "But they're our documents, you dimwit, that they are stealing!"

Just then WW storms out of the Attorney General's office and decides to check on the status of our assassin Reynante Bautista, who is being flown to the farm.

The quandary of espionage through the various embassies versus our State Department prosecuting them is a catch-22. This leaves only one option for WW as he talks to Wes Armstrong about Bautista. "Cut the "GORDIAN'S KNOT."

This is the thought that is going through WW's mind as he speaks to Wes on the phone. He utilized the Black Ops to apprehend the bad guys. Why not employ the Couriers Identification Associates to amass the necessary evidence on the information grabbers?

The various service departments are established and there is no need to reinvent the wheel. Within the US Postal Service department, there is a special branch of Couriers Identification Associates or CIA. How about that? Another branch of the CIA within the Post Office.

There are better than 508,000 full time employees for the United States Postal Service with some 130,000 temporary employees. Now add another 7000 confidential employees registered to the CIA within the Postal service. Their job is plain and simple, gain evidence on what was stolen.

The CIA utilizes primarily three means to gather information through people, devices and satellites. All the information retrieved is maintained in the SAR files or suspicious activity files in a DataMart of SP's, scattered pubs. These pubs were fronts across the nation to house any inferred evidence. A one stop spies haven to store or retrieve information and get a beer. All of this information is synthesized by the Joint Interagency Coalition Operation Center, known as JICOC for combatting future threats.

Now, when it comes to embassies in Washington DC, it becomes a little more abstruse. Most embassies have satellite jamming devices which makes it difficult to listen for threats. Newer satellites operate in higher frequency bands that have transponders, receiver-to-transmitter, aboard to amplify the received signal from the uplink. But most embassies have sophisticated data jamming equipment to jam the uplink signals. Hence, reason enough for why WW is soliciting the aid of the Couriers.

Civilization is all about culture, advancement and enlightenment. More importantly education and expanding the horizon with new information. Whoever controls the information, controls the world. Egypt had it colossal pyramids and literature, Greece gave us democracy and the Roman Empire gave us the rudiments of law and civil engineering but Washington DC is all-encompassing.

From Capitol Hill, the hub of 12 principal avenues leads out like spokes of a giant wheel that encompass the grandeur of memorials, libraries, museums and the government stately buildings and embassies. And in the eyes of WW there are four embassies that are on the target list. As technologies advance, renovations must update these advancements in each of the buildings in Washington.

Two new devices are installed throughout the ménage of buildings that aren't just places of work but residences to many who work 24-7. Security is heavy at most embassies which make it unfeasible to install bug devices or wiretapping. Between the intense security and complex legalities of both, it's impossible for Big Brother to be watching. Unless the slight of hand comes into the picture, the necessary maneuvers to accomplish the task are difficult.

There were two devices used to capture data known as VAL, or voice activated listening and SNOOP, an observation device that snapped photos every minute. The mission impossible task is retrieving the data from these spy devices. Non-detectable devices had to avoid any scanning or bug detectors. This is where the couriers are vital to make a difference. The postal service carrier has an unsuspicious character because they are recognizable. We see them on a daily basis.

Carrie has been a courier for twelve years now. She began her career in law enforcement and worked her way through the hawsepipe to become a detective. Recruited by the CIA in the special task force of couriers she is part of the United States Postal Service.

There were four embassies involved in the espionage to steal vital state documents. The Russian Embassy, the main instigator in the overall plan and the accomplishers of the Nigerian, Philippine and Mexican Embassies. Oblivious to any of the inhabitants of the Embassies and avoiding any of the daily scanning devices; the implants of VAL and Snoop are in all embassies. Typically, any information retrieved from these devices would be handed over to the DDS, the United States Diplomatic Security Service. This federal law enforcement and security arm is part of the United States Department of State.

But the catch-22 comes with not using any of this information to prosecute but to liquidate the bastards. A courier had to be adept and cunning to retrieve the information. The years have seasoned Carrie to accomplish the deed. She nonchalantly entered any of the Embassies, delivered said packages and requested use of restrooms. She had full knowledge beforehand of the architectural layout of each building and if necessary could proceed to her destination blindfolded.

Long before the great rulers of antiquity, rulers like Alexander the Great who was a brilliant, ruthless, power hungry genius, established covert spies to outfox his enemies. Information on your enemy is vital for success.

All governing bodies understand this principle, hence such establishments as the CIA and MI6. Now as Carrie made her way pass the restroom, avoiding detection by security cameras and motion detectors, she removed the snoop retriever from her watch. A microchip that downloaded information and recordings from the VAL's. Timing her steps to the basement, she knew that within four minutes security would be checking on her.

The main controls for the sprinkler fire system were in the basement. All covert retrieving devices were installed in all sprinkler heads throughout the embassy. The access port is installed in the main flow valve. The retrieving skimmer to access the information is in the watch band of Carrie's watch and can download all information in one minute.

While retrieving the information, Carrie looks at her watch and she is beginning her third minute. As she leaves the basement, one can hear the footsteps of the approaching security guard. Carrie quietly closes the basement door utilizing her id card to hold the latch in place, preventing it from striking the plate to make any noise. Then she rushes pass the restroom door just as the security guard comes around the corner. She smiles at the security guard and keeps on walking, thinking to herself, "whew, close call."

A massive network of people is necessary to accomplish all of the tasks. Couriers and translators are needed to retrieve and analyze the information. Then there are the installers of the equipment during the construction of the building. Finally, a special branch known as liquidators which is separate from the CIA agents.

America's military might have four Aces, Seal Team 6, the Green Berets, Delta Force Army Rangers and the 82nd Airborne, besides our five branches of the Armed Services. There is a special covert team known as Trom, in Vietnamese means theft, but Troms steal only one thing, lives of the Viet Cong.

In Vietnamese, "may bay chien dau tang hinh," means stealth fighter who fought along-side our American forces in Vietnam.

These tribesmen won the admiration of our forces. For four years, Special Forces had been training an oppressed minority group in guerrilla tactics. These indigenous Montagnards defended villages against the Viet Cong and served as rapid response forces for covert operations.

The Montagnards, whose named is derived from the French word for mountaineers are a proud people and ethnically distinct from the Vietnamese. In the early 60's better than a million Montagnards lived in Vietnam.

When the United States Special Forces first arrived in Vietnam, the Montagnards were already into an adversarial relationship with the existing government. Tensions arose between the Vietnamese and Montagnards due to bigotry and racism. In 1961 an initiative orchestrated by the CIA and Special Forces moved into the Vietnamese mountains to begin the strategic defense program which included the Montagnards. The Montagnards' forested mountain homeland were prime highways for North Vietnamese forces to move men and supplies. The Montagnards were the first line of defense to ambush and disrupt the enemy forces. Skilled in the art of "dha," a term conventionally used to refer to a wide variety of knives and swords, the Montagnard's camouflaged in mud, would crawl into the North Vietnamese camps and slit their throats. One legend known as, "ma ba'o thu, vengeful spirit, is retold throughout the land. Thirty men of the Montagnard tribe slashed 400 throats of the North Vietnamese. The next day the remaining survivors disbanded the camp.

When the Vietnam War concluded, many of the Montagnard tribes were relocated to safe protection havens in Costa Rica, South America and California. Today there is a small group of Montagnards utilized as liquidators for their superb skill of dha.

WW was burning the midnight oil and contemplating his next few moves. Like a chest game, his next moves were contingent upon what information the couriers retrieved from the embassies and from what the farm could coerce from the terrorists. This would determine the future course of America's resolve.

CHAPTER 11

BACK TO THE FARM

What is heaven you may wonder?

And you may also wonder, what is hell?

Each of us should also ponder the question, what is bliss?

David Hume, a Scottish philosopher once said, "Heaven and hell suppose two distinct species of people, the good and the bad. But the greatest part of humankind float betwixt vice and virtue. My favorite quotes on heaven and hell come from Mark Twain who said, "I don't like to commit myself about heaven or hell for you see, I have friends in both places." He also said, "Go to Heaven for the climate, Hell for the company."

To me, Heaven is bliss because God, our heavenly Father and our Saving Lord are there! And Hell is anguish because neither are there. True Bliss is accepting that fact. The question for each of us in life is simply this; is our faith strong enough to believe in our saving Lord!

The Farm is between earth and hell, how I wish that the need for such a place never existed. The C-130 landed as Reynante Bautista was dragged from the plane and to the barn. Major General Armstrong along with his Black Ops walked over to Bautista's bruised and tired body as his interpreter said in Filipino to the terrorist, "mayroon kang isang pagkakataon. Aminin ang lahat o maging alligator pagkain." Which translated in English means, you have one chance, confess all or become alligator food.

Guillaume grabs the shackles attached to Bautista's ankles and drags him across the barn's rough planks as Boudreaux lowers the winch. Wes Armstrong again talks to him and tells him that this is his last chance. Attaching the winch's hook to the shackles, Guillaume then opens the huge trap door in the floor. Wes looks down and just stares at the dark hole. The surface of the waters some-thirty feet below is dark, calm and silent. One neither sees or hears anything. The dark silence is haunting. Bautista's body is hoisted and positioned over the trap door.

Guillaume then walks over to get the bucket of animal blood and guts and dumps the whole batch into the water. Then like a thunderous roar, the calm waters surge alive with twenty or more alligators thrashing to get whatever has been thrown to them. Wes looks up into Bautista's eyes now bulging with fear, blood rushing to his brain, his body frozen in a panic frenzy not believing what he sees below. Wes signals to Boudreaux to slowly lower the winch.

Reynante Bautista, nephew to the leader of the Sputniks is now screaming in a convulsive agony. His body twisting, withering and jerking upwards as Wes signals to stop the winch. He has the interpreter tell Bautista in fluent Filipino, "ang iyong tiyuhin ay nasa tiyan ng isang croc." Which means, your uncle is in the belly of a croc.

Allowing time for the message to penetrate his mind and the thrashing of the crocs to influence Bautista's attitude, Wes observes the actions of this assassin before he allows the interpreter to ask in Filipino, "Ang gusto mong sumali sa iyong tiyuhin?" Which means, "Do you want to join your uncle?"

Observing such a contortionist fit of dismay, Wes signals to lower Bautista's body to within thirteen feet above the surface of the water to just hang there. With the blood rushing to his head, minutes can seem like hours as Bautista faints and his body goes limp.

Waiting for Bautista to regain consciousness, Wes and the two brothers go to the cabin for a coffee break. A cabin with many amenities which included their distillery for making moonshine, a pool table, a gym with a swimming pool and a library with select reading material on weaponry. It was a two-story building with six rooms upstairs for sleeping accommodations, each with their own bathroom. Down stairs had two 10 x 10 conference rooms for interrogations, two cells for lock-up along with a kitchen and the combo-room of den, gym and library.

The two brothers, Boudreaux and Guillaume were x-military having served with the Green Beret in Vietnam. Both men are proficient in several languages, weaponry and military tactics. Due to their cultural Cajun upbringing and years of duty in the jungle prefer the farm and all of its antics of interrogation to the city life. Wes refers to each of the reclusive brothers as "G" and "B" and nods to them that it's time to head back to the barn.

Throughout the fifteen-minute break, Bautista has been suspended in mid-air. Awakened by the turbulence below, he peers at the dark hole. Occasionally, he feels the crocs below lunge and snap their jaws at his head as he cringes his body and closes his eyes.

Returning to the barn, Wes slides open the vintage door. A picture is worth a thousand words as he looks down the hole towards Bautista's hanging body. Indescribable, a neurotic mess. Crying, shaking and having excrement slide down his body and towards his head, dripping below. The entire scene is wrapped in an eerie darkness.

Wes signals to raise the body and unshackle him. Then it was made crystal clear to Bautista that this is his last chance to tell all or become food for the crocs. He was hosed off and then brought to the cabin where he could shower, dress in a jump-suit and eat a meal. Then he was allowed time to sleep. He awoke within eight hours a little better refreshed.

With a lawyer present for the DOJ, testimony was given by Reynante Bautista that a dirty bomb would destroy the Statue of Liberty and the assassination hit on the President of the United States will be made by a diplomat within the confines of the United Nations. Such startling information can never be taken lightly. The insidious details were unraveled to uncover the entire plan.

What are the steps that lead a person to become a terrorist?

What are the steps in life that lead any of us to where we are going?

It all begins within the steps of our heart. The steps of the heart will discipline the steps of the mind and ultimately lead us to choices of the soul. But once the heart is hardened, our consciousness is closed to making good choices. Then only the darkness abides, and life is neither enjoyable or pleasant on the dark side.

Major General Wes Armstrong is satisfied that he has the complete picture and sends all pertinent information to Wade Washington and Corey Bennett. Once the CIA gets wind of the entire plot, a contingency plan is put in place.

Jackson McKenna lets Rick know that the end is in site and perhaps WW III can be averted. Then he turns and says, “Such knowledge I find extremely disturbing.” And then he asked, “How does such knowledge affect you?”

Smiling and for the first time enjoying the opportunity of our friendship, Rick replied, “The only knowledge that any person needs, is the knowledge of what our Lord said, that he is with us always. That whoever sees him sees the Father!”

Stopping long enough to reflect on those words, Rick then said, “The wisdom in our life is accepting and believing in His name.”

Jackson is completely disturbed that the plot had gone this far and then added, “I need a jack and coke!”

We proceeded to the closest bar.

A C-130 transported Reynante Bautista to Gitmo, where for the rest of his life his sunrise and sunsets will have no meaning as his life sinks into the abyss of darkness.

There is one straightforward way to make sure that the perpetrators cannot destroy the Statue of Liberty, an endearing symbol of hope for so many, and that is to close the island for a few days under the guise of repairs. Extra security is posted on the island and frequent patrols by the U. S. Coast Guard enhance the security until the perpetrators are apprehended.

An extensive review of all dossiers is made to scrutinize each diplomat that represents the various countries at the United Nations. Any new names of diplomats or their entourage will not gain access to the president's speech. Once credulous information comes into the hands of our federal bureaus, the barriers of protection are enforced. This is something that terrorist cannot grasp, they spontaneously assume that one can just walk into our country and do what they damn well please. They all forget that our underlying foundation by our forefathers' states:

We the People of the United States, to form a more perfect Union, establish Justice, insure domestic Tranquility, provide for the common defense, promote the general Welfare, and secure the Blessings of Liberty to ourselves and our Posterity, do ordain and establish this Constitution for the United States of America. Our Statue of Liberty in New York Harbor is Liberty enlightening the world and our Statue of Freedom that stands on top of our Capital building symbolizes that we will in vigilance, uphold, protect and defend to keep us one country under God, indivisible. We as a people should never forget that, and to the world, take note. Therefore, we all need to hold dear in our patriotic hearts our pledge of allegiance to the flag.

Criminal actions, terrorism and violence will never be tolerated. Justice will be done and as Lady Justice personifies the moral force in our judicial system, her attributes are a blindfold, a balance, and a sword and should never be ignored. For wearing a blindfold represents impartiality; the ideal that justice should be applied without regard to wealth, power, or other status. The scales of balance measure the strengths of a case's support and opposition. And the last attribute the sword, represents authority to convey the idea that justice can be swift and final. Although today as the magnitude of violence and crime intensifies, justice is never swift enough. The penalties need to out weigh the severity of the crime in order to obtain justice. The liberals maintain that the death penalty isn't a deterrence to crime. But it does eliminate the heinous perpetrators from our neighborhoods and the overcrowding of our prisons.

The entire complement of our law and justice system were coming together to end this nightmarish ordeal as Wade Washington told Corey Bennett, "Enough is enough!"

Shea Reid is on the prowl for the terrorist and hasn't received word from Pickpocket who has been living incognito on the streets now for the past five years. During that time, one learns of people's habits, routines and can quickly pick out the peculiarities of behavior that send up flags. It is amazing how much information one can gather by observing street culture, something that cameras cannot detect.

Billy Frump had a routine to circulate between train depots, bus terminals, coffee and pawn shops and knew the right people on the street to ask the simple question, "who is new on the street?" People on the street trusted Pickpocket for he had helped many in need and knew the right contacts to render aid to the addict or one who has been abused. As he meandered between the soup kitchens, shelters and the Salvation Army, Billy picked up tidbits of information about a small group of men that despised the people on the street and displayed contempt for such people.

For the average citizen, detestable behavior makes your hairs stand on end. But for Billy Frump it signaled a flag, for Billy knew all too well how terrorist have no compassion for people on the street. He saw the devastation and pain caused by terrorist, having served two tours in Vietnam. The empty apathy of terrorist who could blow-up their victims without considering that they're human beings like you and me. It doesn't matter the place or nationality; all terrorists have a harden heart and a disrespect for God's creation. The vehement hate from within consumes them to either destroy or be destroyed.

Sally has lived on the streets for some two years after serving in Vietnam three successive tours with the Army Nurse Corps. Known on the streets as Sally Two-Bags, because everything she owned could be carried in two shopping bags. Billy tried to help her at times, but she preferred the streets and a life of being alone.

While making his rounds at the 46th Street Salvation Army store, Billy noticed Sally and the bruises on her face as he said to her, "Good morning Sally, how did you get those bruises?"

Sally didn't talk much but trusted Billy, as she said, "These people, foreigners, eight well-dressed men!" Then she started to cry.

Billy had her sit down on one of the benches within the store as he tried to comfort her as he said, "It's ok Sally, this is Billy your talking to, your safe now."

He slowly sat down next to her and said, "Take your time Sally and tell Billy all about it."

Then he handed her his handkerchief so she could blow her nose and compose herself.

She gave Billy a smile which is a rarity among street people and gradually began to speak, "Those foreigners just pushed me down a flight of stairs and laughed!"

Billy decided that this was too traumatic for her to continue talking. He rose from the bench and took Sally's hands to help her up. Then they went for a short walk along the street, stopping at a local McDonalds. He bought her a cup of coffee with a couple of biscuit egg sandwiches.

He let her eat quietly as he sipped his coffee. Then after a short time, he asked Sally, "where did this altercation take place?

She explained to Billy that it was near the Church of the Holy Family. That once they pushed her down, the eight men walked abruptly to the United Engineering Center just around the corner.

Billy then asked her, "How do you know that there were eight men?"

Sally quickly responded, "I was a medic nurse on the front lines and had many casualties! I learned on the battlefield to count quickly for how many safety kits were needed. War is harsh but Vietnam was unforgiving."

Billy then asked, "Can you describe these people to me?"

Sally tried but couldn't really describe the individual assailants to Billy. She looked down upon the ground as she thought to herself. Then looking up towards Billy, an important clue came to her. She told him that they spoke in a foreign dialect. He thanked her for the information and then proceeded on his way to check out the area.

Taking a brisk walk down East 47th Street, he turned the corner onto 1st Avenue and noticed the 18-story building of the United Engineering Center. This is a place to advance the engineering arts and sciences for the welfare of humanity through grants and education.

This is where the character of Pickpocket can blend in and not raise any suspicions as he sat on the sidewalk and held his coffee cup in hand waiting for a donation. He must have sat there for three hours observing people coming and going.

Three well-dressed men stepped out from the Engineering Center and walked right-by Pickpocket. He just starred at the ground holding his cup when one of the perpetrators kicked Pickpocket in his side, laughed and said something in Filipino to the others. This action signaled the appropriate time to call in Shea Reid, who could snoop inside the Engineering Foundation and make positive identification.

Within the hour, Shea Reid along with three plain clothesmen detectives entered the building. Discreetly they mingled and inquired about any new activities by the foundation. There were trade shows on both the second and third floors as Shea's crew split-up to cover both floors.

This is the part of the detective's job that Shea truly enjoyed, sniffing out the culprits and bringing them to justice. The adrenaline pumps a little harder and the sensation of being on the right trail gave him an all-time high like four double-scotches but without the alcohol. But what he couldn't fathom is why here at the Engineering Center.

He always observed from afar to watch people's interactions with others and could always spot a phony a mile away. Never underestimate the devious, cunning mind of the demented terrorist. There is always a backup plan and the dirty bomb which was meant for the Statue of Liberty is now at the Engineering Center. Always prepared to go to the extremes to accomplish their task to destroy, Shea was careful not to alert the terrorists but wanted to find that dirty bomb.

Prepared for the unexpected each undercover cop had an American Society of Mechanical Engineers badge to mingle and move amongst the various booth displays. There was one booth set up for the IEEE, Institute of Electrical and Electronics Engineers that Reid meandered near.

Bending over to tie his shoe, he caught a glimpse of something under the table cloth of the main display table. That must be the dirty bomb he thought to himself! Looking over the table, he noticed three of the eight culprits and nonchalantly looked around the room for the full complement of terrorists.

Making his way to the hallway, Reid radioed a code 9, set up roadblock around perimeter of the Engineering Center and a code 10, bomb threat.

Whenever a Code 10 comes in to the authorities, it signals a silent immediate response without sirens. Perimeter boundary watch is set-up and within sixteen minutes SWAT, local authorities and the FBI are on the premises. No sirens to alert the culprits to trigger the bomb.

Corey Bennett and McKenna were alerted and arrived on the scene a split second behind the SWAT teams. Fire trucks, the bomb squad and Med-Q arrived within minutes to set-up response stations around the entire perimeter.

Hoses are stretched out along the ground as firemen rush connecting hoses to the hydrants. Ambulances arrive and set up two separate stations in anticipation of all contingencies. The bomb squad arrives at the command center and hopefully will have an opportunity to disarm the bomb versus the alternative.

One of the undercover cops has a side exit door open for SWAT to enter. Corey Bennett assigns teams to enter the building along with SWAT. He then signals McKenna to take lead with one of the teams.

McKenna nonchalantly walks up the stairway to the first floor to look around. One of the terrorist in the hallway noticed SWAT coming up the stairs behind him and within seconds this provocative situation inflamed into a shoot-out at the OK-Corral on 1st Ave. Guns started a blazing and one terrorist pulls out a rocket launcher from under the table. Bullets were firing in every direction with people diving for cover as the terrorist stood their ground. It clearly would be a fight to the finish.

Jackson approached by the north door and caught two bullets in the gut as he fell to the floor. He managed to fire two rounds from his chamber hitting the terrorist with the rocket launcher. SWAT team members open-fired on the culprits as two team members carried Jackson out of the building.

Three teams of SWAT moved in with one team heading down the hallway and the remainder two teams jointly rushed into the conference hall ready to apprehend the terrorist. Prepared for the unexpected, one of the terrorist activates the timer on the dirty bomb. The remainder of the terrorist stood fast shooting from behind columns for cover.

The SWAT teams engaged and the battle ensued as the dirty bomb exploded, killing all within the conference hall and igniting an inferno throughout the building.

Mayhem and death erupted like a volcano sending all within the square block into panic as the fire departments responded to an all alarm fire. Shock seizes many as a numbness settles in. Many of the innocent by-standers cannot fathom what just happened.

Simultaneously, extra SWAT teams cautiously move in, Med-Q is on hand to rescue any survivors and rush casualties to the hospital. Firemen approach the scene ready to engage the fire. The FBI are trying to account for all terrorists and not add to the death toll.

Through all the flames, smoke and debris, a cloud of dust arose from Manhattan for all to see. The command center tried to bring some order to chaos, calmness to the ruckus and reestablish some peace to a bad situation.

As the flames were extinguished and the smoke settled, bodies were carried away and the death toll so far reached some

126 victims including seven of the eight terrorists. A frantic Corey Bennett yelling for some accountability of a head count for both law enforcement and the terrorists. Evacuation of the area and testing for radioactivity begins immediately as a new perimeter is set-up to prevent outsiders from entering the contaminated area. Journalist, belligerently wanting to gain access to take pictures and interview survivors to get the scoop of the century were scurrying around like chickens with their heads cut off.

Bennett's concern for the last terrorist consumes him as teams of both FBI and local authorities comb the area. What can one say for in an ungodly world, the unthinkable can happen and does happen. Will we ever turn to Him and believe?

Accountability for the dead reached 131 and one terrorist not accounted for. Shea Reid was killed in the blast along with his associates. Pickpocket was one of the casualties found in the proximity of the Engineering Center and brought to a local hospital and within the day, he died. There were some 46 injured and one Jackson McKenna in a comma holding on by a thread of hope.

The perimeter was maintained for further investigations to be completed and to keep people beyond the contaminated danger. The blockade stopped at 45th Street so access to the United Nations for now was safe. With only a day left until the President of the United States arrives to address the United Nations, the secret service moves in and extra security is set.

That evening Rick visited the Manhattan General Hospital to find out the status of Jackson McKenna. He was still in a comma and there was no comfort in the words from the medical staff that information cannot be given out except for family.

There is only one appropriate place to be when all seems dark and you need to seek His help. Kneeling in the hospitals chapel, Rick did the sign of the cross and prayed the prayer that hopefully would give the both of them some solace. The words to Jesus Christ Crucified:

Behold, my beloved and good Jesus.
I cast myself upon my knees in your sight,
and with the most fervent desire of my soul,
I pray and beseech you to impress upon my heart,
lively sentiments of faith, hope and charity.
With true repentance for my sins and a most firm desire of amendment.
While with deep affection and grief of soul,
I consider within myself and mentally contemplate,
your five most precious wounds,
having before my eyes that which David the prophet long ago spoke about you,
My Jesus: They have pierced my hands and feet;
I can count all my bones,
Oh God, come to Jackson's McKenna assistance,
Oh Lord, make haste to help him.
Amen

CHAPTER 12

TIME IS RUNNING OUT

Too much violence, too much mayhem, too much death!

C. S. Lewis once said, "You never know how much you really believe anything until its truth or falsehood becomes a matter of life and death to you."

There is a harshness to life, there is a beauty to life and both should lead us to God! For our faithfulness is the epitome to the gift of life. And our faithfulness will lead us to our Heavenly Father, if and only if, we utilize our gift of faith.

McKenna's lifeless body disturbed Rick, for his mentor taught this pup much about survival in life and he had earned Rick's admiration and respect. He prayed, reflected and hoped that he would see him again in this life. Rick remembered once watching the Reverend Billy Graham on television and his inspired words of, "It's not the paths of life that are tough, but those damn crossroads with no stop signs!" How many times do we have to come to an abrupt stop in our life before we turn to Him?

The blast at the United Engineering Center destroyed three floors and fire damaged several other floors. The death count is now at 137 and 40 injured with one Jackson McKenna still in a coma.

Eventually the Engineering Center would relocate to Reston, Virginia and a real-estate mogul by the name of a Mr. Donald Trump would purchase the building to make way for the Trump World Tower. Prior to the future construction, many neighbors, including veteran journalist Walter Cronkite, opposed the building due to its height which caused concerns that the new tower would dwarf the United Nations Headquarters across the street.

The day of the blast the USSS, United States Secret Service, moved into the United Nations building to prepare for the security and protection of our President. The blast could not deter the President from making his urgent public speech. Once the United Nations Headquarters was cleared from any radiation fallout, the President said, "I will personally promote SALT II for the safety of the world and to establish détente!"

Desperate times require desperate measures and these times are certainly urgent enough which is the causation of loss of sleep. Especially Wade Andrew Washington, WW as he paces the floor and is fearful. His conscience keeps him awake and fears, "does he have the fortitude of our Founding Fathers."

Like many of the framers of the Constitution, he worried about the capacity of Americans to preserve a republic. But our Founding Fathers understood so well that our Constitution was made for a moral and religious people. It is wholly inadequate to the government of any other. One of the succinct tenets of the amendments is vaguely defined and ripe for abuse. And that is the creation of the presidential office, as Watergate and future atrocities will prove.

WW considers, bomb threats, planned assassinations and the ultimate threat of WW III. He realizes the urgency to assign our best people to protect our president as he reaches for the phone to call H. Stuart Knight.

The director of the USSS, H. Stuart Knight understood all too well the urgency of the message and assigned his best agent to be in charge at the United Nations Headquarters. Andrew Bryan Schuster has been with the secret service now for some twenty-four years and during that time remembers the assassination of President John F. Kennedy, for he was there. President Kennedy's words still ring-out in his ears as he asked, "And so, my fellow Americans, ask not what your country can do for you – ask what you can do for your country."

Inspired by those words, Andy's motto is, "never on my watch will that happen again!"

There are multiple details that go into planning for protecting the president of the United States. Only the best agents are assigned in the field. All new agents start at a field office. Green recruits don't start on protection detail of the highest office. That definitely comes later, once they have proven themselves in terms of work ethics, firearms, and thinking on their feet. Always be prepared for the unexpected. The Secret Service has to be on its game as if it is the Olympics and go for the Gold, second place is never good enough.

Pre-advance checks were done two weeks before the President's speech. Many details have to be ironed out such as visas and passport checks on all visiting dignitaries. Do any of their entourage have weapons permits? These pre-advance checks have to be made whether the president makes the trip or not. Logistics is mindboggling. In order for it to work perfectly, the preparation, coordination and execution has to be flawless to protect the highest office of our country.

The Secret Service can never forget, that there are adversaries that always want to exterminate our top leaders. At the end of each day, in this hectic business, if the president is alive, we have won! It's a good day, plain and simple!

Most people don't realize the staggering details to keep our president safe. There is a safety checklist beginning with clearing airspace during the president's arrival at the airport. Motorcade route checks are critical along with an alternative route to handle all contingencies. Identification of nearby trauma hospitals are put on alert bearing an attack on the president.

There are also behind the scene preparations such as working with local authorities to identify any characters within the area of "Class 3" threats. All threats, verbal, mail or actual attempts to harm the president are kept on file. These are one of the most serious categories of threats because they've threatened the president in the past and have the capability to do so again.

Agents utilize bomb-sniffing dogs to check out suspicious areas outside any building that the president will employ. And canopies need to be set up where the president will exit his limousine, so he isn't exposed.

Even before the president's jet arrives, a backup plane similar to Air Force One will touch down at a secret location in case something happens to the primary mode of transportation. Every time our president moves, thousands of people are involved.

The harrowing checklist causes Andy Schuster to perspire and his ulcers to boil. He has agents perform a complete sweep of any room, restaurant or restroom that the president may use for bugging devices and concealed explosives. Andy thinks to himself, "Thank God the president isn't staying overnight at any hotel!"

That would require another complete checklist. In addition to the floor that contains the president's suite, agents will also cordon off the floors above and below his room. No one, except those in the president's detail, will occupy those rooms.

According to H. Stuart Knight agents will establish three security perimeters around the president; police form the outer perimeter, general Secret Service agents make up the middle perimeter, and the Presidential Protective Division agents provide the innermost shield.

Now as Andy prepares to secure the United Nations building for President Nixon's speech, his eyes scan the General Assembly hall to find the most effective areas to position six sharpshooters. Having been a sharpshooter himself, his keen knowledge of where to position sharpshooters was invaluable and as he learned from the Dallas assassination, simply being there isn't enough. Vigilance means anticipation of the unexpected and at all cost, sacrificing one's life if necessary to stop the perpetrators.

Standing by the podium where the president will give his speech tomorrow, Andy's eyes scan out towards the General Assembly area where 193 nations will be represented and views the seating arrangement, trying to envision the direction of the hit. Before him is the blueprint of the seating arrangement of all delegates as he scans the horizon of seats. Looking at the direction of the Russian seating, he then scans out beyond the seating for any alcoves that would give the perpetrators any advantage.

The numerous agencies have their distinctive purpose to provide layers of protection to act as barriers to uphold, protect and defend our way of life. The secret service was briefed on the conspiracy of the sinister plot from its conception in Russia to the assassination squads from the Philippines. The Russian bureaucracy always act ostensibly as our friends, but as history reveals will always be our adversary.

In the 1930's, Soviet spy rings headed by a Jacob Golos established a company called World Tourists, a firm which posed as a travel agency used by Soviet agents to infiltrate the United States. From spy rings, to the Cuban missile crisis to the present assassination plot, the chess game of espionage never stops between Russia and the United States. Their obsequious intentions have one purpose and one purpose only; to undermine and destroy our way of life. Now Andy's eyes keep scanning the auditorium to anticipate the assassins next move.

This is the difficult part of the job, to anticipate how the adversary will circumvent the many barriers, the system of screening points to commit the atrocity. Not all people share our fundamental beliefs, our core values of a reverence for God, a respect for life, honor to do right and courage to stand firm.

Dishonesty, corruptibility and greed are the horns of the devil, his snares of hook, line and sinker. Already the snares are in place and Andy contemplates the vulnerable points of access to the United Nations. And as always you begin with people, who work at the United Nations and who will need access. A massive cross check of backgrounds, identifications and references need to be conducted to weed out the terrorist infiltrators.

An old acronym of the five P's is applicable to every walk of life, which is "proper-planning-prevents-poor-performance." Andy reflects to himself and is aware of the caution of, "never underestimate your adversary, for that person may be a better chess player then yourself!"

Unaware that Charlie Murphy has worked at the United Nations building for some twenty-six years as a custodial slash maintenance worker. Who would ever suspect that Charlie has a debt problem from a gambling habit and needed money urgently before the bank would foreclose on his home.

An enigma can be construed as a mystery, conundrum or a puzzle to understand, depending on how we use the term. In religion, it is often referred to as the enigma of life, how our savior and redeemer was born, in justice, it is a conundrum how a perfect crime is committed and in this case a puzzle how the terrorist knew about Charlie Murphy.

Never, but never underestimate the enemy. Being clever is one thing but being devious like the devil is another. The terrorist did their homework and a proposition was made to Charlie Murphy. That one hundred and fifty thousand dollars would be deposited into his bank account for a favor or his wife and children would be killed. The choice was his. Now, for most people a flag would be raised, an alert to warn the proper authorities, but Charlie needed the money. This amount would be more then enough to clear his debt and then some, and so decided to perform the deed.

Two packages needed to be smuggled into the United Nations building and placed under the seats of two delegates. One from the Russian delegation and one from the Philippine's delegation. Charlie was too desperate and lacked the acumen to go to the proper authorities. Accepting the devious deed, he sealed his fate and smuggled two small packages into the general assembly area avoiding the scanning detectors.

All United Nation personnel are subject to search and screening, but Charlie has been a fixture there for decades and could circumvent the security with his toolbox as he made his way to the assembly hall.

Charlie normally went about his business doing his rounds. Once he secured both packages under their respective seats, his nerves started to get the best of him. The guilt surged inside Charlie which caused him to see his boss and request for the rest of the afternoon off. The suspicious request raised a red flag and eventually tipped off the authorities as FBI agents went to the home of Charlie Murphy.

All dignitaries that filed into the United Nations building, went through the screening process before proceeding to their assigned seats. The assembly was called to order. A short prayer service was given, and a roll call performed as the Presidential Motorcade arrived with the lead car in front as a guide and buffer for any contingencies.

The Presidential limousine, code name, "Stagecoach," is at the very center of the motorcade package with the entourage of security and protection. There was to be a surprise package today for the assembly of nations for the President along with the vice president and speaker of the house would enter the assembly hall together to show that our solidarity is what gives the United States the credibility and power to overcome any challenges. This preplanned fanfare was arranged to send a signal to Russia that all is well and so far, no assassination attempts have succeeded.

The protocol of introductions is made as President Nixon walks unto the floor and to the podium to present his speech on SALT II. He waves to the general assembly, smiles and before he could begin his speech, two dastardly delegates stood up and aimed their weapons.

Prepared for such contingencies, secret service agents surround the president, using their bodies as shields to protect America's highest-ranking leader. Simultaneously, other secret service agents ushered the vice president and the speaker of the house out of the assembly hall as two of the six sharpshooters fired their weapons.

Two shots to the head instantly killed the first culprit. The second assassin was critically wounded in the neck and shoulder rendering him incapacitated while the remainder of the sharpshooters scanned the assembly hall for other assassins. A third shooter, just as Andy feared, fired from the shadows of the upper balcony to the left of the president.

Three shots which killed two of the secret service men who blanketed the president's body as they usher the president out of the assembly hall. Head shots can only be perpetrated by skilled assassins. They are well trained but by who? Delegates jumping up from their seats and scrambling to the closest exits. Secret Service men scurrying to the balcony.

As Andy and his protective group usher the president to his limousine, one thought raced through Andy's mind, "Where were the two secret service men assigned to that balcony to prevent any assault?"

Secret servicemen moved in cautiously and found one agent down with his throat slit and the other agent prepared to return fire with his assault rifle. Three agents fired simultaneously and hit the culprit in the hip, shoulder and neck. He was down but not out; this bastard was to be interrogated. Agents are well trained when to kill in order to save lives and when incumbent to obtain vital information.

Agent Bill Taget was the first secret serviceman to reach the culprit and kicked the assault rifle away from the assassin. Looking down upon the assailant, Bill couldn't believe his eyes, it was agent Bob Ray. What are the steps taken when an insider becomes a turncoat?

A full court blitz to investigate every aspect of his file, his personal identity checked all the way back to his birth certificate and turn this person inside out. A twenty-year veteran in the Secret Service, sharpshooter in the army and a personal friend to many of the agents. An unscheduled trip for Bob Ray to the farm is ordered by the president of the United States, where Wes Armstrong will uncover a bizarre story.

How the hell did that perpetrator circumvent all three perimeters of security. One of the greatest fears of any security force, whether local or national is an internal security breach.

The Secret Service lived up to their reputation and admirably did their job. The President of the United States is safe, and the entire world knows it.

The date of February 23rd comes in with the sunrise and departs with a beautiful sunset, the blackouts and gridlocks have been foiled, there are no assassinations and World War Three is hopefully averted. But this has left too many grey hairs on so many people.

An emergency meeting of the national security council and the Joint Chiefs of Staff is called and the highest security alert is set. In the future of our destiny, the third world war will be fought on four battle fronts versus the three fronts during the previous world wars. Acquiescence of the security code to all levels is engaged on the land, air, sea and cyber space. If WW III is averted then the proper sanctions will be administered against Russia and the Philippines.

The next morning, FBI agents proceed to Charlie Murphy's home, a split-level house on a quiet street that looks like, "the Leave It to Beaver," neighborhood. Who would ever suspect such a dastardly act from an American citizen? Two unmarked cars pull-up to the front of the house, one parks in the driveway. Two agents from the first vehicle walk up to the front door as the two other agents proceed to the back of the house.

Ringing the door bell, the wife answers the front door and the two FBI agents show identifications and request to see Mr. Charlie Murphy.

The wife calls to her husband but there is no reply as the wife explains to the agents, "We finished breakfast and I'm afraid Charlie wasn't feeling well and went to the bathroom."

Both men withdrew their weapons and asked the alarmed wife, "Which way to the bathroom ma'am?"

Charlie's wife now completely perplexed, points down the hallway.

Ben Ferguson and Frank Devers cautiously walk down the hallway and stand to each side of the closed bathroom door. Ben knocks on the door and speaks clearly, "Charlie Murphy, two FBI agents here, and we are coming in!"

Opening the door, one sees a cord tied around his neck and poor old Charlie is slumped over in the bathtub. The other end of the cord is fastened around the shower head and Charlie appears dead. Frank leans over to feel Charlie's neck for a pulse and just shakes his head towards his partner. The added funds to his bank account won't help Charlie now.

The Russian delegate who was the second assassin, was removed in shackles by helicopter to the federal maximum-security prison in Marion, Illinois. This prison was built to house the convicts transferred from Alcatraz after it closed.

Marion prison is designated the only Level Six institution in the United States. Many prisoners are locked in their cells 24 hours a day. The cells consist of concrete beds, concrete floors and walls with heavy metal doors. Marion has few programs or services for rehabilitation and for many of the prisoners, this is the end of the road in their life.

Long before waterboarding, there was waterlogging where the prisoner is led into an interrogation room and shackled to a chair positioned in a six-foot-diameter tank. Seated in the chair, water is slowly pumped into the tank to the level of the perpetrator's chin. Questions are asked and if the answers are not what the interrogator wants to hear, then more water is pumped into the tank. As the water rises, the prisoners mind races, his senses heighten, his blood surges through his veins as his heart pounds harder and his eyeballs watch the water level rise above his mouth. Then as the water level rises above his nose and before he comprehends that within four minutes, he will drown; his knuckles turn white from gripping the arms of the chair.

He signals with his fluttering fingers to the interrogator that he is indeed ready to talk. The water level is slowly lowered allowing the perpetrator to swallow more water and gasp for air. Choking and wrenching to spew out the remaining water from his lungs, the Russian delegate gasps and shouts out the name of, "Nikolai Podgorny and I have diplomatic immunity."

On the other side of the two-way mirror observing the interrogation were Wade Andrew Washington of the DOJ, Dick

Helms of the CIA, Corey Bennett of the FBI and Sam Phillips of the United States Marshall Service. Expressions on their faces became dire at the name of Nikolai Podgorny who is head of state of the Soviet Union. Leonid Brezhnev is number one of the Soviet Union and Nikolai was their number two-man of importance. This hit was sanctioned from the very top and a vital response is necessary! But, what should such a response be? That will be decided by the President of the United States and his Joint Chiefs of Staff.

Wade Washington flies back to Washington DC to break this vital news to the president. The following day an emergency meeting was called between the president and select cabinet members. Oh, to be a fly on the wall and hear the scuttlebutt within that meeting would burn your ears.

The Russian delegate became a permanent fixture of the Federal Bureau of Prisons in Marion. There is no diplomatic immunity for an assassination attempt.

Perplexed and waiting for confirmation from the farm, WW sits quietly nursing a scotch on the rocks. He wonders if all this conspiracy will ever end? Finally, the phone rings. Wes Armstrong is on the line explaining to WW that Bob Ray is a sleeper agent recruited by the Soviets while studying abroad in Germany. During his college days as an exchange student, Bob Ray studied at the Ruprecht-Karls University in Heidelberg which is ranked 39th in the world for law.

WW sips his scotch before asking, "I personally know this guy and am one of the interviewers to hire him. How could I have been so wrong in his assessment?"

"Director," Wes started to say, "Hell, every day we go out on missions and I ask myself that same question. All any of us ever know about anyone else is what a person reveals about themselves. And if they're an incorrigible liar, we are left to our gut instinct to uncover the worst. And until that happens, we are at their mercy and may God help us!"

WW takes two more gulps of his scotch as he asks Wes, "How did you retrieve so much information in so little a time?"

Wes laughs and replies, "Hell WW, it's not me but those damn alligators! Chomping jaws is the best persuasion."

Now, Wes in his no-nonsense sober personality ask WW, "With all this damn information about assassins, bombs, and WW III, are we winning?"

"Hell Yes!" was WW's only reply.

Both men hang up the phone and go back to their contemplating about life. With the constant threat of WW III on the horizon, what is the epitome to life?

Sleeper agents who have been discovered, like Bob Ray, have often been natives of the target country. They moved to foreign countries early in life and were co-opted either for ideological or some pie-in-the-sky scheme before returning to the target county. Hence, the sleeper becomes an invaluable asset to the sponsor and is less likely to trigger any suspicion.

One of the greatest fears of any country are sleeper agents, whether they are native or implants, who are part of a clandestine cell structure. In a cell structure each small group of people in the cell know the identities of only the people in the cell. This gives support and dependency on each other to bolster their resolve. But if a cell member is apprehended and interrogated, they do not know the identities of the higher-ranking officials outside of the cell.

This is a major conundrum for any of our protective agencies including local police departments. Infiltration of a sleeper agent or clandestine cells is a diabolical way to consummate the destruction of one's enemy.

This is one concept that keeps our top leaders awake at night. Do any of us really know our neighbor?

CHAPTER 13

COUNTERPUNCH AND WALLOP

The term "blitzkrieg" was coined by an English magazine in 1939 in an article about the German army's tactics during their invasion of Poland. A German term for "lightning war," blitzkrieg is a military tactic designed to create disorganization among enemy forces used during World War II.

The Americanization of blitzkrieg is "counterpunch and wallop" and is the code name for our next set of covert operations. Four strategic plans were developed to occur simultaneously on April 5, 1974, the same day that the World Trade Center, WTC, the tallest building in the world at 110 stories, opened in NYC.

Somewhere in the Atlantic Ocean 200 nautical miles from the Gulf of Guinea, a United States aircraft carrier is steaming at about 30 knots, heading into the wind and is prepared to launch four F-14 Tomcat supersonic jets. A giant steam catapult under the deck launches the planes up to 170 mph to provide the inertia for liftoff. Destination, Lagos Logistics plants where the bombs are manufactured. ETA is 0100 hours.

There might be a few stars in the sky, maybe a partial moon above a thick layer of clouds but below that layer, nothing but blackness of ocean. There is an old Naval aviators term used, "Alone and unafraid."

There is a haunting loneliness that only few people have experienced. For most land lovers the saying is, "Where the rubber meets the road." But for flyers this is where the soul of a naval aviator is forged."

Aircraft, whether taking off or returning, are under the watchful radar scopes of air traffic controllers located in what is known as CATCC, carrier air traffic control center. Between the watchful eye and radio chatter it is nothing but space and speed as the four Tomcats fly to their destination.

Aircrew: "Marshall, 101 RS"

Which means to the controller radio silence.

Aviator slang, the lingo anyone is apt to hear in the Ready-Room, on the flightline and aircraft is another language of its own. The air boss, head of the air department on board a carrier rules the flight deck and understands this jargon from morning till night and beyond. The planned landing time aboard a carrier is known as "Charlie" and the air boss will make damn sure the deck is cleared for our four Tomcats. Equipment, hoses and any tools must be off the deck before any return flights to avoid crashes or one may hear "Charlie Foxtrot" phonetics for "cluster-f%*k." And then one may hear over the radio, "Delta Sierra" another phonetic yummy for "dumb shit."

Over the radio in the air traffic control center one hears the talk between the Tomcats.

Aircrew: "ECM," which means electronic countermeasures for jamming enemy weapons, communications and radar.

Aircrew: "Goes Away," which means target is hit with missiles.

The blast could be heard throughout Lagos, Nigeria.

Aircrew: "Tomcat 102 – Tally, three o'clock," which means enemy in sight at three o'clock.

One of the other Tomcats fires a sidewinder missile and hits enemy target and one hears over the radio, "Tomcat 101 – Gomer down."

Aircrew: "Four Eagles, RTB."

A sigh of relief from the air controllers as all four Tomcats return safely.

There are four arresting wires on Nimitz class ships. An arresting hook from the respective aircraft catches one of the four wires which brings the jet to a complete stop within one and a half seconds. Naval Aviators call it a "controlled crash."

When any of the aircraft hits the landing area of the deck, the pilot set the throttles to full power without afterburner. Should the aircraft miss the wires, there is enough power to get airborne again. Failing to catch a wire and subsequently getting airborne is known as a bolter. If one doesn't make it airborne again then there is a whole line of phonetics which isn't worth repeating!

Approximately at about the same time, a C-130 takes off from Clark Air Base on Luzon Island forty miles northwest of metro Manila with four BLU-82B/C bombs nicknamed "Daisy Cutter" used extensively in Vietnam. Destination, the Lapuz-Lapuz cave on the Island of Panay. The 15,000-pound babies had a personalized message written on each bomb which read, "Enjoy the blast – Remember Tala." The Sputnik training camp was devastated, unconfirmed many were killed including the King Cobra snakes.

The next two covert operations required masterful planning, lethal skills and steadfast balls to accomplish the mission. And again, Major General Wes Armstrong and his Black OPS were called upon to accomplish the task.

The most lecherous crap of humanity are the gangs and drug cartels. And what does one do with crap? You flush it! Law and order cannot be maintained by the jurisprudence of a justice system when these groups of criminals circumvent all laws. Declare war on them and exterminate the varmint before they destroy all of humanity.

And that is just what our Department of Justice sanctioned, three teams utilizing three CH-47 Chinook helicopters along with AH-64 Apache assault helicopters with their devastating payload of hellfire missiles, hydra 70 rocket pods and M230 machine guns for close unit support.

Each team would be led by one of three commandos', Major General Wes Armstrong, Colonel Iron-Jaw Macintosh and Lt.

Colonel Stump Carson who was short and barely made the army guidelines for height requirements. The cut-off for height requirements is 60 inches and Stump Carson is four feet eleven and three-quarter inches but could look any man square in the eyes once he kicked them in the groin. He had no fear as he barehandedly took his opponents and bashed their teeth down their throat. Tough, resilient and full of hell-fire his team followed him anywhere including to hell and back.

Mexico, given its geographic location, has been a major source of heroin and cannabis for years and the Mexican drug traffickers had already established an infrastructure to distribute cocaine from Colombia to the U. S. markets, as it became known as the Turkey of the West. Its name comes from the Aztec god of war, Mexitli, and with 31 states and some fourteen major drug cartels within the country lived up to its name for there were many tumultuous battles between the cartels to be number one.

The SAD, special activities division, in the CIA is comprised of the toughest, meanest hombres on the face of the earth. And for good reason because their main mission is complete "deniable" operations. Tired of the cat-and-mouse games of constant pursuit, near captures and repeated escapes, this mission is a liquidation operation. The CH-47 Chinook helicopters would bring in the teams and the AH-64 Apache helicopters were for backup if anything ran amok! Destroy and annihilate! Timing and execution of all three operations had to be precisely engaged.

Camp Pendleton is the staging area to launch "counterpunch and wallop" on three of the drug cartels that rendered support for the Russian conspiracy. Mexican drug cartels were eager to dominate the wholesale drug trade into the United States from the Colombian Cali and Medellin cartels. Russia was a fortuitous opportunity to expand their drug trade and proliferate their holdings with a new supply of weaponry.

Culiacan, Sinaloa is home to a large hacienda of the Alfredo Morelos Gomez cartel and the first of three counterpunches that will take place. The other two teams are already in place to hit two other strong holds, one in Guadalajara, Jalisco where the dreaded Quintero cartel reigns and the Zambada Garcia cartel in Acapulco, Guerrero. Executions take place approximately at ETA 0130 in the wee hours of the morning as all three strongholds are awaken by the blast from AH-64 Apache helicopters decimating buildings, guards and any structure larger than a dog house. Once the smoke settles, the CH-47 Chinook helicopters land with 26 manned teams to search out, annihilate and make positive identification of the drug lords. Wes Armstrong before the landing is reading the passage from the Bible that reads in Proverbs 24:20, "For the evil man has no future; the lamp of the wicked will be put out. And that is just what is taken place, the lamp of the wicked is being blown out and machine-gun down. Hellfire missiles and Hydra 70 rockets exploding as the teams move in and the wrath of justice is unforgiven.

Wade Andrew Washington of the DOJ and Dick Helms of the CIA impatiently wait for the confirmations that all three drug lords are dead. The first twenty minutes is the sound of fury as explosions are endless and both men can hear the activity from the team's microphones and then the search and annihilation from the cameras attached to their helmets as they watch the wallop on their closed circuit tv screen. Finally, after another thirty-five minutes of agonizing waiting two of the three confirmations come in. Two of the teams are heading back to base but Lt. Colonel Stump Carson's team is pinned down by a barrage of gun fire and bazookas from better than a hundred mercenaries paid for by the Garcia cartel.

Apache helicopters rain-down a deluge of hell-fire and brings to conclusion the standoff as the team searches through the debris for Zambada Garcia's body. One of Stump Carson's Black OPS gave a thumbs-up on identifying Garcia's body. Within minutes the deluge of gunfire is over, and the entire team covertly withdraws to head home.

These unconfirmed assaults will not be read in our newspapers or seen on American television.

The last of the counterpunches would require intricate planning, some finesse and a great deal of tenacity. A clandestine meeting took place between the powers to be in the CIA, MI6 and the Russian resistance at a quiet pub in Iceland.

There is a time when a government needs to implement the steps for either détente or war. Sometimes the diplomacy between governments use the tasteless "Persona non-grata" to expel diplomats of unwelcome persons. Then sometimes neither will do. How does one answer the audacity of an assassination attempt unless it is by another assassination?

An Irish statesman and philosopher, Edmund Burke who served in parliament and had much influence on both the American and French revolutions once said, "the only thing necessary for the triumph of evil is for good men to do nothing."

Whether good or bad, a clear message had to be sent to the Russian politburo. And the man for such a job is Mstislav Alexandra. Our old KGB double agent Karpichkov has been in constant touch with Mstislav since the rescue and death of the CIA kibitzer, Trevor.

An assassination can be in many forms depending on the type of execution. It can be subtle with the use of undetectable poisons or accidental which requires much detail and planning or abrupt and poignant like a gunshot to the head.

It would be up to Mstislav whether it be remote from a sniper's bullet or up close and personal. One's chances of escape are better with the former then up close and personal. But exquisite planning is needed for either one. An assassination attempt is better carried out by one person for that one person alone knows the how, when and where to accomplish the task at hand.

And so, the meticulous task of covertly following and outlining the plan in his brain begins. Nothing will be written down, no clues for the police or KGB to follow and with an array of disguises, camouflage his appearance each day. The place and time will be of his choosing and Mstislav wants the satisfaction of seeing the fear in Nikolai Podgorny's eyes.

As head of state, Nikolai Podgorny who reported directly to Leonid Brezhnev, was responsible for the American conspiracy and for many of the present-day atrocities in the Russian penal colony. Mstislav was prepared to carry out this vendetta himself and to his grave if necessary.

His first endeavor is to learn Nikolai Podgorny's daily itinerary like the back of his hand. This will require several weeks of pains-taking, observant stalking to know the how, when and where the assassination should occur. This incognito quest requires to blend into the surroundings and not prompt any suspicions.

The Embassy of the United States is located just around the corner to the government building where Nikolai Podgorny worked. It was better known as the Dom praviteistva Rossiiskoi Federatsii in Moscow or the Russian White House. It stands majestically on the Krasnopresnenskaya embankment of the Moskva River. Mstislav didn't want to alert any government officials so kept a low profile and visited the U.S. Embassy only once to learn some essential facts.

The U.S. Embassy provided a Glock pistol along with explosive bullets that was a prototype and not on the open market yet, designed by the Glock Ges, m.b.H. company in Austria. Because of its unsurpassed reliability, above-average magazine capacity of 17 rounds in the standard magazine and low weight; it became the perfect weapon for assassination. And upon his exit from the embassy learned that Podgorny lived at the five-star hotel of the Baltschug Kempinski located at the very heart of Moscow, in the beautiful historic district of Zamoskvorechye.

The hotel has 227 elegant rooms, including 36 suites of which one is the residence of Podgorny. From his suite, there is a beautiful panoramic view across the river of the Kremlin, Red Square and St. Basil's Cathedral.

The anatomy of a hit is a science of establishing the cognitive, repetitive behavior of an individual to interject at a precise moment the kill. Upon sitting in the lobby of the elegant hotel early one morning, attired in a wig of a white-haired old man, glasses and a goatee, Mstislav observed that at approximately 5:45 am Nikolai Podgorny exists the elevator in the main lobby with two body guards. He walks over to the news stand to purchase a paper and then the concierge tips his hat to Nikolai as he opens the door for him to exit the hotel.

His chauffer is standing by on the sidewalk and opens the door to his official state limousine and is whisked down the avenues towards work. Following at a safe distance on a motorcycle, driving in Russia is not for the faint-hearted for Russian roads are a mixed bag of sometimes smooth, straight dual carriageways loaded with potholes, narrow, winding and choked with the diesel fumes of slow, heavy vehicles.

Most Russian drivers don't use indicators and like to overtake everything on the road on the inside. It was about nine miles to the government office, but the limousine drove by the government building to the De Marco restaurant where Nikolai enjoyed his morning breakfast each day.

Like a cougar on the hunt from dawn to dusk stalking their prey from behind for the opportune time to strike for the kill, Mstislav watched Nikolai's every move. The rest of the morning, he was at the office with lunch at one of three restaurants.

The afternoons changed dramatically from day to day with meetings most of Monday afternoons, practice at the gun range on Tuesdays, Sandunovsk Baths on Wednesday, one of the oldest banyans in Moscow. It looks like a palace with enormous halls, marble stairs and frescos with an enjoyable lounge for drinks.

Meetings all day on Thursdays at the council of ministers building in the Kremlin followed with his busiest day of the week on Fridays. Meetings in the morning at the ministry of foreign affairs, lunch and then meetings all afternoon at the secret police headquarters.

Friday nights and his weekends were Nikolai's favorite moments for that is when he would enjoy his precious Tatiana, "npoctntytka," Russian for prostitute throughout the weekend before starting another hectic work week. Some weekends there would be Tatiana, Tara and Svetlana for a merry-go-round of frolicking affairs. Sometimes he enjoyed the erotic game of roller-coaster where Nikolai rolled over each of his girl's multiple times with all the giddiness of a schoolboy.

Nine weeks have now passed since the stealthy pursuits have begun, time is of the essence to select a place and time. There are very few times that the body guards aren't at his side or within sight. When he is at his suite with Tatiana, there is at least one body guard outside the door.

Many of his meetings are too public with too many people present. There seems to be no time for harmony in his life for as the adage verse used to say, "harmony in life is simple with work, play, pray, family and worship." Mstislav takes a moment to reflect how both men are in the same boat. There is no family, prayer or worship and too much time for work but very little time for play. A sad truth as Mstislav sees his one opportunity to pull off the hit, possibly without a hitch.

On some Sunday evenings late at night, Nikolai enjoys a solemn, quiet stroll from his hotel along the meandering Moscow River, over the bridge and a few more meters to the solemnity of Red Square. No bodyguards, just himself to his thoughts and the peace of the night along with the twilight of the stars.

John Muir once wrote, "In every walk with nature one receives far more than he seeks." But it wasn't just nature alone that enthralled him but the history of Mother Russia that seemed to come alive which intrigued Nikolai as he eyed the panoramic view of the Kremlin, Moscow's historic fortress and the center of Russian life since the time of the Muscovite prince, Ivan the Great.

Lost to his thoughts and unaware that for every one-step that Nikolai took, Mstislav hastened his pace and is now only ten paces behind him. He withdrew his Glock and calls out to Nikolai, "tonight is your last." Nikolai turns and becomes frozen in his footsteps as his eyes squint in fear before Mstislav fires his Glock twice to the head.

The body falls limp to the ground, motionless with eyes wide open. The heart finally ceases and with no pulse and no more breaths to take, he dies to the world.

Mstislav with the deed done just stares down upon Nikolai's lifeless body. He then walks towards the Moscow River and tosses the gun into the flowing water, as he once again disappears into oblivion.

News of the deed spreads like wild fire throughout the world agencies of espionage. Mossad is the first to learn of the truth.

WW has mixed feelings about the deed, euphoric that the bastard is dead for he promoted so much mayhem. He was a major thorn in WW's side but knew down deep that the misery of espionage roulette is about to begin. Once any major player in espionage is assassinated, the game of "tit for tat" begins. Retaliation to eliminate spies was instantaneous around the world.

The United States in 1917, prior to entering WW I, passed the Espionage Act to deter espionage and better enforce our criminal laws. But trying to enforce these laws on foreign countries is like trying to bring justice to the crime syndicate. It would be easier to pull teeth out of the jaws of a shark with a pair of pliers.

In the underground world escape routes are well known, as if on a tour guide map. They're not that difficult to learn. Avoid all major means of travel by car, bus, train or air. These means of transportation can easily be intercepted for a thorough search. What does that leave?

In most countries that leaves the passageway of rivers. Russia, among its 100,000 rivers contains some of the world's longest especially the Volga that runs throughout central Russia and into the Caspian Sea. The winding pathways of the estuaries in Russia became known as "Mstislav's maze" of escape.

Every nautical craft imaginable from barges, ferries and ships sail upon the Volga. No passports or ID's needed. If one has the money, you pay; if not you work. The only difficulty arises in the dead of winter when parts of the river freezes for three months. Otherwise it's a piece of cake or in Russian "kekc."

Predictably, WW's fears surface, as agents around the world begin to vanish. In the world of counter-espionage there are no secrets, everyone knows everybody. WW turns to none other, then our man in the CIA, Jackson McKenna who has recovered somewhat and is 85% back to health.

Long before Mstislav concocted the assassination plan, he sent word to WW that he wanted asylum in America. The opportune time arises when McKenna submits his paperwork for retirement, but WW intrigues him with one last mission. Rescue Mstislav!

CHAPTER 14

RESCUE MSTISLAV

The CIA wrote the encyclopedia from "A" to "Z" on espionage, if they hadn't, they would have collapsed or been demobilized a long time ago. WW conveys the urgency of Mstislav's dilemma to McKenna. He would not allow his old friend to die by the hands of those vodka drinking fanatics. Jackson Mckenna with a flare of gallantry turns to WW and with a hand shake, a farewell scotch on the rocks and five million dollars in his private Swiss account, disappears to rescue his old friend.

Mstislav after the dastardly deed, walked down the Moskvoretskaya Embankment along the Moscow River for about a hundred yards. He then jumps on a Russian houseboat moored to a piling. Once onboard the boatman untied the rope and meandered down the winding river as sirens could be heard in the distance.

The two boatmen are his old compatriot fighters, Dmitry and Vadim who know the anomalies of the river. The sirens got louder as police vehicles raced by on the streets above and Mstislav watched intently while thinking to himself, "they must have found the body of Nikolai."

Officials found the murdered body too soon and Mstislav wondered if they would escape out of Moscow. Perimeter searches are activated on all roads, buildings and means of transportation. How long before the searches will include the river?

Dmitry handles the tiller while Vadim watches the current from the bow of the houseboat. The boat is extremely slow between maneuvering the many bends in the river and with the old motor sputtering to a stop. Vadim goes below to restart the motor.

Early diesel engines fitted for installation of narrow boats around the turn of the 20th century was manufactured by either Bolinder or Lister engine companies. Unlike a petrol engine where fuel is ignited by a spark plug, diesel engines use very high cylinder compression to start the ignition process. There are no spark plugs which make the trouble shooting process easier.

Vadim checks the engine and notices that a tripped governor caused the engine to shut down. Troubleshooting the engine, he traces out the shaft from the engine to the gearbox and realizes that a broken coupling is the culprit. Fortunate for them that they always carry a few spare parts that included a spare coupling. Within twenty minutes, the coupling was replaced and the engine restarted as the houseboat regained speed.

The houseboat meanders along the eastern edge of the city. Not wanting to be ostentatious to alert authorities, they cruise down the river without any running lights and without any sound for the engine is shut down. Leaving Moscow and the old bastions of the Kremlin, Mstislav began to relax and went below for some shut-eye.

Awakened from his slumber by Dmitry, Mstislav is alerted to trouble ahead. Approaching the city of Kolomna where the Moskva or Moscow River joins the Oka River, there is a blockade with two police patrol boats.

Vadim, who now steers the boat, maneuvers to the shoreline and allows Mstislav to jump ashore. Then steers the craft downstream towards the blockade. A Russian beleaguerment is the way of life in the motherland.

The acrimony causes Mstislav to grit his teeth and seethe inside as he walks away from the river. He looks towards the lights of the skyline from Kolomna, one of the most appealing cities of provincial Russia. Picturesquely situated at the confluence of its rivers with the silhouette of many monasteries reflecting the rich ecclesiastical heritage. Such a dichotomy existed between a life of fidelity to a harsh perverseness of intransigent rulers in Moscow, some 60 miles to the north.

Mstislav hides in the bushes and watches in anticipation of the worst for his comrades as their boat approaches the blockade. Two patrol boats with machine gun nest in each bow and armed guards along their respective sides. Search lights come on and monitor the boat as it comes along side. An officer and six armed guards jump onto the houseboat.

The officer in charge ask, "How many aboard?"

Dmitry responds, "Just the two of us."

The officer demands for both men to come forward as Vadim shuts down the engine and climbs topside.

Then the officer demands to see their papers and ask Dmitry, "what is your destination?"

Dmitry smiles and responds, "No place in particular, we're on a vacation jaunt enjoying the freedom of a cruise along the river. Fate will decide our destination."

Two of the military guards unsling their machine guns and climb below to search for any other personnel. With their paperwork in order, the officer allows the houseboat to pass the blockade as the two patrol boats backwater.

Dmitry handles the tiller while Vadim once again checks the engine and the new coupling. They cruise along and before entering the Oka River, Dmitry pulls in towards the riverbank to allow Vadim to jump ashore and find Mstislav. Then he proceeds onward and hopes for the best.

Mstislav gets weary as he walks along the bank of the river. In the far distance he sees a patrol boat approaching. He stops awhile to rest and sits behind a large cedar tree with his back against the trunk of the tree. A patrol boat passes by slowly with searchlights scouring the banks of the river. While sitting there to catch his breath, he daydreams of fonder times and wonders how did the milieu of our beloved country deteriorate into such hostile times? Extremely tired, he physically falls asleep but his mind is still racing.

"Evolution, revolution or both, what shaped the opinions and attitudes of a people into servitude of such extreme measures?"

History has never been kind to its people from the savage cruelty of Ivan the Terrible, the first Czar of Russia, to Peter the Great and onward through the heinous dictators of the present. From the many gulag prisons, censorship and newspapers that only print propaganda, truth has not survived.

The doctrine of Karl Marx called religion, "the opiate of the people." The founders of the Soviet State therefore, opposed all religious worship. Remove truth, hope and freedom from life and the outlook becomes quite dire. The teeter-totter of life dips through the highs and lows of harassment, interrogation and incarceration.

The dreams are of a time when Mstislav remembers his dad, Bogdan, the name means a gift from God. Russia was largely an agrarian society, a life of farms, fields and hard work in the early fifties. Four out of five Russians were peasants and a typical family size is five to eight children. The fundamental and most stable feature of Russian history is the slow tempo of her development. Mstislav thought that we were clones for everyone wore the same clothes, ate from the same bowl, slept in the same room and wore hair cut's all alike. He fondly remembers playing a game called "Fipe" similar to our game of tag in America. Sometimes his dad would be the leader and close his eyes as he counted to 50. All the children would run away and hide from the leader. As his dad searched and found each of the children, he would allow the younger ones to slip away and tag one of the older children to be the leader.

They were beautiful times of laughter and love but they were also painful times of hard work and loneliness. Ideas shape our society and ideals shape politics but it is the family unit that builds a foundation of love, perseverance, caring and sharing. Nostalgia, that wistful yearning for memories past to keep our sanity from the harsh realities of the present, brought tears to Mstislav's eyes as he awakes from his dreams. For he also remembers the bitter times when his dad was arrested during the riots as a result of shortages of food and provisions, as well as the poor working conditions in the factories.

The unrest began when Nikita Khrushchev raised the prices of meat and butter throughout the Soviet Union. Then under a new harsher economic plan, the minimum production quotas for each worker at the factory were increased. Riots, labor strikes and discontent abounded that led to police arrest and shootings by Soviet Army troops killing many, including Mstislav's dad. History has a somber way to repeat itself for Bogdan's dad, Mstislav's grandfather was also killed during the Bolshevik revolution.

Mstislav steadies himself as he stands to continue on his way. A loud thunderous roar echoes from above as a Mi-24P "Hind" helicopter whizzes by. He hugs the tree to blend in with his surroundings and surmises' that the search has expanded to the waterways. Indeed, the KGB are determined to find the assassin who killed Nikolai Podgorny with every means possible. For the first time Mstislav wonders if he will be able to escape.

He walks stealthily through the woods and stops his clandestine approach to the city of Kolomna, which is some two hundred feet ahead of him. The sound of the dogs in the distance makes him nervous and he wonders if the helicopter had FLIR, forward looking infrared cameras on board.

The sound of the dogs gets louder as he quickly enters the cold, flowing river and swims away from the bank. Some thirty feet out, he turns and sees flashlights flickering in the woods and the sound of the dog's barking getting louder.

The water is too cold for Mstislav as he lowers his face into the water and does the breast stroke. He closes his eyes and concentrates on every painful stroke, for every five strokes, he raises his head out of the water to take a breath. What seems forever, finally gets him to the opposite side of the river.

He climbs out from the frigid water and up the bank rubbing his arms and legs to keep his blood circulating. The agonizing pain and loss of some feelings in his extremities from the numbness of the cold causes him to tire quickly. Thinking to himself, "keep moving," he walks along the bank. His memory failing him as he tries to remember the location of the safe house in Kolomna.

He uses every effort to concentrate on the name of the street, "Ulitsa Isayeva." He remembers that just beyond where the Reka River enters the Moskva River and before the Moskva empties into the Oka River, there is a safe house. IF only he can keep walking, there is a safe refuge not too far from here.

Mama and Papa Lebedev run the safe house and were compatriots from the old war. Now due to their infirmities and age, they run the safe house and keep pigeons to cook and send their covert messages. Infact, it is a pleasant delicacy eating pigeons for many Russian peasants, like Americans eating pumpkin pie, a delicacy of shear delight.

Mstislav's bones ache from the chill and he doesn't know how much further he can walk. Step by step he continues to move but tires from shear exhaustion and feels that he may not make it to the safe house.

Vadim finally catches up to his comrade before he collapses to the ground and says to him, "let me help you," as he wraps his burley arms around Mstislav for support. Together they proceed to the safe house.

The aroma of food permeated the night air along with the scent of cedar wood burning in the wood stove. Mstislav is energized from the nostalgic smells of his boyhood days and walks faster towards the safe house. Vadim helps Mstislav along and opens the door for him as both men are greeted with warm smiles.

Mama and Papa Lebedev a derivative from the Russian word, Lebed meaning swan, for many family names are of indigenous birds, help the two men to their table. Warm bread, stew and a hearty drink brings color back to both men's cheeks.

Mstislav as he eats, watches the elderly couple who are now in their eighty's. Both still spry for their age, papa moves gingerly with a cane and mama still cuts firewood with an ax. During the revolution in their younger years, they were the dynamic duo as compatriot fighters. Now Mama prepares a hot bath for Mstislav and gathers some dry clothes for him. Papa goes out with their pet dog, Freedom, for a walk and heads down towards the river bank. He walks along until he finds the moored houseboat to give Dmitry a message.

Freedom, just the name in itself says it all, enjoys his walk but also is the protector of the couple as he growls at something in the bushes.

Papa says to the dog, "Tishe, vse v poryadke." Which means hush, it's ok.

Spies are bountiful in Mother Russia and a typical way of life within the State Duma. The peasants feel that if they turn in their neighbor, there is a better chance of acceptance into the political party. It is a sad reality that the state officials could care less; for peasants are peasants and are no better then a door mat. But as history teaches us whether it is the peasants, pioneers or immigrants; they were the builders of yesterday.

As Papa returns to his pigeon shack and attaches a coded message to one of the pigeons, he hears a noise from behind the shack. He always kept a sawed-off shotgun under his work bench. While reaching for the shotgun, the door to the shack comes flying open and two state officials rush in to apprehend Papa. But Papa was prepared and fired off two rounds from his double barrel, killing both officials.

Mstislav and Vadim come rushing out from the house at the sound of the shotgun to see what is happening. Papa eyes the two men and just smiles as Mama comes out of the house behind them with another shotgun prepared to fight to the end. Old compatriots are always ready and will do whatever it takes as long as they are able. Mstislav just smiles and says to Vadim, "Can't teach an old dog new tricks, because they know them all already!"

It may seem an archaic way to send messages but it works for the underground fighters as Papa releases the pigeon and sends a message. Who knows how many relays the message will make or its destination except Papa. Word is relayed of a final destination for Mstislav and a pickup point for a rendezvous.

Once both men are refreshed, Mama packs a picnic lunch for them and Dmitry as well. Mama even packs more food for their excursion for she knows the way to a man's heart is through his stomach. The houseboat is moored by a jetty just pass highway M5 and it will be a difficult jaunt for both Vadim and Mstislav. Before they leave, both of the state officials are buried by the river bank.

Blockades are not prevalent on the Oka River but searches continue with helicopters scouring the riverbanks. The hunt for Mstislav has definitely expanded. The Oka has more bends then the Mississippi River and Mark Twain would have enjoyed both the Oka and the longest river in Europe, the Volga River.

Jackson McKenna is at the naval base in Rota, Spain aboard the USS Alexander Hamilton SSBN-617, one of the submarines used for CIA covert operations. He is collaborating with the chain of command preplanning the extraction of Mstislav which has been sanctioned by the State Department.

All submarines in the United States Navy are nuclear-powered of three major types; attack subs, ballistic missile subs and cruise missile subs. There is a catch-22 for nuclear deterrence and that is assured nuclear destruction. As more countries enter the arms race, this pushes humanity towards annihilation. The essence of the times has pushed us beyond the "if," and the only question that remains is when?

The USS Alexander Hamilton has performed many deterrent patrols admirably and is preparing for a covert defection. In the chess game of the cold war major defections is a check on either side. Weighing the balance of forces with more, better, and longer-range ballistic and cruise missiles lulls us into a false security blanket of "perceptive warping" of our human subjectivity and spirituality. If the big push ever comes, may God help us and have mercy on our souls!

For now, with all of our satellite surveillance, it is the pigeons informing us of Mstislav's moves. Satellite coordinates are programed to observe critical areas of deployment or to ascertain a person's location. Coordinates and a time reference for Novgorod at the confluence of the Oka and Volga Rivers were activated along with the districts of:

- Kazan
- Ulyanovsk
- Podstopki
- Novokuybyshevsk
- Volgograd

A reference time line of positioning has to be fine-tuned to determine the availability of an extraction.

The odds of success are slim to none for Mstislav. There are two many checkpoints along the 2294 miles of the Volga River along with two known blockades within the crescent shape of the river between Podstopki and Novokuybyshevsk.

It's a nine-hour transit along the Oka River to Novgorod, home to many shipyards for repair and commercial hauling. The underground fighters have arranged for Mstislav to work passage on the "Padeniye Zvezda," Falling Star, if he can make the rendezvous in time. The difficulty in any peregrination throughout Mother Russia are the Oblast or administrative regions in many cities. Each Oblast had their own military police to search, seize and incarcerate anyone that looked crossed-eyed.

The satellite pictures show Mstislav's arrival into Novgorod. This satellite detection triggers when the USS Alexander Hamilton should transit out to sea. Destination is somewhere in the Mediterranean Sea. Lines are cast off and hatches are buttoned-up as she glides out of the harbor. Once underway, then ballast tanks are filled with water as the USS AH sinks to a depth for "Silent Service." The world of the U.S. Navy submarine operations may be shadowy, but this steel bus has colorful terminology to express everything in two term phraseology. Down bubble, trim tanks, zero bubble are terms one hears and you many wonder who is chewing the bubble gum.

McKenna is in the control room and is holding on for dear life. This land-lover likes level ground under his feet, as the sub slips silently and swiftly beneath the sea. As the sub trimmed her tanks, Mckenna trudges to the conning tower to deduce the GPS coordinates for the rendezvous.

The houseboat safely transits the winding river to Novgorod evading a couple of helicopter searches by hiding under bridge overpasses. Mstislav, aboard the Falling Star, a commercial freighter will become a deck hand and hopefully arrive at his final destination.

McKenna radios a message to his contact in Istanbul to contact their bush pilot in the region. The message says,

> "Package pickup, stop."
> "Delivery date to come, stop."

There was a cantankerous old fart from the Vietnam era who flew too many missions for the CIA. They named it and he flew it, from helicopters, Cessna's, to C-130's; the best damn pilot in Asia. His code name, "Micky Mouse," coined for getting out of any tight hole that arose! His only problem being a dry drunk, dysfunctional from abuses of booze, drugs and women! He gave up the drugs and the drinks but not the women! No one could stand him for any longer than two hours. Needless to say, he lived alone and couldn't hold down any job except excursion flights for the CIA. McKenna and Micky Mouse got along fine together as long as McKenna could drink his Jack. Whenever there was a tight dilemma, McKenna turned to Micky for help.

Meanwhile the freighter, Falling Star, left port and is heading in a southerly route down the Volga River. Mstislav is assigned to the engine room as the ship heads towards Volgograd to load tons of barley grain. At the appropriate times he will stand on the flying bridge of the ship for satellite detection as the ship passes the ports of Kazan and Ulyanovsk. The satellite images will be retrieved on board the USS Alexander Hamilton somewhere in the Mediterranean Sea.

There is a time delay and blanking interval for receiving the signals from the satellite. As the signals are received aboard the USS Alexander Hamilton, McKenna studies the pictures and time reference. Cruising at a depth of 300 meters, the hull is withstanding thirty atmospheres of water pressure. McKenna's nerves were rattled. He had withstood many battles in both WW II and Vietnam and been shot-at on many occasions for the CIA but confine him in a tin can under the sea and it was "Bonkers-Ville" for him.

It was safe passage for Mstislav until the Falling Star approached the canal locks at Tolyatti. Before any ship entered the double sets of locks to transcend the river around the Samara Bend, a military shakedown occurred. The captain being prepared for such contingencies signaled Mstislav to climb aboard one of the tugboats that nudged each ship into the locks. He climbed down the Jacob's ladder from the port side of the ship as soldiers climbed aboard on the starboard side. The search for the murderer of Nikolai Podgorny is still prevalent and extends beyond Moscow.

The shakedown lasted for four hours before the Falling Star could proceed through the locks. Military shakedowns have to account for the entire crew and check all compartments from the bow to the fantail twice, as well as the paperwork. All the "I's" were dotted and the "T's" were crossed, as the soldiers thoroughly searched the ship.

Once on board the tugboat, Mstislav hid in the wheelhouse. Passage around the Samara Bend there is a beautiful transition zone between the broadleaf forests of the north and the grasslands to the south. Two reservoirs form the north and southern borders of this park. The river pilot of the tugboat revs the engines to full speed and maneuvers along a strip of land known as the isthmus of Perevoloki. Mstislav must cross through the narrow part of the isthmus to rejoin the Falling Star on the Volga River.

He is dubious of what lies ahead and wonders if there are any soldiers guarding the isthmus. Time is pressing and he understands the consequences of not rendezvousing with the ship. The tugboat maneuvers close enough to the edge of land for Mstislav to jump ashore. Now, survival instincts awaken inside him from his jungle warfare training. He easily walks through the forest from tree to tree but suddenly stops from the silence of the birds. With his back against a large coniferous tree, he inches his way around the large trunk.

Peering through the overgrowth of vegetation, no guards are apparent but why have the birds stopped singing. He thinks to himself, "am I the culprit to cause the birds to be silent or someone else?"

He looks up and notices about forty feet off the ground, a tree stand with guards aloft. Carefully he retraces his footsteps back to the other side of the isthmus and walks further down to find a safe haven to meet the ship.

The Falling Star has made passage through the first set of locks and is approaching the second set. Then, an hour transit around the crescent of the Samara Bend. Hopefully, there will be enough time for Mstislav to make his trek to meet the Falling Star.

There are more canals at Balakovo, Russia usually with minimal security and if he makes it, then safe passage along the Volga to the last set of canal locks at Volgograd where security is exorbitant. Every ship that transits through Volgograd must have their crew disembark the ship for a complete shakedown. Soldiers board each ship for a thorough search and if one person is found onboard, then they are shot. No questions asked!

Mstislav has no time to enjoy the beauty of the land as he proceeds steadily to make his rendezvous. Engagement with the enemy is not an option. This would endanger the crew of the Falling Star. He hurriedly picks up his pace to find an escape route to the ship. Moving a thousand meters southerly through the forest, he crosses eastward towards the river and none too soon. His eyes scan the forest and then the riverbanks before stepping out of the forest. The Falling Star is maneuvering around the bend as Mstislav cautiously walks to the edge of the riverbank.

A bow lookout with binoculars surveys the river banks and once he sees Mstislav, the lookout signals to the bridge by walkie-talkie, "Man on starboard side riverbank."

A lifeboat is lowered and Mstislav is retrieved back aboard the Falling Star. It will be another day's journey to reach the canals of Balakoro and then on to Saratov. The captain contemplates what precautions are necessary to conceal Mstislav for when they arrive at the next set of canals.

Latitude 36.878 and Longitude 27.500 are reference point locations for the USS Alexander Hamilton as she sits on the bottom of the Mediterranean Sea. At the appropriate time the submarine surfaces to periscope depth and surveys the area. A fishing trawler is cruising towards their position. Name of trawler is the "Mavi Kaz," Blue Goose.

The captain gives the command, "Blow ballast tanks."

The USS AH surfaces and the captain gives a thumbs-up to Jackson McKenna to climb aloft. He quickly climbs aloft through the sail and up to the bridge. The hatch is popped open and it seems good to breath fresh air again. The Blue Goose, a covert trawler for the CIA, pulls alongside. A happy McKenna climbs aboard the trawler. When the appropriate time arrives, new coordinates will be given to McKenna for retrieval of the package. A submarine never sits in the same position for too long.

The waves are a bit choppy but the forty-five-minute trek to Bodrum was peaceful especially since Jackson could now drink his Jack Daniels. Infact, on the flight to Istanbul he finished his Jack and needed to buy two more bottles.

It was a bizarre meeting between Micky Mouse and Jackson McKenna. Two war time cronies' both CIA undercover agents, one drinks, the other one doesn't, one is taciturn and the other is loquacious. They say opposites attract and that is just what happened because there is a bond between brothers of war!

Micky brought Jackson back to his bachelor pad which was above the "Dans Bacaklar Salonu," the Dancing Legs Lounge, which turned out to be splendid for both men. Micky had his women and Jackson his drinks! The two men didn't mind each other for it had been too long living alone for Micky Mouse. Jackson, who is an inveterate, skeptical person never trusted anyone but always seemed to trust and enjoy Micky's company. But not for long, if they were to deliver the package safely. The following day both men fly in Micky's Piper PA-23 Seminole to Hopa and wait for further instructions on the package.

The Falling Star approaches the canals of Balakoro and safely transit through without any delays. There is no shakedown this time and the captain knows that the Volgograd canals will be harsh and unpleasant. As the ship approaches the city of Saratov, Mstislav once again climbs to the flying bridge so satellite imagery can detect him. The ship will pull into the port of Saratov and offload some agricultural equipment which will take six hours before resuming down the Volga River.

The message is relayed to Jackson, "Package ready for pickup."

It will take six hours for the Falling Star to offload cargo and another six hours to cruise to the canals of Volgograd. Within twelve hours Micky can make the flight to Volgodonsk airport to refuel and then on to a remote field near the Volgograd Dam and canals.

The plan may seem too elementary but an assassin cannot be ushered through the regular diplomatic channels of an embassy. Hence, a simple covert operation with deniability and no Black-Op's involvement is a good plan. The Piper PA-23 is registered to a manufacturing plant in Istanbul for surveillance flights. The rescue of Mstislav is highly improbable. If, and it is a big if, Micky and Jackson can retrieve Mstislav and get him to the drop zone; it will be a miracle.

The airplane takes off from a remote airport in Hopa, flying in a northeasterly direction towards Volgodonsk, Russia while the Falling Star is off loading their cargo in Saratov.

The haggard expression on the captain's face reveals a life of torment from constant searches, seizures and incarcerations. Depending on the situation and gravity of the predicament, this can lead to internment and torture or worst yet one of the many gulags for life. The captain has experienced two internments, one for two months and one, for a very long year. A life of formidable enforcement to gain control of the people never builds any trust. This constant aggravation wears a person down as Mstislav has learned so well throughout the years. One either fights, submits or dies! Two people and two very different choices as Mstislav fights the bureaucracy and the captain is reconciled to accept it.

The Falling Star finishes offloading their cargo as Micky lands the Piper at Volgodonsk. The constant security searches of passengers in any of the transportation terminals whether by bus, train or air causes one to become torpid to life's caustic dilemmas. But there are no lines, identification checks or any of the security barriers to refuel a plane. Within twenty minutes, the piper takes off and heads on a perilous mission to retrieve Mstislav. It is a quiet, somber flight as both Micky and Jackson contemplate the future of the unknown.

The field where Micky will land the plane is a couple of klicks due west from the Volgograd Canal. There is a dam across the Volga River and he circles a wide arc around the dam to get his bearings. Micky will land on a narrow road leading to a farm storage facility and hopes that no vehicles will be on the road.

One of the compatriot fighters that works at the collective farm ensured Micky that it will be a safe refuge for their covert rescue the last time they spoke. But that was yesterday and everyone knowns that there is no relevancy in Mother Russia from day to day.

The landing was safe and sound. Micky and Jackson climb out of the Piper and look around. As Micky checks over the tires of the plane, one of the compatriot fighters approaches the men and talks to the both of them of their plans.

This is where the rescue plan becomes a bit shaky, for the rest of the excursion is completely improvised. Micky retrieves his tools to check the engine as Jackson confers with the compatriot fighter, Ilia, about directions. Then Ilia cautions Jackson to be weary for there are many eyes upon them. He then bids Jackson to come with him for a short jaunt on the tractor due east towards the dam. As they approach the dam site, the compatriot lights up a cigarette and hands it to Jackson as he explains the consequences of the shakedown.

"This is highway R226 that transverses over the dam," Ilia explained to Jackson.

Then he said, "On the other side of the dam is the canal where all ships pass. Your friend will disembark the ship with the entire crew. As soldiers search all compartments of the ship, others will check the crew for their papers. Your friend," Ilia coughs and clears his throat before continuing, "will hide in the fire box that houses hoses and extinguishers. The search will last for two hours and if all goes alright, then the ship and crew will sail through."

Ilia who has trouble catching his breath from asthma gasp for air and then continues by saying, "Once the soldiers are done, they'll head back to the barracks until the next ship appears. Then your friend can leave the confines of the fire box."

Jackson thanks Ilia for his help and ask, "where do we wait?"

Ilia smiles and says, "where else?" and takes him to a local pub down the street.

There is a bird's eye view of the canal from the pub as Jackson enjoys a brew and offers Ilia a swig of his Jack. Jackson intently watches the canal as Ilia takes a swig of Jack and then says to Jackson, "YA predpochitayu vodku!" which means, I prefer vodka.

Finally, the arrival of the Falling Star approaches the canal. Tension mounts as Russian soldiers line both sides of the canal. The crew disembarks and the search begins as the clock is ticking precious seconds for Mstislav. Two tedious hours pass and the search is completed of the Falling Star, the crew once again climbs aboard and the soldiers disperse. The ship proceeds through the canal.

Ilia and Jackson leave the pub and proceed cautiously towards the railway viaduct to retrieve Mstislav but when they get to the canal and open the firebox, "There is no Mstislav in sight!"

Both men look about and see the fantail of the Falling Star vanishing out of sight down the Volga River. Now, the two men scurry haphazardly looking in boxes and any barrel in sight that could hide Mstislav from the authorities. From the distance it must have looked like the silent film follies of "Buster Keaton" as they bounce around and jump from container to container. Empty handed and exasperated the two men return back to the tractor and head towards the farm.

Jackson's insides are twisted like a knot as he wonders where his friend may be. Driving along R226, they cross over the dam and about a quarter of a mile beyond the dam notice a spry Mstislav walking along. The tractor stops long enough for Mstislav to climb aboard as Jackson asked, "You gave us a damn scare!"

Mstislav replied, "You a scare, I opened the box and nobody was around, no ship, crew or soldiers! I nearly shit my shorts!"

At that comment, all three men laughed.

The tractor backfired and Ilia proceeded back to the farm with the package safely on board. Micky had the Piper ready for takeoff as the tractor appeared. With a couple of quick handshakes for Ilia, both men climbed into the Piper.

It was a bumpy takeoff as Micky hit two potholes in the road shaking their inners and some cursing words from Mstislav as he said, "YA chuvstvuyu sebya kak tsyplonka s otrezannoy im zadnitsey." Which means, I feel like a chicken with his ass cut off.

Both men were laughing because both Micky and Jackson understood some Russian as Micky said, "I think he means like a chicken with its head cut off."

Our English language may be difficult to learn but some of our colloquialisms are more difficult to understand.

The return flight was anything but uneventful as Micky experienced troubled with the carburetor on his Piper PA-23. Heading in a southerly course Micky looked over his navigation charts to find a safe place to land his craft. The engine is sputtering and the plane is losing altitude as Jackson asked, "What the hell is the problem?"

Micky shaking his head replied, "Loss pressure and the engine is spitting, sounds like the carburetor is acting up!"

Always more questions than answers Mstislav ask, "Will we make it?"

As the plane makes a nose dive Micky yells, "Hell, I don't know!"

As the plane quickly descends, Micky pulls up on the throttles and decides to glide land on a remote field on the outskirts of the farming community of Pyatigorsk. The name Pyatigorsk means five mountains which is of the Caucasian range overlooking the city. This is one of the oldest spa resorts in Russia with delightful mineral springs and beautiful, frisky peasant girls.

The piper bounced along the ground as Micky tried in vain to steady the plane along the furrows of the field. The emergency landing broke up the daily monotony for the peasants tending the field as they all waved and rushed towards the plane.

Relieved with the safe landing, the three compadres disembarked from the plane and were greeted by many well-wishers. Micky hurriedly checks the piper's engine.

All farm land within Russia was owned by the state. About two thirds of all farmland was worked by collectives. The farms often produced enough food but getting the food from the farm to the consumers was a major problem hence there was much spoilage which infuriated the political leaders.

The interruption of the uninvited guests caused a work stoppage, as all came flocking to the plane; tractors, haulers, workers and all within eyesight of the emergency landing.

Micky climbs down from the piper with an oily carburetor. The carburetor has two swiveling valves above and below a venturi known as a choke and throttle. Apparently, the throttle valve was busted which caused the plane to lose power and take a nose dive. Luckily for them there were plenty of tractors available of the DT-14 and Belarus vintage which had similar carburetor parts. And since the state owned all the equipment, the peasants were all too pleased to furnish any parts needed. Within the hour, the carburetor was repaired and our happy crew were taking off with a cheery send-off from the crowd and plenty of fruit to eat.

Their return trip to Hopa, Turkey to refuel and then proceed on to Istanbul was a welcomed relief. Once in Istanbul, Jackson McKenna contacted the Rota, Spain Naval base and received a new set of instructions. The instructions were clear and concise, "Get to Antalya – 2 Days - contact – "Mutlu Trol," which meant Happy Trawler in Turkish. Apparently, the USS Alexander Hamilton is in a new waiting zone off the coast of Southern Turkey.

What should have been an ostensible rescue turned contrary as KGB agents surrounded Micky's pad and riddled his apartment with machine-gun bullets. Thank our good fortune that all three compadres were in the Dancing Legs Lounge just below the apartment. They definitely weren't counting their drinks but instantaneously sobered up, once they heard the ruckus upstairs.

All covert agents have their own idiosyncrasies and one of Micky's is always keep a get-away jalopy two blocks down the street. No sooner had the sound of machine-gun fire erupted and they retreated out the side door. They raced down three alleys and crossed two streets before the KGB were aware of their movements.

The jalopy started and like a bat out of hell, Micky shifted into gear and raced to the D100 highway. This baby was a 1955 Pontiac with a V8 – 287 engine. Mstislav climbed into the passenger seat and Jackson climbed into the back that had no seats. He had to sit on the floor with his back against the front seats and his legs straddled around a 7.62mm, M60 machine gun. The trunk hood was removed and this baby stuck out four inches. Cartridges were loaded from a disintegrating belt of M13 links with armor-piercing rounds. This baby was ready for war!

Micky using every known curse word in the universe as he said, "Damn, Friggin, F%$k- - g, Asshole, bastards, how did they ever find us so fast?"

Mstislav is bent over in laughter as he says, "never underestimate the KGB!"

Jackson yells, "Where to, Micky?"

Micky yells back, "Always be prepared!"

He looks out his side view mirror to see if anyone is following them before replying to Jackson, "I always have two jalopies, two planes, two guns and two women!"

He again checks his side and rearview mirrors for a tail and then says to both men, "I have another Piper plane at a small airfield between the towns of Silivri and Corlu. We should arrive there within the hour."

With the peddle to the metal the engine is roaring with all eights at maximum revs. At the junction of D567 and D100 there was a blockade of three Lada cars straddled across the lanes.

Mstislav yells, "KGB Bastards!"

Micky yells to Jackson, "LOCK AND LOAD!"

Micky slams on the breaks and spins the steering wheel to the right as the Pontiac spins around. He now throws the car into reverse and backs the V8 as fast as she will go.

Jackson McKenna fires the M60 spraying bullets and the fury of hell. KGB agents are scrambling and ducking. One of the Lada cars blows-up as Jackson continues to fire igniting the gas tank.

Micky slams on the brakes and cuts the steering wheel again doing a 180 and crashes through the other two flaming vehicles. He continues racing his big Pontiac jalopy down D100; it's only a quarter of a mile to the exit for the Dhmi airport where Micky houses another P-23 Piper in the northwest hanger at the end of the runway.

Turkey is the funnel for everything; every type of contraband, human trafficking, money laundering and the biggest circus of espionage for the right price. Israel, Iran, Russia and even the United States are some of the performers in this circus of life. The tides of the cold war brought much disharmony into the world, but it was a better alternative than another world war.

Racing down the privately-owned runway, Micky slams on the brakes by the hanger's doors. Jumping out of the Pontiac, Micky helps a disheveled Mstislav to the hanger. Mstislav says to Micky, "I hope the damn flight isn't as rough!"

Micky laughed as he looked back and yelled to me, "Are you coming old man?"

Feeling every bone in my body after this fiasco, I slowly climbed out of the car and realized that the decision for retirement is the right one!

With all three of us on board, Micky revved up the P-23 engines and proceeded down the dark runway. Halfway down the runway he tapped on the signal from his plane to turn on the runway's lights as we lifted off.

Two fast moving vehicles were approaching the runway as we lifted off the ground. Mstislav turned to Jackson and said with a shake of his head, "Probably more KGB!"

Micky adjusted the altimeter setting and then adjusted the GPS for Antalya and wondered what was in store for them? For now, the KGB didn't know our destination, but it wouldn't be long before a trace on our plane pointed the way.

Antalya is the largest Turkish city on the Mediterranean coast with hot-hot summers, beautiful naked women on the beach which is an area shielded from the northerly winds by the Taurus Mountains.

We landed by sunrise, hailed a cab and sped off to the docks where the Happy Trawler was moored. The HT was our covert boat for the CIA and Jackson McKenna was very familiar with the captain. Captain Horatio D Skinner, the "D" stood for damnation for hell and fury was his game. The three of us climbed aboard as two deck hands prepared the line and tackle for bluefin tuna. The helmsman veered the trawler out to sea. Everything had to appear kosher for a fishing trip and most catches of the Atlantic bluefin tuna are taken from the Mediterranean Sea. This 40' trawler was equipped with the latest surveillance equipment and CCTV system along with sophisticated sonar and radar detection.

Jackson's memory faded a bit as he tried to remember the coordinates for the rendezvous with the submarine. He gave the coordinates to Horatio and hopefully they were the correct ones as the trawler gained speed. About two miles out from the pier, another trawler was approaching us fast from the west.

The captain signaled for one of the deck hands to stand ready with a FIM-92 Stinger which is a shoulder launched weapon used for either ground or air targets. The other deck hand was below listening on the sonar for our submarine. This trawler was well equipped for a four-man crew.

Looking through high-powered binoculars the captain scanned for any markings to identify the boat and noticed machine guns mounted on the gunwales. The captain realizing that the range of any good machine gun is 800 to 1000 meters, he barked the command to his deck hand, "Top side and fire when ready!"

The mate quickly ascended to the top deck, steadied his stinger and fired, hitting the trawler broadside. The seas were calm with moderate three to five-foot waves. Another trawler was bearing down upon us from the east as the captain called out to the second mate to ready another stinger.

Jackson thinking to himself, "where is the AH when you need her?"

No sooner had the thought materialized when we witnessed the second trawler torpedoed to smithereens. Three hundred yards off the port bow the USS Alexander Hamilton without any fanfare surfaced and was a beautiful sight for sore eyes. With a smile on his face, Jackson gave the captain a thumbs-up as the helmsman steered the trawler towards the sub.

There was such a feeling of exaltation for the three of us, as we climbed aboard the submarine. For myself there was an accomplishment to save Mstislav and contemplate retirement. For Mstislav to achieve asylum and a life of true freedom and peace is now possible. Micky was the only one that felt anxious and troublesome! For he was leaving his bungalow, his two women and a what he considered a life of liberation. Starting anew would be arduous for Micky but life would be too precarious to stay.

While Micky and Mstislav were shown to their quarters, I went to the captain's quarters for a briefing. He divulged more than I bargained for. Captain Dinsmore explained that there is a pending mission and a week's delay to get the three of us back to the states. The captain began by saying, “While the Cold War itself never escalated into direct confrontation, there are a number of conflicts around the globe instigated by it.”

I looked at the captain quizzically and replied, “Go on.”

He quickly explained, “This cat and mouse scenario is diplomatically daunting and for our leaders extremely demoralizing to the point that it jeopardizes peace. Just imagine the jockeying that occurred between Russia and the United States during the Cuban Missile Crisis. Thirteen days without sleep that closely pushed us to the brink of nuclear war.”

The captain stopped long enough to take a drink of water before continuing,

“There is another diplomatic game known as “Global Roulette” where there are only six major players. Six countries deploy nuclear subs:

- United States
- United Kingdom
- France
- Russia
- China
- India

And as you know, Russia never starts something directly, there is always a middle country!”

Now the captain gets up from his desk and walks around his cubicle and is within an inch of my face and says, “Top secret, for your ears only McKenna!”

I quickly replied, “Aye, aye sir!”

The captain sternly questioned me, “Are you aware of the Western Sahara conflict between the Kingdom of Morocco and the Polisario Front?”

I replied, “Yes I am!”

The captain’s face got rigid as he said, “Russia is supplying arms to Mohamed Abdelaziz Ezzedine’s Front movement with SAM’s as part of the arsenal agreement. This will directly upset the balance of power in Northern Africa.”

I quickly responded, "What about the United Nations?"

Captain Dinsmore vehemently responded, "The UN, those candy ass bastards don't intervene or do a damn thing!"

He gritted his teeth as he said, "Those bastards recognize Western Sahara's right to sovereignty and don't have the balls to stop this bullshit!"

Now the captain is shaking his head and rubbing his hands over his forehead and continues by saying, "Hence, the reason for our covert involvement."

Now I understood the whole picture and could empathize with the captain as I thanked him and returned to my bunk. Quarters are tight on a submarine and the best that could be done is a bunk for the three of us. Hence, we shared and rotated our sleeping habits over three shifts. When one was in the rack, the other two were in the mess hall.

I went to the galley for a cup of Joe and laughed to myself about how certain words stick around in the navy. Has anyone ever wondered why the slang term for coffee is a cup of Joe? It dates back to WW I when president Woodrow Wilson was in office. It was coined after the secretary of the Navy who under Woodrow was Josephus Daniels. He implemented strict moral standards for naval life such as cracking down on prostitution at naval bases and banning alcohol. A cup of Josephus Daniels was meant as an insult and I surmise better than shooting the bastard. At least the coffee is pretty good and hot 24/7.

I sat there drinking my coffee and reflecting on what the captain had said. And I wished I had my bottle of Jack. I guess covertly the best way to orchestrate this assignment is through the Navy seals. The most lethal delivery any submarine can execute before the use of torpedoes, Tomahawks and D5 missiles are the effective weaponry of Navy Seals.

The captain couldn't rest and prepared for their next covert operation. In two days the USS Alexander Hamilton would be off the coast of this sandbox known as Western Sahara. Navy seals would infiltrate two warehouses that stockpiled SAM's, surface to air missiles and blow them up.

On our arrival day off the coast of northern Western Sahara, the USS AH deployed two teams of six-man units. Destination coordinates 27.16 /-13.21 to blowup two warehouses. Off the port of El Aaiun' the SDV, seal delivery unit, left the USS Alexander Hamilton and approached the coastline. Two reconnaissance seals swam ashore from the SDV to find the best point of penetration. Once both teams surfaced two scouts were dispatched to find the warehouses. That left one 4- manned unit to set the demolition at the warehouse in El Aaiun' and the other team to follow the scouts to Laayoune where the other warehouse is located.

The captain waited anxiously for both teams to return while the sub sat quietly on the bottom of the oceans floor. The silent service lived up to their reputation as ships passed overhead.

The first demolition team set the explosives and set the timer for four hours. The second team should be within Laayoune in one hour, locate the warehouse and set explosives in the four-hour time allotted. The seal teams did their job and did it well for both teams returned to the warm coastal waters. Submerged and out of site, they swam back to the SDV as two gigantic explosions erupted sending reverberating soundwaves throughout the surrounding countries.

Both teams made it safely back to the submarine. The next command was periscope depth to witness a plume of smoke a mile high. Then the command was down bubble as the USS Alexander Hamilton skedaddled to the big abyss of the Atlantic Ocean.

The captain in the control room is looking over navigational charts on the computer screen. Every commander of a submarine knows most of the bottom topography like the back of their hand but continually review their navigation charts so not to screw-up.

The bottom topography of the Atlantic Ocean is characterized by a huge mountain range known as the Mid-Atlantic Ridge. It extends from Iceland in the north to the very tip of South America at the 58 degrees south latitude. The North Atlantic has a weird "seascape" of lofty ridges, seamounts, deep trenches and broad abyssal plains which become the chess board of the deep for all submarines. Always be aware of enemy subs in the area, for the opposing players are the commanders of each vessel. A check means our sub is within their firing range and a checkmate is annihilation.

Depths, currents and thermal layers come into play in this game to outfox the enemy in an ocean with a maximum depth of 27,841 feet.

The following morning the captain called Jackson to his quarters and handed him a notice from the State Department which informed about the relocation of Mstislav. The USS Alexander Hamilton had a destination for contact and transfer of the package.

Now the cat and mouse game begin as contact is made of an enemy sub within range of our sonar. Passive sonar has a greater range than active sonar and allows the target to be identified without giving away our position. The next command came from the captain, "Control, TMA."

Which means for communication to do a target motion analysis. The range of most passive sonars, if the listener is good at filtering out ambient noises, is from 100 to 1000 km. For those land lovers, 1000 km equals about 621.37 miles. This means it is time to move, evade and escape using the bottom topography as our camouflage. Passive sonar is stealthy and very useful. However, it requires high-tech experience and that intuitive instinct for the technician to become one with the sea.

Once a signal is detected in a given direction it is possible to zoom in and do a narrowband analysis. No matter how quiet a submarine's engine may be, every engine makes a certain acoustic sound to identify the target. Databases are continually updated by the Navy of unique engine sounds known as ACINT, short for acoustic intelligence. The captain knew now he must evade and hide. If this action doesn't succeed, then the next command would be to engage.

On one of the thirty-eight deterrent missions, Captain Dinsmore learned of a trench within range of the USS Alexander.

Approaching the trench, the captain then gave the command to bottom bubble and coffin rest.

The coffin rest command means lie and wait or lie and die! No explanation needed as all faces of the crew turn dire. The next command is, "DS." Dead silence. More often than not, a modern submarine is tracked by their "transients," or noises generated by the crew. This vigilance toward doing everything quietly is the reason submarine duty is called "the silent service."

Two days we were in that trench, Mstislav rested, Micky climbed the bulkhead and I got the heebie jeebies.

The captain enjoyed these gunslinger fights, matching wits with the enemy energized his survival instincts. The army had their battles, the air force their dog fights but below the deep, subs had their gunslinger moments.

The captain gave the command for up bubble and leveled at 400 km. At 640 feet below the sea we listened and searched with passive sonar. Did the target lie and wait or did the target move out of range? Time will tell!

The next maneuver is "MEET" or move, evade, engage and tackle. God Almighty did the captain enjoy this confrontation. Within another day the USS Alexander Hamilton utilizing the swift currents maneuvered to the western side of the Mid-Atlantic Ridge.

At 2100 hours two targets were identified and the USS AH received active pins from both targets. Immediate counter measures were enacted. Our sub was fair game in the open of the basin plateau. The active pins meant one thing that our enemies have found us and are ready to do battle. As transparent as glass we were found and they were waiting for us. The nefarious bastards of the USSR uncovered our covert missions in both Russia and Western Sahara. It is now high noon and its payback time.

The warm currents of the ocean create thermal layers and the captain would utilize these layers to our advantage. In order to thwart the enemy's sonar detection, even briefly, he had to maneuver the sub through the various levels of thermoclines.

To serpentine a submarine where the levels merge is no easy maneuver.

It is extremely critical to monitor water temperatures between the 55-degree Fahrenheit and the 39-degree Fahrenheit levels and then rise and fall between the layers which breaks up sonar detection. This boggling effect frustrates even the most experienced sonar technician. A submarine beneath the thermal layer becomes almost undetectable until the adversary sub duplicates levels to monitor. If the captain is experienced of keeping his sub out of sync with the enemy's sub maneuvers, then he creates a black hole and escapes.

That is just what Captain Dinsmore did to out-whale his adversary. But time is of the essence and he must gain knots and out distance his wake from the other two adversaries. Once the Russian subs lost sonar contact, they immediately began a serpentine pattern to locate the Alexander.

The next command from the captain in the control room was loud and clear, "Full speed ahead."

The captain figured that he needed a twenty-minute green-light from the other subs to send an emergency message to SOSUS. An acronym for sound surveillance system which is a chain of underwater listening posts located around the world to monitor the enemy. With enough time gained, Captain Dinsmore sent a coded message of CLS with their coordinates and bearings. Once the message was received an alert is sent to other United States Subs on station. The CLS stood for "Custer's Last Stand" which meant an American sub pursued by multiple enemy subs.

Within fifteen minutes a return coded message was received that said, "FA" with coordinates and bearings. This coded message meant funnel approach and location. Checking the navigation charts the USS Alexander Hamilton was one hour and thirteen minutes from their intercept.

In submarine warfare the funnel approach allows the ally through two defending subs and then fires upon the approaching enemy. Once the ally is through the funnel, then it will maneuver the dolphin shuffle and come about to render backup support. During the cold war four such scuffles occurred and three submarines were sunk. History didn't repeat itself this time, as the two enemy subs aborted mission, tucked their fins and skedaddled.

Attitudes can become tendentious, but American commanders are the best because of the core values held by each one of them. Down deep there has to be a reverence for God, respect for life and courage to defend.

The USS Alexander Hamilton proceeded to their destination and it was clear sailing the rest of the way. The sub finally surfaced off the coastal waters of Maine. I climbed through the hatch to the flying bridge and the fresh air felt great! Micky followed me up the ladder and seemed unsettled as I said, "What's the matter?"

He looked at me and just said, "I'm lost, I cannot return home!"

I leaned over the gunwale, breathed in plenty of fresh air and contemplated on what Micky said. Then I turned to him and put my hand on his shoulder to give him some reassurance, before saying, "You know Micky that I bought a pineapple plantation in Costa Rica with some 20,000 acres. And I very much need a dependable partner to help run the operation."

He looked at me and said, "It would seem that you need a crazy flyboy!"

I smiled, we shook hands and that was the beginning of our partnership.

A designated trawler named the "Happy Hooker" cruised out to the submarine and Mstislav climbed aboard. Micky and I climbed onboard as well for I had some unfinished business to do. The state department made all of the arrangements for Mstislav and the papers were signed at the Blaine House, home to the governor in Augusta to make everything kosher.

There are several islands off the coast of Maine and one of them is the home of Mstislav where he enjoys the sunrise and sunsets over Casco Bay. Some say he enjoys an occasional drink and the scrumptious culinary meals at the Jamison Tavern in Freeport.

CHAPTER 15

VENGEFUL GHOST

WW and Dick Helms were sitting at a table enjoying a couple of drinks and a good steak in their favorite restaurant. Both enjoying the camaraderie and light conversation over a mutual passion of sailing instead of business. An aide walked into the restaurant and handed over some papers for WW to sign along with a note from McKenna addressed to both men. The note read, "Mission accomplished, retirement begins!" and it was signed "*JM*."

That left one more account to be completed. In the world of espionage there are many players, the couriers, assassins, diplomats, plumbers and the most despicable the moles. How does one clean so many loose ends? WW didn't want any remaining unfinished business, especially where the Russians were concerned.

The impalpable calls for devious finesse to circumvent all political means and WW arranged an incognito visit. The seeds of evil, heinous crimes, malicious corruption and the inconsequential culpability of murderousness has to be dealt with at some point. One must have consent of the President of the United States and congress to declare all-out war and the authority of the president to act upon any divisive act that threatens the security of the United States. Then a warrant for search and seizure by a federal judge on federal matters. But when it come to counterespionage matters, the DOJ had the CIA to vacuum and clean-up many of the espionage messes.

Travel aboard the DOJ's aircraft can be for "mission-required" purposes or "non-mission" purposes. According to the GOA, Government Accountability Office, the Department of Justice owns, leases and operates a fleet of airplanes and helicopters. This includes a growing number of unmanned drones for counterterrorism and criminal surveillance.

Presently WW is on one of those flights to a destination that no one but the state department is cognizant of. He opens his brief case to sensitive material that is marked with a heading, "For your eyes only." After reading the first page of the dossier, he sets it down and lays his head back against the seat to contemplate his next ominous moves.

Our American history hasn't always been so gallant! Yes, we have won many battles and wars to achieve and preserve our precious freedom. But there are circumstances within each war that are infelicitous and don't warrant any accolades or parades. Our apathetic feelings towards the American Native as tribes were continually pushed west and treaties continually broken. The racial insensitivity that led to a civil war. The one that perturbed WW, because it happened on his watch, is the one concerning the Vietnamese tribesmen who fought alongside our American Special Forces.

The indigenous Montagnards, recruited into service by the American Special Forces in Vietnam's mountain highlands, defended villages against the Viet Cong and served as rapid response forces. That bond between America's elite fighters and their indigenous partners has persisted into the present. There were several million Montagnards in Vietnam and roughly only half-a-million remain. Unlike the general populations of Vietnam, Laos and Cambodia who were granted a blanket of sanctuary by the U.S. State Department, no such opportunity awaited the Montagnards.

A small group of the tribesmen that were the mainstay of many CIA missions were resettled with their families in North

Carolina, Northern California and Costa Rica. None of the social deviations arguably reflect our troubled history of human relations more than the genocide on a mass scale. This is one that haunted WW especially now, as he contemplated requesting their aid on one more mission.

He remembered back to when he was in Vietnam in 1964 of a stellar example of their courage. A collaborative effort between sixty of the indigenous troops and a dozen Green Beret along with three CIA operatives repelling a thousand North Vietnamese. WW was one of the CIA operatives. He would not be alive today if it wasn't for the Montagnard fighters. When the United States Special Forces first arrived in Vietnam, in the early sixties, the Montagnards were promised protected lands by the French that vanished with their withdrawal. Undeterred, their loyalties turned to help our brave special forces.

Now as his plane landed at the Chico Municipal Airport some ninety miles north of Sacramento, he wondered if his old friend Dac Kien Phan will be pleased to see him. Chico became the perfect home for the Montagnards which was founded by one of the first wagon trains to reach California in 1843. This town was the starting point of the "Koncow Trail of Tears" and became home for many remaining Indians around the Sacramento Valley. An area of diversity, friendship and peace and a welcome relief for some of the remaining Montagnards.

A warm welcome and a special banquet greeted WW as he disembarked from the plane. Dac Kien Phan along with his brother Huynh and the leader of their village Quang Nguyen stepped forward and were eager to see their old friend. Their custom to come together and share in the breaking of the bread and drink is an old tradition throughout many religions and an opportunity to rekindle old friendships. It wasn't until the following day that WW could get down to business and reveal the reason for his visit.

Among the ancient traditions of a ninja, shinobi and chien si, the functions of espionage, infiltration and assassination are accomplished. And like the samurai warriors, the stealth fighters of the Montagnards were highly skilled in the art of guerrilla warfare. Proficient in multitudinous forms of self-defense and assassination skills, they are vigilant in the act of revenge.

The following day WW meets with the leaders of the Montagnards to parley a "moi thu truyen kiep giu'a hai ho," vendetta against our enemies. His recollection of the first time when he met Dac Kien was a blessing in disguise. Both good and painful! His ambivalent memory was crystal clear as if it was yesterday. Any POW wants to forget the horrors of war but the bitter-sweetness of the truth, that is how our good friendship began.

WW was a prisoner of war at the ruthless hands of the Viet Cong and still has reoccurring nightmares of his torture on many nights. Tiger cages, beatings, baronet cuts, leaches, rats, hunger pains and the list are endless. Countless torture and prolonged solitary confinement and their will to break our will, made our resolve firm, "Never give up."

Three hundred and sixty-four days in hell, just shy a year. That is when a raid by the Montagnards saved our battered lives and the day I met Dac Kien's smiling face. WW was in a state of shock and hadn't spoken for days but when Dac Kien lifted him out of the pit, he uttered, "Thanks be to God." They saved us from the "Snake Pit Prison" and the rest is history on a mutual everlasting friendship.

Present circumstances are still ominous with ongoing moles, espionage, and pending perils as the two men smile and greet each other over morning herbal tea. WW presents a sealed package to Dac Kien containing forty-four names with dossiers on hitmen, couriers, suspected moles, and diplomats still remaining in the Washington DC area to be eliminated. Both men conclude their tea, bow towards each other and then depart with WW flying back to Washington.

Dac Kien Phan a former Buddhist monk for twelve years has experienced a varied life. Vietnam has a rich and colorful history that evolved throughout the centuries of 500,000 years of culture clashes with the Chinese, the Khmers, the Chams and the Mongols. Scars from many battles from warring factions left the infants of Dac Kien and his brother Huynh without parents as they were brutally murdered from marauding raiders from the north. An uncle whisked them off to a monastery for their protection and a life of religious upbringing.

Sometimes it's an edgy, cultural insight delivered with biting irony of life, death and rebirth so a person can begin anew. For the two brothers this transformation blossomed with a rigid formation of prayer, worship and contemplation that originated from the Tibetan Lamas that predates the time of Marco Polo's historic visit. The tradition of the Buddhist mystics is upheld very strongly in Myanmar a neighboring country to Vietnam where the brothers were taken to the monastery at Amarapura a bit south of Mandalay. There they both learned the disciplines of the Chinese martial arts of Kung Fu, 功夫 , and Wushu, 武術:武, along with the intricacies of the spiritual realm.

Both brothers grew strong, wise and insightful in the spiritual realm of "tinh than di bo," spirit walking. Novice monks learn through prayer and meditation to transcend all boundaries and dimensions of time. Every Buddhist Burmese boy between the ages of seven and thirteen is expected to enter the monastery as a novice. In due time each novice has a choice to return to life outside the monastery or stay within the disciplines of monasticism.

The brothers returned to their native country as the war escalated and the Montagnards were being exterminated. They were trained as rapid response fighters and fought along side our special forces in many battles.

Fundamentally, all details are left to Dac Kien as he studies the list and meditates on the how and when along with the necessary vitals to exterminate these individuals. WW will not know any of the details for the sole purpose of deniable culpability.

Both brothers lived in a culture where they learned about the art of nature. The good, the bad and the ugly. The selection process is not easy to learn on which plants and creatures are poisonous and what are the antidotes for such venomous creatures.

Darwin once described nature as a material system in which all living things are kin and the key to life. Dac Kien and Huynh learned about such things and knew how to utilize the toxins of the puffer fish that can be 1200 times stronger than cyanide. Or even harness the bite of the Vietnamese pygmy centipede. Nature fascinated them for it was a different adventure every day.

It was nature that taught the boys to coexist harmoniously with the seasons. The animals and creatures taught the brothers to adapt themselves to their environment. And it was the monastery that inspired the boys to transcend the spiritual mountains, plateaus and valleys of life. The discipline of the mind and body only brings people to the midpoint of life; the spiritual takes a person beyond oneself. Then and only then does true progress begin, for the spiritual expands beyond the boundaries of our horizon.

The ritual of spiritual walking requires the fourteen steps of truth. The brothers Dac Kien and Huynh first must wash their bodies to purify the outside and then spend three days of fasting, prayer and meditation to purge the mind, heart and soul. These are the first four steps that the brothers observed.

Since only the two brothers will observe the "moi thu truyen kiep giu'a hai ho," or vendetta, a special prayer had to be said for each of the forty-four persons. A special prayer is said for each person because whether good or bad, all are created by the super being. Then forty-four effigies were carved of each victim that supposedly has a soul to start their journeys to "Dia nguc," hell! The seventh prerequisite is to burn each effigy symbolizing the fires of hell and the purging of mother earth of evil.

The next seven steps of truth are extremely onerous for they test the courage and virility to accomplish the vendetta. Then and only then will they be able to pass through the "passage of spirits."

Dac Kien and Huynh must hold a burning ember in their hands as they recite the prayer of truth and touch each ember to their lips for purity of the spoken breath. Finally, they bring the embers to their chest over their heart. Most monks fail this trial for purity of heart is held by very few souls. If and only if they survive the burning of the heart, then they will successfully complete the rest of the steps.

A bed of daggers to walk across and ignore the penetrating pain and hold a poisonous snake in their mouth and not be bitten brings them to the pinnacle of the fourteen steps. Both will recite the prayer of "Transcendental Passage" the words are known and understood by very few monks. As the words are recited, the clouds above part and a hole appears as both men are drawn within the "passage of spirits." The very admittance means that their deeds are accepted.

While within the passage hole of spirits, the dimensions of time are nonexistent and the two brothers cannot be seen or heard. All the victims will meet their scourge and the vendetta will be consummated.

The first victim is not prepared for the riggers of hell as he comes home expecting to go to bed for a good night's rest. Yuri Konstantin, a KGB agent and one of the Russian diplomates for twenty-two years, lays down his head as the potent toxin of the puffer fish is wiped across his lips by Dac Kien. He doesn't see, hear or even realize that the spirits of Dac Kien and Huynh are above, looking down upon him.

The toxin paralyzes his body within a few minutes, he cannot move and wonders, "what the hell is going on, am I experiencing a stroke or heart attack?" Then very carefully Huynh removes four of the pygmy centipedes, better known as, scolopendra subspinipes. They are small reddish-brown arthropods with many yellow-orange legs. They craw very steadily millimeter by millimeter as he places one in each ear and each nostril of Yuri Konstantin. Yuri immediately feels the centipedes crawling but cannot move his hands to wipe them out or toss his head to displace them. He can't even blow out his nose due to the paralyzing effects of the toxin. He wants to scream but cannot as his eyeballs look out of his body, now a cell of hell!

The bite of the centipede is not deadly but extremely excruciating and the pain very agonizing as it crawls millimeter by millimeter biting flesh and bone. Their destination is for the culinary delicacy of brain matter.

Imagine lying in bed, unable to move, scream or yell, as the race is on in each of your ears and nostrils with the villains crawling devouring flesh and bone within their path. This isn't the worst of the ordeal. They finally penetrate into the brain matter and begin feasting for the victim is now in zombie hell.

Each agonizing bite of the brain's thalamus or the switchboard of the brain that sends out 911's, but there are no responses. The other centipedes devour the hypothalamus which regulates many body actions, the cerebellum involved in coordinating muscle actions and finally the cerebrum or thinking portion of the brain. Now the body is brain dead and only seconds away from the heart to stop pumping and the reflexes twitching. The centipedes feast and gorge themselves until they no longer can crawl. Their auspicious life has ended inside the brain as the centipedes die of gluttony. For even in the animal world there are seven deadly sins.

Eventually the bodies are found as the authorities scratch their heads and wonder on the how's, the what's and the why's for the rest of the puzzle. The coroners perform their autopsies but never cut open the brain and so do not discover the grotesque centipedes.

The next diplomatic duo were a husband and wife team and one of the most bizarre double espionage stories ever told. Brigit and Claude Dechambeau were more than just partners in crime but ambassadors for the French diplomatic corp. When one speaks of the twist and turns in life, they did all the contortionist's turns possible.

They both had an enormous, insatiable appetite for the finer things in life. A chateau in the French Riviera, a yacht that needed a crew of twenty-five to properly manage all the details of the boat and a night life of socializing in Cannes, Saint-Tropez and Monte-Carlo. Huge appetites that required substantial play money of the Big-ones!

The conniving twosome sort political careers after obtaining law degrees from the College De Droit De Montpellier. Conveniently located in the south-eastern part of France, they hopscotched to their favorite nightlife spots and rubbed elbows with the jet set.

Brigit enjoyed her men and made sure that they enjoyed her as she met, fell in love and pursued one of the legal partners of the prestigious law firms of Bredin Prat which represented antitrust litigation both at European and national levels.

Her lover throughout the college years, Claude Dechambeau pursued his interest with the law firm of Kramer Levin Naftalis & Frankel LLP; they provided creative and pragmatic solutions for top companies in corporate takeovers.

The combination of working for prestigious law firms and hobnobbing with the right clientele cemented their careers to be appointed to represent their country within the diplomatic corp. Brigit Dubois became ambassador to Russia and Claude Dechambeau became ambassador to the United States.

Once both became entrenched in the diplomatic corps and their acquaintances renewed, it was wedding bells and a blissful time for the twosome. Their marriage became vows of not only "I do's" but also, "I want it all!" Together, they plotted and connived the most diabolical scheme to garner massive Swiss accounts by selling trade secrets to both Russia and the United States.

Their amorous affairs, licentious parties and debauchery led them down the path to hell! Together they went through the ranks of diplomats, judges and politicians and no one dared to point the finger. Top diplomatic officers have full immunity, as do their deputies and families. That means ambassadors can commit just about any crime, from jaywalking to murder and still be immune from prosecution. They also can't be arrested or forced to testify in court. A neat package that has been wrapped that became their catch-22.

This game of theirs of selling trade secrets went on for about a decade and their wealth skyrocketed. WW gets wind of their malicious scheme when the husband and wife diplomats change from selling trade secrets to national secrets. In plain English, they pissed off the wrong players!

Whenever national secrets are sold, there are too many people involved to point the finger. This is when WW decides to handle the delicate matters outside the walls of justice. The choice was simple, implicate a bunch of people, fight immunity or eliminate the culprits.

A party of the notorious type was to be given on the Dechambeau yacht at sunset on the lovely Mediterranean Sea. Wine, food and debauchery as the couples mingled and their inhibitions gave way to promiscuities of the evening. Many of the names attending that party were on the sealed list that WW gave to Dac Kien. The rest would become collateral damage. Once again, the spirits of Dac Kien and his brother Huynh transcended the boundaries of space and time and float above the people on the yacht as they enjoy their sexual innuendos. There is an immoral insipidity to orgies that leaves a certain credence to the vindictive act that was about to take place.

Dac Kien and Huynh floated above all of the participants. From above the entangled bodies that resembles the copulation of a rhumba of snakes, the two spirits disperse the potent toxin of the puffer fish and within seconds all of the active bodies become paralyzed. None of them can move, twitch, scream or call for help.

Their bodies become entombed in a heap of flesh and bone and are not aware of what is happening. Each of them looks out from their bodies and wonder about, "the horror they are experiencing?"

Unable to fathom what is happening; the worst excruciating pain is about to be unleashed. The pygmy centipedes are released with their many yellow-orange legs beginning their trek through the ears and nasal passages of the victims. The arthropods begin to bite and devour flesh, bone and any matter that is in their path.

Oh, to lie there paralyzed and suffer the continuous agonizing bites will cause one to go insane. One can feel each tortuous infliction of severe pain and do absolutely nothing. Once each centipede reaches the boss of your body, the brain, they begin the trail of horror to devour the wrinkly, gray sponge.

The biggest part of your brain the cerebrum makes up 85% of the brain's weight. It controls your thinking and voluntary muscles. But as the centipedes eat, your legs, arms and entire body functions go limp. Then your thinking goes from hazy, light headed to dimming out like the TV set losing its signal. Now the memory fades to nothing. Now one is in the "Twilight Zone" of utter horror!

The brain is like a computer that controls the body's functions and the nervous system is like a network that relays messages to all parts of the body but now you are nothing but a blob!

Journalists and foreign correspondents had a field day with this story. Major headlines from top news agencies and newspapers around the world read, "Invasion of the Body Snatchers - Mysterious deaths of multiple victims in Washington DC and around the world."

This isn't impending news for our zombie legislators who do nothing!

Law enforcement agencies throughout the world were at a loss for there was no evidence, fingerprints or even perpetrators to arrest. The next headlines read, "Buffaloed Again! Law Enforcement Stymied!"

This mystery would never be solved for once Dac Kien and his brother Huynh entered the spiritual realm, there is no way for them to return to the physical life.

CHAPTER 16

HALLOWED BE THY NAME

From our mother's womb, we learn to crawl and from our father's strength we learn to stand tall. And from our Lord and God we receive the call as God speaks to each one of us through our heart and soul. If one takes the time in our busy lives to pray, contemplate and listen, then and only then do we spiritually hear.

Each of us have been created to enjoy with wonder and awe the magnificence of God's creation but more importantly of God himself. Sometimes people seldom seem to do that. They seldom enjoy praying and thinking of God and talking to Him. We are too caught up in the menial daily task of life. But Rick needed more than just that; he needed space in his life to expand his horizons and enjoy the many-splendored mysteries of life and especially of God and His Son who showed us the way.

No one knows what his eyes have seen, his ears have heard, what his heart has felt and the pains that he has endured except, for the One that has given us the gift of life. It is that very call that led him to the monastery, a contemplative life of prayer, worship and listening to God.

Jackson McKenna always recited an old Irish Blessing that went something like this, "May the road rise up to meet you. May the wind be always with you.

May the sunshine warm you always till we meet again!
Christ before you, Christ behind you.
Christ in every heart that knows you.
Christ to shield you, Christ be with you.
Christ be with you now and always."

Rick resigned his position with the CIA and with the help of the military chaplain went on another spiritual retreat. This became his impetus to enter a Benedictine monastery. Upon entering a Benedictine Monastery, he had only one regret. "If he could see Jackson McKenna one more time and enjoy a Gentlemen Jack together." That would have been grand and to hear another one of his Irish verses would have been marvelous.

He began his spiritual trek as a postulant; a probationary candidate for membership in a religious order. A period of twelve weeks and a day to search, pray and contemplate the religious path of obedience, silence and humility. How appropriate the number twelve for in the religious life numerology has its place and symbolized the twelve tribes of Israel and the twelve Apostles of Christ.

Life's pathways are as plentiful as the stars of the sky and we humans squander so much time searching for meaning in the wrong places. One's entrance to the religious life is known as a "Flight" for one is not running away from but running towards a great light.

This gives some time for soul searching within himself and a snapshot of his inner character to others. Eventually, all the religious at the end of Rick's postulant period would vote to either accept or deny his entrance. They observed his mannerisms, his patience and perseverance for each monk had to discern his sincerity to enter a holy life to seek and serve. This was accomplished by casting either a white or black marble for acceptance or denial, hence the term, "black- ball."

The soul-searching task is no easy endeavor for either the postulant or the other monks. From infancy we are taught to always do. Crawl, walk, run, grow strong. As we mature we learn that the most important functions that we can perform are to pray, meditate, worship and contemplate to deepen our bond with God.

The word holy-life may seem like an oxymoron to most people in the real world. And for Rick the entrance to a Benedictine way of life must have seemed like "Mission Impossible!" On his first occasion for penance in the confessional, the Abbot recommended for a fresh start and leave no stone unturned. There was a newly ordained priest within the monastery and the abbot thought that this is a good opportunity for the both of them. Sometimes the best intentions turn out to be the worst ideas.

Rick had experienced a side of life that most people weren't used to. Unabashed and sometimes too provocative, he stepped inside the confessional, kneeled and began with the customary, "Bless me Father for I have sinned!" He began with his escapades in Panama. Then he continued through the various episodes in his life along with the countries that he sojourned in. Before he concluded with the happenings in Turkey and moved on to Copenhagen, Rick heard a "thud."

"My God," he thought to himself, Father Florian had fainted!

It took the next week for the both of them to recover from that episode. The Abbot in turn recommended one of the older monks who had been a military chaplain to be his next confessor.

The daily horarium of the contemplative life centers around the Divine Office of the community meeting several times a day to pray. The prophets from antiquity once said, "Seven times a day have I given praise to thee." The monastery observes this sacred number of seven by giving their service in prayer at the hours of Lauds, Prime, Terce, Sext, None, Vespers and Compline. Within the monastic horarium there is a harmony between the Divine Office, study and manual labor with spiritual guidance by four main members of the community.

From the very first day of your inception, one is obsequiously immersed to a holy life worthy of absolute devotion to the One that gave us the gift of life. There are four key mentors that guide you throughout the spiritual journey. The Abbot who is a man worthy to rule a monastery. He is believed to be the representative of Christ within the monastic life and according to the words of the Apostle in Romans chapter 8 verse 15,

"For you did not receive a spirit of slavery to fall back into fear, but you received a spirit of adoption, through which we cry, Abba, Father!"

The Spirit itself bears witness with our spirit that we are children of God, hence, heirs of God and joint heirs with Christ. The Abbot is head of the monastery and personally gives spiritual guidance to each new candidate.

The second in command is the Prior who teaches monastic history and then there is the novice master who teaches the Rule of St. Benedict and will be our teacher throughout novitiate if we so choose to persevere. Then as a postulant and throughout your novitiate one is assigned a confessor for the soul cleansing duty of confession.

His confessor was a Father Patrick O'Mahoney Finbar born in Bantry Cork, Ireland in the year of 1918. Oh, how I, Jackson McKenna, would have enjoyed his wisdom, antics and delightful brogue. He once told Rick, in his delightful brogue, that a box has eight corners but that he possessed twelve and needed to constantly work on his rough edges. I laughed a heap when I read that in one of his letters that he wrote to me from the monastery a year down the road.

There was another young candidate seeking entrance at the same time and it seemed good that he wasn't alone in his spiritual endeavors. For our world does not lend itself to the spiritual but if one takes the time to appreciate God's creation and presence, one sees evidence of a loving, patient God. God only knows that it took Jackson McKenna many more years to learn this truth. A truth that this young pup, as I called him, learned very well.

As one withdrawers from the secular life, there are those things that you hold dear and come to miss in the wee night when your alone and have time to meditate. A fine cigar, female companionship, family and a jack & coke and not necessarily in that order. But as one withdrawers, it is not so much a running from but a running to a spiritual quest.

Study of the Rule, the Divine Office, manual labor, worship and meditation in the cloister rounded out each day. Each day began in the wee hours of the morning as the younger monks took care of the older ones. Especially in performing their duties in the crypt saying Mass at one of the twelve altars. Since they were too old or infirm to concelebrate in church, they faithfully administered their daily worship in the crypt.

He enjoyed each aspect of the cloistered life, the seeking, the sharing, caring and of rendering his will. This is no easy task for anyone. The only explanation that I, Jackson McKenna can give, is that he must have received a true calling.

Each community member came from a different walk of life and together aspired to seek and serve. He enjoyed each of the fathers and brothers who brought a unique part of themselves to become one in community to share, care and contribute in worship. Even the manual labor of cutting fire wood for the community room, planting in the garden and washing the refectory floors were good for the soul.

The meals were eaten in silence and one listened to the weekly reader as he first read from the Rule of Saint Benedict, then the Holy Bible and finally from an approved novel.

The rigors of life mold each one of us to either bend and shape our will or accept His will. Our most precious gift is the gift of life. But our most beautiful gift is the gift of faith. This along with the most powerful gift of prayer where we learn to communicate to our Creator and balance the tightrope of life. For learning the facets of prayer is like learning to ride a bike when we are young children. The discipline of practice is a life long journey. The daily practice of prayer gives us balance in our hectic lives.

Rick found the ways of the monastic life both enthralling and inspiring as he learned about the four steps of lectio divina or prayerful reading. First, there is Lectio or read a Scripture passage aloud slowly. Pause in silence. Then the next step is Meditatio, to reflect on the word and move on to Oratio, reading the word aloud and allowing it to be your prayer or response to God's gift of insight to us. Finally, Contemplatio, read Scripture aloud a fourth time, but now listening to God's response in silence.

It was St. Ignatius of Loyola that revealed in his Spiritual Exercises that when your own will is aligned with God's will, you shall know great consolation. Each day the monks took the time to reflect in the cloister and within the covered walkway, spiritually empty themselves, knock on the heavenly doors and listen. Rick spent much time in the cloister and yes, he prayed, meditated and listened. But he also thought about Danny, Sinclair and Trevor. These memories haunted him as he prayed for the souls of each one. He also thought about Jackson McKenna and just wondered about him!

Today the abbot, novice master and the two postulants took a walk around the grounds of the monastery. Established in the late 1800's as a priory from an archabbey in Pennsylvania it grew from a private secondary school to a four-year college. The Benedictine spirit was predominant throughout the campus as the monks taught and administered to the college along with ministering to seventeen mission churches.

There were also two nunneries on the campus; Joan d'Arc sisters who did the culinary and housekeeping duties for the monastery and the Benedictine sisters who ran the nursing department for the college and at one of the local hospitals.

There have been many upheavals within our church history caused by its lofty ideals. The crusades, schisms, inquisitions and reformation were the impetus for major change within the world. Ideals and core values have always clashed causing paradigm shifts within humanity. The postulant's studies of church history, spirituality and the Rule of St. Benedict inspired them to look deeper inside their heart for a sincere pursuance of their vocation. For the spiritual journey is a lifelong endeavor.

Studies may enrich the mind but it is the Holy Spirit that enriches the soul through the grace of God. Rick was inspired by the story of St. Benedict that at one point of his spiritual endeavor got frustrated with the system and left the learning centers in Rome for the desert mountains of Sublacum, nearly forty miles from Rome. Near this place the saint met a monk of a neighboring monastery, called Romanus who gave Benedict the monastic habit and some instructions. In a nearby cavern he pursued his spiritual endeavors. Benedict didn't want to lose his fervor for Christ and so chained himself within the cave to pray for the rest of his life.

One day, a passing hermit found Benedict and asked him why he was chained. When Benedict explained his reasoning for the chains, the hermit became appalled. The hermit scolded Benedict and told him that one truly sought God with the chains of love and not with the chains of iron. From that day forth, Benedict broke his chains of iron and never lost fervor for God but went on and founded many monasteries as houses of prayer and established a rule for monks.

In order not to diminish the zeal of a monk, there is much manual labor to counterbalance the rigors of continuous prayer and religious study. Both postulants were assigned to a Fr. Wolfgang who tended the garden for the monastery because man cannot live by bread alone but needs vegetables and potatoes too. He was a man in his mid-seventies and somewhat a gruff character but a very pious one.

He drove the monastery's van like a bat out of hell, which was loaded with implements, garden hoses and a rotor tiller. With a lead foot, the one-thousand-yard trek from dead stop was made in thirty-six seconds. The postulants just looked at each other bewildered, as the rotor tiller came crashing towards the front of the van.

Indeed, Fr. Wolfgang was a diligent, hard worker and had a green thumb to prove it as he produced enough vegetables for the entire campus. And I mean that literally for his fingers were actually green from tending the many tomato vines. Daily, his routine to diligently scrub his hands clean and sandpaper the stained fingers caused them to become callous. But as callous as his fingers where, he had a heart that was pure, compassionate and magnanimous.

His father died when he was still in high school leaving a surviving widow with five sons. Fr. Wolfgang, being the oldest boy quit high school and went to work in the local factory. He graciously supported his mother and put the remaining four brothers through college. Then upon the death of his mother, entered the monastery and completed his schooling, college and ordination to begin his new life.

The more Rick got to know each monk, he became enamored with what kind of men God called to the monastery. Men of heart, humility and vigor for God sent His Son to do and die for each one of us and God wanted men that would pursue and follow unswervingly. Each monk brought his own set of scars, struggles and spirit and pursued the heart of Christ.

The afternoon was spent tying up vines, tilling the rows and repairing the outer perimeter fence to keep out the raccoons. More supplies were needed as Fr. Wolfgang raced off in the van to retrieve them from the monastery. The horn in the old jalopy didn't work. As Fr. Wolfgang raced down the pathway to the monastery and found any monks out walking, he would stick his head out of the van window and yell, **"Hey!"** All the monks would quickly disperse to the side of the path without giving it a second thought.

Upon his return, he noticed that he had forgotten some extra wire. Fr. Wolfgang asked the two postulants if either one of them could drive a standard? Rick quickly acknowledged in the affirmative. He told him to go to the east wing of the monastery and find a workbench in the basement and bring back some wire and an extra set of wire cutters.

Rick jumped into the van, started the jalopy and shifted into first and put the pedal to the metal. Quickly shifting into high gear, he noticed the abbot and some of the brothers walking down the pathway. He stuck out his head through the window and yelled, "Hey!" And the monks dispersed to each side of the pathway. Brother Aloysius noticed that it was one of the postulants driving and exclaimed to the abbot, "My God, there are two of them!"

After the three of us finished our chores, we loaded the van and headed to the refectory for our afternoon snack. The nuns made fresh pastries daily and God, did we look forward to trying each one. Then it was time spent in the cloister for meditation followed by Lectio Divina in our cells. As the rule states, "A monk must learn to love his cell." He was beginning to understand why.

The following day they were having a lecture by Fr. Procopius on "The Core Values of Life!" He began by asking the pertinent question, "What are the core values?" Rick remembering what his dad had taught him replied, "They are reverence for God, respect for life and honor to do what is right."

Fr. Procopius was pleased with Rick's answer and then asked, "But where do these core values come from?" And as quickly as he asked the question, he went to the blackboard to write down the answer. He wrote down the 10 Commandments and quickly highlighted the first three that dealt with reverence for God. Then he circled the next three of honor your mother and father, thou shall not kill and thou shall not commit adultery which are inclusive for respect for life and the final four commandments deal with honor to do right. Then he turned to both of the postulants and said, "They come from God and they are definitely relevant today as when God gave them to Moses!"

Fr. Procopius paused for a moment and then asked the question, "What happens to people that do not live up to the core values?"

This question wasn't so easy to answer as Fr. Procopius continued with the question, "What causes a volcano to erupt?"

Now this question really intrigued Rick as he replied, "Pressure, internal pressure within the earth builds and causes a volcano to erupt."

"Precisely," answered Fr. Procopius as he continued, "In life we need outlets of prayer, the sacraments, worship and a belief in God to defuse the pressures of life or else we could erupt and make the wrong choices of murder as Cain killed Able, suicide or other heinous choices."

Rick thought to himself, "Dad was right-on about the core values and decided then and there to persevere and give it his best effort to try and follow in the footsteps of the monastic life.

It is difficult to comprehend that twelve weeks and a day of complete devotion have passed, and it is time for the community to come together and cast votes for two new brothers. Brothers who will take the names of Brother James and Brother Kurt, for once they enter novitiate, one is to give up all personal possessions including your own name. Fifty-four monks will cast a vote and the tally showed some fifty-four white marbles.

Tomorrow evening at Vespers in a quiet ceremony for no outside family members will be present; he will enter novitiate on the same day that Richard Nixon announced his decision to resign as President of the United States.

He will be cloistered for a year and a day with the tools of good works of obedience, silence and humility. Twelve weeks to determine if he wanted to persevere and a year and a day to discover if he has what it takes to become a monk.

It takes three years to make simple vows and six years to affirm final vows for a monastic life of continually seeking and serving is no easy endeavor. I Jackson McKenna had the pleasure of knowing this young lad and admired his faith.

Vespers, evening prayer to give thanksgiving for our blessings throughout the day and for Brother James and Kurt to pledge their obedience to the Abbot to enter a spiritual life-long journey. They processed into the church with the newest members of two novices leading the procession. There was a short, solemn ceremony. During Vespers they professed their obedience to the Abbot.

The church doors flew open and some stranger proceeds through the Nave of the church and walks towards the Sanctuary to sit in a front pew. As I approached closer to their stalls, which were to the right and left of the Altar, Rick became aware of my presence. Surprised at the sight of me our eyes met and he was pleased to see me. He saw with his own eyes that Jackson McKenna is alive, well and still kicking.

As evening prayer concluded, they filed out of the church. I was proud to be his mentor, friend and know this lad as I stood, smiled and gave him a thumbs-up. Life is not easy and for the both of us we had choices to make. For me to retire and for him to persevere, God willing in a spiritual life.

We accepted our choices. That was the last time that I saw Rick or Brother James. When these four young kibitzers entered the CIA, everything seemed so surreal, that when one is thousands of miles away from home, it is easy to lose your way. Perhaps now he will be able to put some of the pieces back together in his life. For in my life there are too many broken pieces and as the "Act of Faith" prayer beckons Him above,

> "O my God, I firmly believe that You are one God in three Divine Persons, The Father, the Son and the Holy Spirit. I believe that Your Divine Son became man, and died for our sins, and that He will come to judge the living and the dead. I believe these and all the truths, which the Holy Catholic Church teaches, because You have revealed them, who can neither deceive nor be deceived."
>
> Amen

I learned from this young pup and as I now watch the sunsets, remember back to the beginning. There were four young kibitzers, one disappeared and was tortured in the Russian penal colony, two were murdered and one entered a Benedictine Monastery where he found some solace in the daily prayers,

> "Oh God, come to our assistance.
> Oh Lord, make haste to help us!"

THE END